HOW TO LOSE A Fiancé

HOW TO LOSE A *Fiancé*

STEFANIE LONDON

Entangled Publishing, LLC
2614 South Timberline Road
Suite 105, PMB 159
Fort Collins, CO 80525
rights@entangledpublishing.com

Indulgence is an imprint of Entangled Publishing, LLC.

Edited by Liz Pelletier and Heather Howland
Cover design by Bree Archer
Cover photography by
Q-stock/Shutterstock
zhudifeng/Deposit Photos

Manufactured in the United States of America

First Edition May 2019

To Nan, for all the hours you spent at the library with me and for paying the fines because I never wanted to give the books back

Chapter One

No. No, no, no, no, no.

It was something Sophia Andreou said in her head a lot more than she said aloud. Chalk it up to having a control-freak father who was an expert in getting his way, with an arsenal of techniques up his sleeve to make sure he had the last word. Voicing her opposition was unheard of.

Until now.

Because *this*…this was taking it too far.

"Dad, you can't be serious." Sophia tried to laugh, but the sound had a razor edge to it. "Marriage? To a guy I've never met?"

She looked over to where her mother sat on the windowsill of their Brooklyn brownstone, studiously avoiding Sophia's gaze and picking at an invisible piece of lint on her skirt. As usual, she said nothing.

"To a man who will save this family," her father corrected. "Dion Kourakis is willing to buy our company and put the necessary funds into reviving it. Without that money, we'll be—"

"Nothing." The quiet word slipped from her mother's lips, but then her eyes immediately darted over to her husband. Sophia knew her mother would never question the head of the family, because for as long as she could remember, he'd always known—and done—what was best for them all.

But she was *really* struggling to see how marrying her off to a stranger as part of a business deal was the best solution.

Besides, why did everybody want to be *somebody*? She suppressed the urge to roll her eyes. Sophia would have been perfectly happy to leave New York and live a quiet life somewhere green and peaceful with a small army of furry friends. Somewhere far, *far* away from her father's influence.

Did she love her father? That was a complicated question about a complicated man. But Sophia valued being part of her family, valued the lifestyle her father had worked hard to provide, and valued the fact his decisions were born of the best intentions, though she could have done without his steamrolling. So she'd been a good daughter. Everything he'd ever asked for, she'd done. Like a good little princess. Well-mannered and well-behaved, that was her in a nutshell. But now it appeared they'd reached the point where she would have to put her foot down.

Delicately, of course.

Before she could say another word, her father tapped his finger on his desk. "Dorothy, leave us for a minute. I want to talk to Sophia alone."

The command was enough to have Sophia's mother on her feet and exiting the room without so much as a backward glance. So much for reinforcements.

Her father turned to her. "This isn't the time for you to be doubting your loyalty to this family."

Sophia's lips tightened. She was *nothing* if not loyal. She always put her father's requests ahead of her social life. She always dropped her own needs to care for her mother when she had one of her bad spells. Doubting her loyalty? Seriously?

Clearly, she was the worst person in the world because she didn't want to be sold off like livestock.

She reined in her emotions as best she could, but her blood had started to boil. "My loyalty is not the issue. Aren't you concerned about a guy who wants a wife thrown in with a business deal? I'm not a gift with purchase!"

Whoops. That had not come out as calmly as she'd hoped it would.

Her father's eyes narrowed.

That was a mistake. She knew better than to raise her voice when negotiating with Cyrus "the Greek" Andreou. Anything that could be classed as insubordination was like flashing a cape at a bull. Sophia sucked in a slow breath, composing herself.

"I didn't mean to yell," she said before he had the chance to blow up. "It's just…marriage? What's so wrong with this guy that he's using a business deal to leverage a wife?"

Cyrus folded his arms across his chest. "He didn't."

She frowned. "What?"

"It was my part of the deal. My request."

Sophia reeled as if she'd been slapped. Wait, *what*? Her father could be a bully, sure, but she never thought he'd pimp her out like she was a piece of property. "You asked *him* to marry *me*?"

"I didn't ask." Her father's black, bushy mustache bobbed up and down. "I told him if he wants this company, then you are part of the deal."

"Why?"

"Because, my dear child, when I sell the company to him, it's gone."

Realization seeped like ice through her veins. "The marriage will mean our family retains a claim on the company."

The return smile was calculating. "Smart girl."

She gripped the edge of her seat, nails biting into the soft leather until she felt it dent under the pressure. Was the company so important that he was willing to sell off his only daughter in order to keep a handle on it? Of course he would do it. In his mind, it was the best move for their family.

Everything he did was in the best interest of their family.

Sophia glanced around her father's office. The room wasn't big, but it was packed with as many status symbols as he could possibly fit in: a Montblanc pen in a fancy crystal holder, a shiny new laptop—which was a glorified paperweight, since he barely ever used it—a precious antique painting, and classic novels lining the bookshelf behind his desk.

The wealthy, sophisticated veneer was a lie, however. The Montblanc pen was a fake—high quality, but a fake. The laptop was of dubious origins, meaning it had come from one of her father's shady business acquaintances. The painting was a replica, and the vintage collection of classic novels, which made her father appear educated and well-read, was a sham. He'd never even cracked one open.

Needless to say, the Andreous weren't some upper-crust blue-blooded family. Her mother grew up in a house with more mouths to feed than there was food to go around. And her father was a glorified blunt instrument, the muscle who'd gone on to inherit his boss's property development company after the man's untimely death.

So her father had switched steel-toe boots for pinstripe suits and wanted a reputation to match. But that didn't change who they were underneath it all. Or her father's "do whatever it takes" personality.

"Can't you start a new company with the money from the sale?" she asked. "Wouldn't that be better? You don't need to hang on to this one. You could have something of your own with *your* name."

For the first time in as long as she could remember, her father's hard mask slipped, and she glimpsed the weary face of a burdened man beneath it. "When I took over the company, I had no idea Aristos had racked up so much debt. The sale will barely cover everything he owes. If I sell it now and don't have money coming back in, then your mother and I will have nothing. *You'll* have nothing."

Sophia wanted to point out that their house was worth a small fortune, especially since her father had owned it for years. But he wouldn't see it like that. They needed to keep up appearances, maintain their picture of success and wealth. Selling the house to get by would make them look bad. Like failures.

And she was their only cash cow.

Her breathing came quicker. What had started off as a laughable suggestion suddenly felt like a nauseating reality.

If it wasn't for her mother, she would have taken off years ago to chase her dream of a quiet, happy life of independence and solitude. She'd been busting her ass working as a virtual assistant for over two years now to save for a place of her own. She loved her work, loved helping people get their lives in order, and she had a good chunk of her deposit for a place of her own set aside. Better yet, her father knew nothing about it.

The only thing stopping Sophia from acting on her dream was her mother. The older woman was gentle. Vulnerable. She wasn't emotionally strong enough to stand up for herself. Not only did she suffer spells where she couldn't get out of bed, but even in her "good times," the older woman didn't have much confidence. She didn't see her worth.

Sophia would always shield her mother from the brunt of her father's temper and his need to control everything. But that responsibility was like a pair of hands around her throat, squeezing. Drawing up a fluttery panic her stomach.

"Do you really want to leave your mother with nothing?" he asked.

The man had always known her weak spot.

Sophia slumped in her seat. "Of course I don't want to leave her with nothing," she said, massaging her temples. There had to be another solution. Something that would keep her family safe and secure while not landing her in a loveless marriage with a stranger. But what?

"It's not like I'm marrying you off to some disgusting old pig," he added. "Look him up on Tweet Face or whatever you kids use these days. He's young, and he's Greek, which gets my mark of approval, and he's as rich as a king. You'll be living on an island in the Mediterranean. It's not going to be a difficult life. Frankly, he's a better option than what you could have found yourself."

She gritted her teeth. Okay, *that* was uncalled for. At twenty-six, she'd hardly been concerned with finding a husband. Especially since anyone she dated had to meet her father's high standards—a feat she thought impossible until Dion—or be willing to sneak around behind her father's back. That left only the guys who had a death wish or had no idea what they were getting themselves into. Needless to say, pigheaded and stupid were not qualities she looked for in a potential love interest.

"This isn't open for negotiation. Your mother is counting on you." He twisted the knife further, leaning back in his chair and folding his arms across his chest with a self-satisfied air. "Your flight is already booked. You'll leave for Corfu early next week."

Heart thundering in her chest, she pushed up from her chair. It felt as though the world was tilting beneath her feet. How could she possibly get out of this? One glance at her father's stony expression told her that arguing now would only end up in the worst possible scenario: him railing about it to her mother until the woman dissolved into tears and resigned herself to bed for the week. The last time it happened, it'd taken Sophia days to convince her mother to eat a full meal. Even longer to leave the house and face the world.

And this time, she'd be stuck in Corfu, unable to fix it.

She bit down on her lip. She'd tried so many times to get her mom to leave—begging and pleading and offering a simple, uncomplicated life. They'd find a way to make it work, Sophia was sure of it. But her mother steadfastly refused, not even willing to consider it. Was it out of fear? Pride? Something else?

All Sophia knew was that she wouldn't leave her mother, and her mother wouldn't leave her father.

Which meant she was trapped.

"We're very proud of how you always put your family first," he said, assessing her calmly. Could he read the riot of emotions swamping her? "It's an admirable quality. I'm sure your future husband will appreciate it."

Sophia nodded numbly and excused herself from the room. As she walked through the house, the chunky heels of her pumps echoing against the wooden floorboards, her stomach rocked in time with each step.

Marriage?

More like a prison sentence.

By the time she got up to her room, her hands were shaking. She pulled her laptop off her desk and settled onto her bed. Slowly, she typed Dion Kourakis's name into Google. The image that popped up made her blink. Her father hadn't been joking. He wasn't a disgusting old pig by any stretch.

"Well, he *might* still be a pig," she muttered to herself. "But he's not an old one."

In fact, the man who stared back at her could have

been cut right out of a GQ fashion shoot. Hair like polished onyx, deep olive skin, and a sexy five o'clock shadow. Dark, mysterious eyes and full lips that had the most subtle quirk, like he was laughing at a private joke.

He was hot. Superhot, even. But that didn't change things.

According to Wikipedia, Dion Kourakis was thirty-one and a self-made billionaire. Born and raised in Corfu, Greece. He gave to charity on the regular and was well-known in the community for his company's program to provide underprivileged residents with employment opportunities.

Okay, so he was superhot *and* a good guy.

Grumbling, Sophia folded her arms across her chest. That still didn't change things. The last thing she wanted was to go from being under the control of one domineering man to another. And a man who was willing to marry someone for the sake of a business deal was bound to be domineering, right? Never mind that he seemed like a good guy. Was it worth the risk?

Sophia groaned. Didn't anyone marry for love anymore? Was that such a ridiculous notion? She wanted the kind of marriage that was founded on things like trust and mutual respect, on genuine feelings and equality. And, of course, on love.

Because, as much as she adored her mother, she'd be damned if she followed in her footsteps. No way would Sophia end up tied to a man who didn't view her as an equal, least of all one who seemed willing to use her as a pawn for the sake of money. Not. Going. To. Happen.

Resolved to find some flaw in the man, Sophia scrolled through page after page on Google Images of Dion in an array of well-tailored suits, attending charity balls, cocktail parties, ribbon cuttings, and premieres. Even a shot of him shaking the hand of someone in royal dress.

In the images were a rotating bevy of stylish dark-haired

women on his arm. Okay. Clearly, he had a type. Sophia frowned at the reflection staring back at her from her vanity mirror. Her very *brunette* reflection. Darn it.

She lifted her chin. Whether she was his type or not, a man like Dion would need a wife befitting of hanging off his arm. A wife who would be okay with the spotlight, with having her photo taken, and who could dress well and shine beside him. A woman who could look pretty but stay quiet.

In other words, the woman she was raised to be, with her ability to assume an outwardly demure personality and her closet full of stylish clothes. Problem was, she didn't want to be that woman any longer.

And she certainly didn't want a man who felt entitled to those things.

But it wasn't like he knew her. She could be anyone…

Sophia gasped as the solution hit her like a bolt of lightning. She wouldn't have to refuse her father's wishes if Dion decided *he* didn't want to marry *her*. After all, she couldn't be blamed if her husband-to-be wasn't happy with the merchandise. If he rejected her, then she could return home, absolved of her "duties" to her family, without worrying her mother would take the brunt of her defiance.

Then she could get back her plans for building her perfect life. All she wanted was to find a house somewhere quiet, somewhere green, where she could work her own hours, be her own boss, and wake up each morning with a view of nature. Then she could convince her mother to come live with her, and the two of them would be happy and free forever.

Guilt immediately curled in her stomach at the thought of lying to this stranger, of deceiving him. But what other option did she have? Her father would never bend, never waver. His word was final…always. If she showed any ounce of resistance, he'd march her onto the damn plane and buckle her into the seat himself. Or worse, fly to Greece with her.

And really, wasn't this for Dion's benefit, too? He seemed like a decent guy. Upstanding. A good member of his community.

He shouldn't be steamrolled into a loveless marriage, either.

That meant none of her beautiful clothing or fancy shoes or her perfect-wife personality would be coming to Corfu with her. If Cinderella had ditched her rags to go catch a prince, then Sophia would simply do the opposite.

Chapter Two

Dion Kourakis leaned against the back seat of his Audi and closed his eyes. The soothing flow of air-conditioning skated across his skin, easing the tension in his muscles and luring him into a state of relaxation. He checked his phone for what must have been the hundredth time that day, refreshing the screen with Sophia's flight details. He'd found himself counting the minutes like an insomniac counted sheep.

It was a good thing Dion was a master at appearing at ease and in control, even if his mind was a mess. He had a feeling that would serve him well in the next twenty-four hours.

His phone buzzed, and he wearily brought it to his ear. "Hello?"

"Has the mail-order bride arrived yet?" Dion's business partner and best friend, Nico, asked with a chuckle. The question wasn't meant with any malice, but it didn't stop Dion from rolling his eyes.

"That's not what this is," Dion replied. "And you *know* it."

"I remember when you told me that getting married out of obligation was old-fashioned and unnecessary," the other man said. "Not all that long ago."

Of course, his best friend was taking every opportunity to rub that one in his face. He should have known those words would come back to bite him. "And look how that turned out for you," Dion replied smoothly. "A gorgeous wife, a bouncing baby girl. You'll have another one on the way before you know it. I'd say it worked out well in the end."

"Yeah, it did." A rare softness smoothed his friend's tone. "Does that mean you're hoping for a similar outcome?"

"Absolutely not."

Marriage wasn't something Dion had wanted for his future. The whole institution was a sham. And even though there were people like Nico who ended up with something real, the marriage part of the equation had nothing to do with it. After all, Nico and Marianna had barely known each other when they'd exchanged vows.

They had something real because they loved each other, *not* because they got married.

"I'm under no illusions that this is anything but a transaction," he added. "I need her father's company, and, in return, I'm going to give her the best life I possibly can."

"Does it strike you as odd that her father is using her as a negotiating tactic?" Nico asked. "I know you and I aren't exactly experts on family dynamics, but doesn't that seem off?"

And why would *Sophia* agree to an arranged marriage? Cyrus had refused to back down on that condition, so Dion had hoped his daughter would protest it. No such luck. And when Dion had emailed so they could get acquainted, she'd merely responded that she was very happy to be coming to see him and to "partner their families."

Dion was certain he knew what Cyrus Andreou's motives

were. The older man had tried to act like he wanted a good life for his daughter and that he wanted to get her away from some of the shady dealings lingering after the death of his former boss. Dion wasn't an idiot. Cyrus wanted to keep a close watch on the family business, and if Dion married his daughter at the time of the sale, it would be very difficult to use a prenup to ensure he kept the company should the marriage dissolve.

Cyrus Andreou was making a mistake if he thought Dion would play along. He *would* make this marriage work with Sophia Andreou because there wasn't another choice. Dion's father was a bastard who left him to grow up alone and unloved in an orphanage. Who left him in the hands of strangers when he could have had a family. Scum of the earth would be a fitting title. Or maybe world's worst dad. But now he was dead, and his company had gone to Cyrus Andreou. But it *belonged* to Dion.

And he would take great pleasure in getting his hands on it so he could rip it apart, piece by wretched piece. He would rid the world of his father's mark and ensure that the name Aristos Katopodis faded into nothingness.

Not that he would tell *anybody* about his plans. Not even his best friend.

"Maybe, but that's not my issue. Having a wife won't be the worst thing in the world. If we're going to broaden the influence of Precision Investments, then having the cofounders look family friendly is hardly a bad thing."

Nico snorted. "Who would have thought the two unwanted orphans would grow up to be family friendly?"

"Especially not you," Dion teased.

"You should see me now. I have a baby on my lap and a wife snoring on my couch." He laughed. "And I couldn't be happier."

Though the two men had looked out for each other from

childhood, as they'd both assumed blood brothers might do, they weren't blood. Regardless, they'd stuck together and started their own company, Precision Investments. Nico had always been reticent about touchy-feely stuff, until recently. Becoming a father and falling in love had changed him.

"I'll take success over happiness." Dion grinned. "But I appreciate the sentiment."

Dion's driver, Silas, looked up and caught his attention in the rearview mirror. "Miss Andreou's plane has landed."

"Gotta go," Dion said to Nico. "I'll see you tomorrow night."

He disconnected the call and shoved the car door open. Outside, the air was thick and balmy. Dion had come straight from the office, so he was still in his suit, but he ditched his jacket on the back seat of the car, along with his tie.

"You can wait here, if you like," Silas said. "I've got the sign. I can bring her out."

"No." Dion shook his head and shut the car door. "She's come to a new country and doesn't know anyone. The least I can do is be here to greet her."

Silas nodded but didn't say anything further as they walked to the terminal. His staff didn't know the whole story behind Sophia's visit. In fact, Nico was the only person who did. As far as Silas and the others were concerned, Sophia was the daughter of a business acquaintance. In the emails he'd exchanged with her, they'd agreed to keep the engagement quiet at first.

Dion's approach was to bring Sophia to Corfu, give them some time to get to know each other, and then have a quick, private wedding out of the spotlight. There would be no love, no real emotions. Which was precisely why the thought of marrying someone he didn't know wasn't all that perturbing to him.

Besides, he'd done his homework. There wasn't much

of Sophia Andreou online (which was a plus), but from the little bit of information he could glean, it was obvious she was the kind of woman he'd want by his side. She worked in her father's business doing bookkeeping, so she must have a head for numbers. And she was on the volunteer page of a Brooklyn hospital, her face beaming like a ray of sunshine as she held a chubby-limbed toddler in her arms. Aside from that, he'd come across a few older pictures of her and her parents at upscale events posted to her rarely used Facebook profile.

He'd be lying if he said he hadn't found her attractive. She was petite with long, dark hair and high cheekbones befitting a model. Not to mention wide eyes with heavy lashes. Definitely pretty. Stylish, too, from the few photos he'd seen. She would fit right into his busy, social lifestyle.

Since it was peak tourist season, the inside of the Corfu International Airport arrivals terminal buzzed. The rattle of suitcase wheels mixed with the din of people chatting in all different languages and the somewhat distorted sound of a gate-change announcement over the speakers.

Dion glanced around, searching for Sophia's face. He'd seen enough photos to know what she looked like, but he didn't recognize any of the people coming in from the baggage collection area. Silas unfolded the thick piece of paper, which had *Andreou* neatly printed in block letters.

"She shouldn't be too long," Silas said. "Are we heading straight back to the house?"

"Yes. Kristina is making dinner, and I'm sure Sophia would like to freshen up after her flight."

He continued to watch the terminal. With the warm weather, people were dressed comfortably for their flights. Even those carrying briefcases weren't wearing full suits. Out of the corner of his eye, Dion noticed a woman in an outfit so bright and garish it made him blink.

She wore a boho dress in some mind-bending shades of orange, mustard, and lime green, with the kind of polyester fabric that was a breeding ground for static. On her feet were a pair of worn Birkenstocks over a pair of thick, white socks. Layered on top of the dress was a chunky cardigan in baby-poop beige that was the approximate texture of a pot scrubber. To make the outfit even more obnoxious, she'd layered a few strands of mismatched beads in hot pink, yellow, and blue.

The look screamed *little kid raiding eccentric grandma's dress-up trunk.*

"That's quite an outfit," he said under his breath.

He'd been flying private for so long—since even before Precision Investments had its own jet—that he'd forgotten how strangely some people dressed for travel. They got their share of backpackers in Corfu.

Still, there was backpacker style, and then there was… that.

The woman looked at him, her eyes narrowing for a second before a big grin broke out over her face. She started walking toward them, a carry-on bag slung over one shoulder and a larger black suitcase rolling along beside her.

Dion averted his eyes and checked his phone. The last thing he wanted to do was engage a stranger in conversation. He was starting to wonder why he hadn't pushed Sophia harder about coming over on his private jet.

"Hello!" The cheerful voice made him look up.

Up close, the outfit seemed even brighter…if that was physically possible.

"Hello," he replied with a tight smile before looking down at his phone again.

"That's all you've got to say?"

God, give him strength.

"Don't you know it's not good to talk to strangers?" he drawled.

"Ha! That's a good one." She tried to elbow him in the ribs. "But you owe me something else."

He did *not* have time for this right now. Perhaps the airport had an issue with people pretending to be passengers so they could go around asking for money. It wouldn't surprise him. There'd been an increase in unemployment in the city over the last few years, which was something his company had worked hard to combat by increasing job opportunities for people who hadn't been fortunate enough to go to university or even finish high school.

Dion pulled out his wallet, rifling through the cash so he could hand the woman a few hundred euros in the hope that she would leave him alone. "I'm not sure you're supposed to be doing this here," he said, holding out the crisp notes. "You'll get in trouble with airport security. But this should be enough to get you into the city and find a place to stay for a few nights."

The woman cocked her head but took the cash from him and slipped it under the neckline of her dress and into her bra. "Or I could blow it all on partying."

He raised a brow. "That's not a very long-term strategy."

Silas looked at him like he'd lost it, but what the hell was he supposed to do? Dion had been groomed by a mentor who had taught him to be warm and friendly at all times. Without exception. He could practically hear the old man's words in his head:

Every interaction is an opportunity to make a fan.

Only this woman didn't look like someone who would use Precision Investment's services. He wondered if the suitcase was a ruse so she didn't get stopped by security.

"Maybe not," the woman said. "Or I could stay with you. We can split the money and have a good time."

"I'm in a relationship at the moment," he lied.

Well, it wasn't *quite* a lie. Ever since he'd started

negotiations with Cyrus Andreou, he'd made his bed a ghost town. And that was even before he'd said yes. It seemed wrong to think about potentially marrying one woman while courting another. And he really didn't want to be dealing with this when he was supposed to be meeting Sophia.

"Oh, come *on*. You find me attractive, don't you?" She batted her eyelashes.

"If you'll excuse me, I'm trying to find a friend at the moment."

A strange expression flittered over her face. "A friend, huh? That's very kind. You're Dion, aren't you?" She pointed to the sign. "Andreou. You're waiting for Sophia Andreou, right?"

Dion's blood ran cold as he searched the woman's face. Regret hit him with the force of a sledgehammer. The wide, doe-like eyes, creamy skin. The petite yet curvy frame hidden beneath those hideous layers. The dark chestnut brown hair. The accent.

"It's me!" She grinned and stuck out her hand. "*So* nice to meet you."

No fucking way.

He'd mistaken his wife-to-be for a beggar. For a second, Dion didn't react. Couldn't react. His brain was stuck between gears while it processed what in the hell was going on. How could this outlandishly dressed woman be the very same Sophia he'd seen online? The very same woman he'd agreed to marry?

He pasted a smile onto his face. "Sophia, I'm sorry I didn't recognize you." His tongue felt heavy in his mouth, disbelief slowing him down.

"You're in a relationship, huh? That's going to be awkward." She handed her bags over to Silas, who looked as dumbstruck as Dion felt. "You expecting to keep a mistress?"

Silas looked at him sharply, but Dion shook his head and

waved his hand. "Silas, why don't you get the car? We'll wait for you out front."

He motioned for Sophia to walk with him toward the terminal exit, and she slipped her arm through his and held him close with a vulture-like grip.

"I meant you," he clarified.

"Oh." Her smile seemed a little tight.

"As far as I'm concerned, we're now in a relationship, so I wasn't about to accept an invitation from another woman."

"A true gentleman," she said. Then she stuck her hand into her bra and fished the money out, shoving it back in his face. "Then this is yours. I only wanted to see how long I could fool you into thinking I was some random stranger."

A couple walked past with raised brows at the sight of Sophia shaking a wad of cash in his face. "Keep it," he said. "There's plenty to see in Corfu, and I'm sure you'll want to go exploring."

She eyed him for a moment before shrugging and stuffing it back into her bra, almost giving another man an eyeful as they walked into the valet waiting area.

"Did you have a good flight?" It was the most benign thing he could think to ask.

"Yes, I did. Thank you for putting me in first class. It was very kind of you to offer the private jet, but I'm scared of small planes."

He didn't bother to correct her false assumption that the Precision Investments company jet was small. "Understandable."

"They had the fanciest champagne on the flight." She beamed up at him. "Normally, I'm used to champagne coming out of a can, so that was a real treat."

Champagne in a can. He didn't even know such a thing existed.

"Well, I guess it's not *technically* champagne. Sparkling

wine is probably more accurate, because it has, like, flavors and stuff mixed in. Champagne actually has to come from Italy, right?"

"France," he said. "From the Champagne region."

"Oh, they named their town after the drink? Cool!"

Was she for real? Dion cast a sideways glance in her direction, confused that Sophia was *nothing* like what he'd imagined. Nothing like the sophisticated, intelligent woman her father had described. He tried not to jump to any conclusions—maybe she'd taken sleeping pills on the plane and was feeling a bit off-color. Or maybe she was nervous. *That* was entirely possible.

Or maybe Cyrus lied to you. And anyone can present a better image of themselves online.

They walked through the airport's exit and out into the parking lot, Dion numbly putting one foot in front of the other, wondering what the hell he'd gotten himself into.

• • •

This was going even better than Sophia could have imagined. Dion had clearly been shocked, which meant her costume was on point.

Thank you, Goodwill!

Of course, she'd pass the euros on to someone who needed them, like a shelter in the city. She had no interest in Dion's money.

Sophia stifled a yawn. Even a properly reclining seat, fluffy pillow, cozy blanket, and abundance of free champagne hadn't been enough to lull her into slumber during the flight. Her mind had whirred like a motor without an off switch and she'd used the sleeplessness to catch up on work for the clients of her virtual-assistant business. Working made her feel productive and in control of her future, which was something she *desperately* needed right now. And, as long as she was squirreling away on newsletters and content plans and events for her clients, she could pretend that everything was okay.

At some point, she would crash, but not yet. Right now, she had to prioritize her mission.

She'd been surprised that her "future husband" had come to collect her himself. After all, a guy like that would have an army of people at his disposal. Chauffers, maids, cooks. The works. Why would he waste his precious time picking her up from the airport?

As they waited for the driver to return with the car, Dion seemed physically repulsed by her. She clutched his arm, fighting against how good he smelled. How delectable. He was hotter than the pictures she'd seen online—dark hair, sharp jaw, and full, kissable lips. Shoulders broad enough to carry the world. Not to mention an arrogant swagger that told her he knew how to use what he had, how to move his body. In another life, she'd be fanning herself. Fantasizing about kissing him…and more.

But not in this life.

Unfortunately for both of them, her attraction was going to have to be squashed like a bug, because Sophia was going to do her best to make herself as *un*appealing to him as possible. Hence the whole champagne-in-a-can thing. That was a stroke of spontaneous genius, but the raise of his brows told her she'd done well. Maybe he was a food guy? If that was the case, then she could add pretending to be totally uneducated in that area.

Every little bit would help her end goal.

The biggest risk of this plan, however, was that Dion would report back to her father. It would be a delicate balance, trying to make her newfound quirkiness feel so real that she didn't tip him off. Sophia looked down at her outfit and frowned…maybe the beads and sandals with socks were a bit over-the-top. She might have to tone it down next time. If it felt like a ploy, then he'd be more likely to rat her out. If she nailed her performance, however, then hopefully he'd feel so awkward about the whole thing that he'd back out of the deal and find another company to buy.

Well, that was the hope, anyway.

"So, where to now?" she asked. "I'm guessing you'll want to introduce me to lots of people."

"I thought we might have a quiet night," he replied. Was that the original plan, or had he decided on that after meeting her? It was hard to tell. "Dinner at home so we can get to know each other."

On the surface, it sounded like the perfect option. The lack of sleep was starting to catch up with her, and if they went out to a restaurant she might face-plant in her meal. Funny as that would be, she didn't want to risk drowning herself in a bowl of soup on night one. But the idea of spending time alone with Dion unnerved her.

The longer they stood there, the more *ridiculously* good-looking he seemed to become. The photos were a poor reflection of his magnetic pull in real life. His dark hair was thick and shiny, and the way it curled ever so slightly over his ears made her fingers itch to brush it back. His face had all the right elements. He was probably one of those rare people whose face was perfectly symmetrical.

That's why you're attracted to him. It's nothing but symmetry and evolution making you see him as a viable mate.

Oh god. Viable mate? Sophia swallowed and whipped her head in the other direction so he wouldn't see the heat rushing to fill her cheeks.

Do not, under any circumstances, think about Dion Kourakis as a mate. In fact, don't think about mating at all. With anyone.

Alone time was a bad idea.

"You know, I'd love to get out and see Corfu. If this is going to be my new home, then I don't want to waste any time at all in getting to know it." She squeezed his arm and stifled a smirk at the resulting flinch of his muscles. "I want you to take me to your most favorite restaurant."

"My most favorite," he echoed.

"The one place you would recommend people to go if they were visiting."

"Okay." He nodded. "If that's really what you want."

Not even a little bit. "Yes. It's what I want."

It'd been hell emailing Dion last week, saying she was excited to meet him. Excited to "join their families." Ugh, gag. But Sophia's father had read her emails in the past, and she couldn't risk anything giving her plans away.

"You sure you're not too tired after the trip?" He looked down at her, a charming smile on his lips. She had no doubt that smile convinced a lot of people to do a lot of things.

Sophia would need to be immune to that smile. As far as she was concerned, Dion was as much a barrier to her freedom as her father. So, no matter what, she had to resist him.

"Suddenly, I feel full of energy," she lied. "A shower would be great, and then we can hit the town."

He nodded.

"I wasn't expecting you to meet me at the airport," she said. Now why on earth did *that* pop out of her mouth?

"I thought it might be nice for you to arrive to a friendly face."

Dammit. Guilt twinged low in her gut. She felt bad messing with this unsuspecting guy who, from their brief interaction so far, actually seemed like a decent person. She didn't want to hurt him, and she hated lying. But they were in opposition, and Sophia wasn't going down without a fight.

"Yours is a *very* friendly face." She batted her eyelashes

at him.

"Thank you." Dion brought a fist up to his mouth and cleared his throat.

"Is this, uh…the first time you've done this?" All her curiosities were bubbling away, like champagne that had been shaken and uncorked.

Or un-canned…if that was even a word.

He was hot as heck, and he didn't seem to have the hallmarks of a complete asshole. So why was he saying yes to her father? Surely the man was capable of finding his own wife. There'd be a line around the block if he said he was looking for someone to fill that role. And why would he want her father's company if it was so riddled with debt? Unless that wasn't true. She wouldn't put it past her father to lie to her.

Dion's eyebrows rose. "Met a woman at an airport?"

"No, I mean more about the whole arranged-marriage thing." Was it her brain's way of trying to find something out about him that might help her continue this charade uninhibited by her conscience? "Have you been married before?"

"No. Have you?"

"No."

Never will be, either.

Before the conversation could go any further, their car arrived, and Dion extracted himself from her grip. Was it her imagination, or was there a brief flash of relief in his eyes?

He pulled the door open and motioned for her to go ahead of him. "After you, Sophia."

A shiver ran the length of her spine at the sound of her name on his lips. The gently-accented English was like a drug winding its way through her system. If only she were here under different circumstances, she would have been thrilled to be on this beautiful island with a gorgeous man all to herself.

But that was a fantasy for another day. She was determined not to be her father's bargaining chip. She would get out of this mess, take the money she'd saved, and start her new life.

That's right, keep thinking about your dream cottage with all the beautiful trees and singing birds.

Solitude, peace. Being her own boss. *That's* what she was working toward.

Unfortunately for Dion, she had a whole list of weird and wacky things that would make her look like the fiancée from hell. Dion Kourakis was about to wish he'd never agreed to marry her.

Chapter Three

Dion slumped in his office chair and rubbed his palms over his face. After bringing Sophia back to his house, he'd shown her to a guest room, and Silas had brought her bags in. Currently, she was showering before they were due to go out to dinner. But Dion was already having reservations about anyone seeing him in public with her.

Perhaps she was trying to dress comfortably for the trip?

He doubted it. The itchy cardigan couldn't possibly be comfortable on anyone's skin, let alone for a long-haul flight. No, there had to be more to it than that.

Dion never liked to think of himself as a shallow person, and he knew that the value of a person came from the inside—from intelligence and personality and humor and loyalty. But the fact was, appearances *did* matter. At least in his world. As the "face" of Precision Investments, with more than five thousand people employed across Europe and a further two thousand elsewhere in the world, he needed to be presentable at all times. Hence why Nico claimed that he was the brains and Dion was the beauty.

Joking aside, there was some merit to it. Not the beauty bullshit, of course, but how he presented to the world was a reflection of his company, a reflection of the job security his employees enjoyed. As he was one of the wealthiest men not only in Greece, but in all of Europe, he was subject to scrutiny. Heading out for a night on the town with a woman who dressed like she'd rifled through a dumpster wasn't going to attract the kind of attention he needed or wanted.

What would Elias say?

Dion's business mentor, a man who'd been like a father to him over the years, would say that perception was reality. What people thought of you was what they would believe to be the truth.

It was the mantra Dion had built himself upon. Creating the perception that he was confident, savvy, and worldly hid the fact that he was still the orphan boy who'd grown up unloved and unwanted. That he wasn't worth anything to anybody. He'd *made* people see him as worthy, and then over time he'd *become* worthy.

Perception. Reality. The two were inexorably linked.

Which meant he would need to deal with the Sophia situation carefully. He needed Cyrus's company—needed to know that everything his father built was gone. Razed to the ground. He wouldn't be able to get closure and move on until he knew that there was nothing left of the life Aristos Katopodis made when he abandoned his only son and moved to the United States.

And all of *that* was to say that he couldn't call Cyrus Andreou and say his pride and joy wasn't good enough… although now Dion was starting to understand why the other man was trying to get a marriage deal thrown in with a business contract.

Dion reached for his phone and dialed the number of his favourite restaurant. "Ersi? It's Dion. I need your help."

He detailed his plan to the woman who ran Vlahos Taverna. He'd known Ersi since he was a teenager, when he'd gotten by washing dishes and waiting tables once he'd left the orphanage. Ersi and her husband ran the restaurant and had treated him like one of their own, always making sure he had a hot meal. When he made his first million, he'd cut her a check big enough to take care of the restaurant's rent for a year. When one million had turned into ten, he'd bought the building outright and let her run her restaurant rent-free.

She didn't hesitate to let him cash in a favor.

Dion stashed his phone in his pocket and wandered out in the main area of the house. It was mostly silent now. He'd dismissed Kristina for the night, given Sophia had requested to eat out, and the other staff had gone home hours before. He'd even sent Silas home.

Sophia must still be getting ready, because her bedroom door was shut with a telltale thin beam of light shining through the crack at the bottom.

Dion drummed his fingers on the wall unit where his turntable sat. He'd inherited a Linn Sondek LP12 from Elias when the older man had been cleaning out a storage unit after his divorce years ago. He'd shown a young Dion how to use it and how to care for the vinyl records that went with it. For a kid who'd never had a radio or an iPod growing up, hearing only music selected by the sisters, which was mostly church hymns and traditional Greek music, this gift had been an entrance into a new world. Being able to erase silence whenever he wanted made him feel in control of his life for the first time.

Silence had been the sound of his childhood—be quiet for prayer, be quiet for bedtime, be quiet for lessons. He'd envied the families outside the grounds of the orphanage, envied the sound of squealing and shouting and laughter. Envied the music floating out from houses and car windows, everything from nineties grunge to electro-pop and the old, soothing crooners of bygone eras. Since then, he'd never let himself dwell in silence for too long.

"I'm ready!" A cheery voice grabbed his attention.

Sophia was dressed in a brown dress that hung down to her mid-calf, above the Birkenstocks from earlier that day. This time there were no socks, but her toenails were painted a retina-searing acid green. With glitter. The cherry on top was her hair. She'd teased her brown hair into a puffy ball on top of her head. It looked like one of those pom-poms you might find on a hat at a ski lodge.

Dion forced in a breath. "I hope you're hungry."

"I am." She rubbed her stomach. "And I hope you've got a special place picked out. I want to get to know *all* of your favorite things. If we're going to be married, then I need to know everything about you."

He'd expected some hesitation from her over the marriage thing. Hell, he'd hesitated himself. It had taken him a full two weeks to process Cyrus's offer—or, rather, ultimatum—and come to grips with the idea of marrying a stranger. Seeing his mentor hooked up to half a dozen different machines after having a fall in his home, with tubes coming out of every orifice, had finally pushed him over the edge.

The old man still had a twinkle in his eye, despite his nurses buzzing around him like protective bees. He'd still had enough breath to tell Dion that he believed in him. That he was worth something. If not for Elias, Dion might never have found his way in life. Certainly no thanks to the man who'd gotten his poor mother pregnant and then decided he didn't want to deal with the consequences after she died.

Closure was now within Dion's grasp—he could shut the final page of his father's book. He wanted that feeling so bad he could taste it…so bad he would marry a stranger.

"We have plenty of time to get to know each other." Dion

motioned for her to follow him outside. "Your father told me that you've been working in the family business."

"That's right. I've been doing some general admin," she replied. "And I have my own virtual-assistant business, too."

Outside, Dion's white McLaren—the car he liked to drive when he wasn't being chauffeured by Silas—sat in the driveway. The sun had set some time ago, but the lights dotted around the garden brightened the front of the house. He unlocked the car and held the door for her.

"Ah, so you're a businesswoman. I'm sure we'll have a lot to talk about, then."

"Sure, although it's not my *real* passion in life, to be honest." She looked at him expectantly, as though waiting for an invitation to elaborate.

"What would you rather be doing?" he asked.

The car's engine rumbled as he pulled out of the circular path in front of the four-car garage. A warm breeze carried the salty tang of the ocean into the car.

"You know, I'm really passionate about taxidermy." Sophia nodded as though this was the most natural thing to say. "There's something about animals that fascinates me."

"Taxidermy?" He frowned. "Like, stuffing dead animals?"

"Stuffing or mounting," she said. "It includes both."

Was she…joking? Her expression didn't reveal even a sliver of amusement.

"I see it as a way to prolong an animal's life," she explained. "I know it might seem a little strange, but trust me. When I bring my collection over, you'll see how wonderful it is."

He gulped. "Your collection?"

"Yes, I have a huge collection. Squirrels and racoons and a couple of cats. I even have a fox. She's a real beauty. I was thinking we could put her in the living room. Or maybe the foyer, so she can greet guests." She clapped her hands together. "Baroness Sasha Foxington III would absolutely *love* that."

Baroness. Sasha. Foxington the fucking third.

Was he in a nightmare right now?

"I, uh...saw you've done some volunteer work at a children's hospital," he said as he steered the car along the winding road that ran the length of Corfu's coast. He'd driven it so many times he knew every curve. But tonight, the road seemed to stretch on forever, as if time had been slowed down and he was trying to drive through sludge.

"You've done your homework," she said with a nod. "Impressive."

"I wanted to make sure I'd recognize you at the airport." He cringed as soon as the words popped out, but he covered it by rubbing one hand over his jaw. "That's a very admirable line of work."

"Do you like children?" she asked.

"I guess so, although I've never had any in my life before. But my business partner recently had a little girl, and she's adorable."

She nodded. "Are there any hospitals or medical centers here in Corfu? I would really like to keep up my volunteer work."

For the first time since she'd arrived, he detected a sweetness in her voice. A sincerity. "Yes, there is. I'm sure they would love to have another volunteer."

"That would be great."

After a stretch of awkward silence, Dion pulled the car into Vlahos Taverna. But rather than parking in the front with the rest of the restaurant-goers, he continued down a small path that lead to the back of the building and pulled up next to a simple red sedan.

"This is it." He opened his car door, and Sophia followed.

They entered the restaurant through the staff door at the back, and he waved to Ersi, who was busy ordering her staff around with a voice he knew could strike fear into the hearts of grown men. When she looked up, her face split into a huge grin, and suddenly her tone was soft as butter.

"Dion!" She threw her arms open and enveloped him in a hug.

"This is Sophia." He'd already told Ersi that Sophia didn't speak much Greek and requested they converse in English so she felt included. "She landed in Corfu today."

"Welcome. Any friend of Dion's is a friend of mine." She hugged Sophia. "Come, come. I have the best table in the house set up for you."

Ersi lead them through to a small room that was nestled between the kitchen and the main restaurant area. It was intimately set for two, a candle burning in the center and cutlery gleaming on a blue and white table cloth.

"This is our private room. We use it for functions and important guests, so please make yourself at home," Ersi said. "I'll have Alex come in shortly to get you started."

"A private room, huh?" Sophia said as she took a seat. Her dark gaze tracked his every movement. "You sure know how to pull out all the stops."

If only you knew.

But this was a Band-Aid solution. Tomorrow, there was a cocktail party with important business associates and some of the senior staff from Precision Investments. Dion's life was a public one, and that meant he couldn't hide his future wife away in private dining rooms for the rest of their lives.

He needed to figure out how the hell he was going to tactfully help Sophia Andreou step out of the dress-up bin and into the role of wife of a billionaire. Shopping. Lots of women loved shopping, right?

He made a mental note to get his assistant to contact a

personal shopper tomorrow. He *would* make this work. As he unfolded his menu, a genuine smile curved his lips for the first time since meeting his fiancée.

• • •

Stunning gray fox taxidermy. Freestanding, life-size. Not mounted on a stand or plaque, but could be mounted if you choose to do so. The fox measures 26" long (tip to tip) and 16" tall.

Thick winter fur including a beautiful full tail and stunning face. Perfect for any distinguished home.

A very nice fox taxidermy for your collection.

Sophia couldn't believe she was going to pay almost five hundred dollars to buy a stuffed fox on eBay. But when she'd planned out her "persona" during the flight to Corfu, the most disturbing thing she could think of for a hobby was taxidermy. Must have been stuck in her head after her friend had emailed her some disturbing images from the Bad Taxidermy website, one of which included a fox wearing a strange expression and a three-piece suit.

And so Baroness Sasha Foxington III was born.

Which meant she needed to acquire a stuffed fox. Sophia hit the buy button and completed the shipping details with Dion's address, forking out extra for express shipping. She swallowed back her guilt and found the website for a Corfu animal shelter, making an anonymous donation to find some karmic balance.

Unfortunately for her, desperate times called for desperate measures. Her guilt would have to take a back seat, since it looked like Dion wasn't going to be as easy to dissuade as she'd hoped. He seemed to really be making an effort to get to know her.

Last night, he'd totally foiled her plans to dive straight into embarrassing him in public. The whole "private dining" experience was brilliant. He managed to get out of having to be seen with her without giving her a damn thing to complain about. Either the man was already wise to her plans or he was so smooth her amateur con-lady moves were bouncing right off him.

He'd acted sweet and attentive, too. If it was a real date, she would have been thoroughly charmed. In addition, the food had been incredible, since the chef had done a tasting menu—thus messing with her plans to order weird and disgusting food combinations—*and*, to make matters worse, she'd found herself enjoying Dion's company as the night went on.

Which absolutely had to stop.

Sophia wiped her internet history and stashed her laptop under a layer of clothes in one of the drawers in her bedroom. Thankfully, Dion hadn't done anything outrageous like try to suggest they share a bedroom. At least this way, she had a little privacy in which to conduct any reconnaissance work.

Like ordering weird shit off the internet.

She glanced around the room. The "guest bedroom" that Dion had given her was probably bigger than the apartments most people lived in back home. Along with a giant king-size bed covered in linens that felt like they were spun from the clouds in heaven, the room contained a reading nook, a dressing room, and a stunning antique vanity unit that had been thoughtfully filled with all manner of useful things. A small note told her to use anything she liked, and the drawers contained hand creams and body lotions, bottles of perfume, and an entire skin care regimen from some fancy-looking French brand, all with sealed boxes.

You will not be won over with cosmetics.

Still, there weren't too many opportunities in life for someone to be treated like a VIP. Sure, her father tried to make sure they had that facade whenever they were in public, but there was a big difference between someone like Dion, who was truly wealthy, and her father, who simply appeared to be.

So far, only her mother had made contact by asking if she'd landed okay and wanting to know if the weather was good. No mention of Dion or the whole arranged-marriage fiasco, mind you. Her mother was a gold medallist in sweeping things under the rug. Usually Sophia could rationalise it was a "survival mechanism" born out of dealing with a temperamental and bullish husband. But this time it had Sophia's blood boiling. Her mother could pretend she'd sent her daughter off on some fancy vacation if she liked, but that didn't change the fact that they were trying to sentence her to a life without the freedom to make her own choices.

"Sorry, Mom," she muttered under her breath. "I love you, but I can't be *like* you."

Tonight, a cocktail party was being held in Dion's lush and expansive backyard. A party in her honor, apparently. He'd informed her over dinner last night that he wouldn't be announcing their engagement immediately. Rather, he would introduce her as a family friend and give her a chance to settle in before he broke the news.

"How kind," she muttered.

Whether people knew she was here to be married off was irrelevant to her plans. If there was a gathering of people, then she would be putting on a show.

She looked down at the oversize balloon-style pants made of red and yellow satin. They were almost as outlandish as the silk blouse with tiered ruffle sleeves. Sophia stifled a snort as she looked at herself in the mirror.

She couldn't quite tell what was more ridiculous: the fact that she looked like a couture version of Krusty the Clown or that these pants had cost almost five hundred euros. But Dion wanted a high-fashion wife, so she was going to be high fashion.

Dion's "personal shopper" had taken her out today on what was clearly meant to be a "make sure she dresses well" trip. Ha! Sophia had allowed the lovely woman to take her out, to help her pick some glittering, strappy sandals with a pencil-thin heel. But the demure black dress was tucked away in her closet, tags still swinging.

Sophia adjusted her hair, which she'd left in its wildly curly, natural state—rather than smoothing it down with a flat iron like she usually did—and sucked in a breath. After spending her entire life doing everything possible to look like the perfect daughter she was, wearing such an outlandish outfit in public was intimidating.

"You can do this." She stared at her reflection. "You *will* do this, because then you can go home."

Home. To the mother and father who were treating her like cattle. To her life of unfulfilling work under her father's thumb. To the house that was a glorified prison.

"You're going home to make a new life. *Your* life. Running your own business from your dream cottage." She swallowed. "And then you'll never have to answer to anyone insisting they know what's best for you ever again."

She flung open the bedroom door and cringed at the sound of string instruments floating up the staircase. It sounded like one of those fancy parties where people sipped champagne and wore the kind of outfits Sophia would wear back home. Little black dresses, pencil skirts, diamond studs.

Gripping the handrail, Sophia took the stairs carefully, her movements slowed by the teetering Jimmy Choo heeled sandals. They were a ploy to make the outfit look intentional—

like this was some huge fashion trend in New York that he knew nothing about.

Dion would likely be outside wondering where the hell she was. Sophia had never been late for anything in her life, especially not on purpose. But the "big reveal" had to occur when the party was already in full swing. That way Dion couldn't shuffle her off into a quiet room and demand she change. She needed the moment to be public so he'd have to grit his teeth and bear it. And be planning how to dump her after the party.

There's no way he'd be able to see her as wife material after this.

When she got to the bottom of the staircase, she could see all the way out to the back garden through the wall-to-ceiling windows in the house's main lounge area. She could see it all—Dion's dark hair and tanned skin, his bright smile and warm handshakes and kisses on the cheeks of his guests. She could see the softly glowing lanterns and the sparkling night sky and the glistening pool. She could even see the trees shifting in the breeze, their leaves fluttering and trembling.

Dion's perfect, polished life was about to have a wrench thrown in the works.

As if he sensed her, his head snapped up, and his dark eyes cut through the glass door leading out to the garden. Was it her imagination or did his jaw tighten? Any minute now, she would find out.

"Three, two, one..." she whispered under her breath as she pushed the door open. "Showtime."

Chapter Four

What the actual fuck?

For a moment, confusion addled Dion's brain. Was she wearing…clown pants? What happened to the shopping trip his assistant had organized? What about the instructions he'd given her?

Chic. Sophisticated. Elegant.

She was wearing fucking clown pants.

"Sophia?" He blinked, trying not to let the shock twist his face. What the hell kind of game was she playing?

Eyes turned toward them left and right, whispers gathering steam as everybody looked on. The yard was filled with his employees, business acquaintances, high-profile clients, and close friends. Dion's cocktail parties were legendary in Corfu, and he'd built this house with entertaining in mind. From pool parties to networking events to chill weekend afternoons, Dion's house was the place to be.

He'd planned to introduce Sophia to everyone tonight. They weren't going to speak of their agreement to get married yet, but he still wanted her to get to know people so she felt at home here.

"Dion." She waved, a collection of gold bangles glittering at her wrist. The clown pants were worn with a white blouse that had frilly sleeves. If worn with a pair of jeans, it might look fun and cute. But with red-and-yellow striped pants…

"I almost didn't recognize you," he said. "Again."

Maybe because I was told to expect a little black dress.

Behind Sophia, Iva was looking at him with wide eyes while she shook her head and shrugged. His assistant, who prided herself on being in control at all times, looked as though she was about to have a meltdown.

"I guess my new outfit is working, then." She came up beside him and looped an arm through his. The stares and whispers continued.

For some reason, Dion started having flashbacks to the orphanage. That one time the bully kid named Stav decided to pull Dion's pants down in the middle of Mass. Instead of going beet-faced like most kids would have, Dion had waved his pants above his head, making it seem like he was in on the prank.

They'd both been given a ruler over the knuckles.

"I fear my outfit isn't quite as impressive as yours," Dion joked. "In fact, I feel boring as hell by comparison."

She snorted. "You're hardly boring."

"The pants are…something."

"Right?" She looked up at him with wide eyes. "You know, these are all the rage back home. Hot off the runway."

"Really?" He quirked a brow.

"Think of it as a backlash to traditionally uncomfortable things that women wear to impress men. It's a bold fashion statement." She squeezed his arm. "And I like to be bold with my fashion choices."

That certainly seemed in line with what he'd experienced so far.

"You're not embarrassed, are you?" She cocked her head. Was it his imagination, or was there an edge to her voice?

You're definitely imagining things.

"It takes a lot to embarrass a guy who has no shame." He shot her his most charming grin.

"I know my style isn't for everyone," she replied, though her smile seemed a little brittle. "My friends back home would always say you could never tell what I might do in any given situation."

"Duly noted. I will be prepared for anything."

For a moment, Dion questioned his initial assessment of Cyrus Andreou's motives. Maybe the marriage component *was* about finding his daughter a husband, rather than trying to keep claim over the business.

Regardless, the second they were married there wouldn't be a business left to argue over.

"Want to introduce me around?" she asked.

"Absolutely. You're the guest of honor."

Sophia looked at him as though perplexed.

Dion led her over to Nico and his wife. His friend's new daughter, Katherine, was still in Nico's lap, her chubby hands clutching tightly at his finger. "I'd like to introduce Sophia."

Nico raised a brow in open disbelief while Marianna smiled politely, her hands knotted in front of her. Katherine gurgled.

"Sophia, this is my business partner, Nico. We run Precision Investments together. This is Nico's wife, Marianna, and their beautiful little girl, Katherine."

Sophia's expression softened. "She's adorable."

"It's lovely to meet you." Marianna held out a hand warmly and then glared at her husband until he did the same.

"What's with the pants?" Nico asked, and Marianna shot him another look and then rolled her eyes. "What?"

"Honestly," Marianna said. "I can't take him anywhere."

"Why not dress up?" Sophia lifted one shoulder into a shrug. "Life's too short for boring outfits."

"Indeed," Marianna agreed. "I think you look fabulous."

"Thanks." Sophia's reply didn't sound all too cheery.

"How long are you staying in Corfu?" Marianna asked.

"Actually, I've moved here." She smiled up at Dion. "No end date."

This was off-script. They weren't supposed to be announcing anything as yet, although Nico was the only one who knew about the impending marriage. Which meant Marianna would likely know about it, too.

Still, he'd have to keep an eye on what she was telling people.

Marianna clapped her hands together. "How exciting!"

Dion took that opportunity to steer the conversation away from Sophia's reason for being in Corfu. "Sophia was asking about our local hospital last night. She did a lot of volunteer work back home, and she's hoping to find that opportunity here, too."

"You're a hospital volunteer?" Nico nodded, his earlier reserved expression morphing into one of respect.

"Yeah, I am." She bobbed her head. "I used to take part in a sick kids summer program every year."

"That's lovely." Marianna pressed her hand to Sophia's arm.

"Marianna teaches English at the Corfu Town Language Center," Nico added, "but she also volunteers with a refugee support program."

"We're always looking for extra people to help out. If you want to give your time to a nonprofit, we would absolutely love to have you."

A small circle had gathered around them. People were eager to meet the new guest and, of course, have time with Dion. Perfect timing. Because now they were hearing about

Sophia's volunteer work, which would overshadow any clothing choices she'd made.

"I'm sure your hospital back home would be thrilled to give you a reference," Dion said. "They've got your picture up on their website, so they must have been pleased with your work."

Sophia nodded tightly but didn't say anything.

How many more strange quirks was Sophia Andreou going to reveal to him? She'd been chatty last night, talking ad nauseum about her taxidermy hobby. Then today she pulled a bait and switch with her outfit. Now she was suddenly shy and quiet.

What could he possibly expect next?

• • •

Dammit. Dion and his slick moves were humanizing her, making her out to be some Mother Teresa type rather than a tacky princess wearing couture clown pants. How did he do that?

It was a smart move, shifting the focus to her volunteer work. A very smart move indeed.

She remembered the first time she'd asked her dad if she could have a month off work to take part in the children's hospital program for sick kids, and he'd looked so baffled she might as well have asked him if she could borrow his car to drive to the moon. He didn't understand that helping others could be a rewarding experience.

"I'd love to take you out and show you around Corfu," Marianna said. "I've totally fallen in love with the place."

"She knows all the good spots." Nico looked at his wife with pride.

He was handsome, with sharp eyes and thick, dark hair. Along with Marianna's sweet face and large, brown eyes, they made a striking couple. Had Dion been hoping to find someone like that, someone who complemented him?

Sorry to break it to you, but that ain't going to happen with me.

As Dion introduced her around the party, he continued to make reference to her volunteer work, to the fact that she loved helping children. At one point, she'd offered to hold Marianna's little girl, and someone had snapped a picture of them playing together while the baby shrieked with joy.

So much for giving herself a bad reputation in Corfu. It felt like every time she made a move, Dion was quick with a counter, easily dodging her attempts to embarrass him and deflecting with something that made her look good. She'd expected that he might have wanted to shove her into a corner so people wouldn't see her. But he'd seen her move and pivoted with cat-like grace, never letting his charming smile slip for even a second.

After a while, several of the women at the party had asked her where she bought the pants and about the fashion in America, and it became clear her getup wasn't working the way she'd hoped it would. Excusing herself from the party, she slipped inside to clear her head and try to think of her next move.

"You made quite an entrance tonight."

Sophia caught sight of a tall man leaning against the wall inside the hallway. She scanned her memory for his name, but it didn't spring to mind. The introductions all blurred together, face after face, name after name. She wasn't very good with either, unfortunately.

"Theo," he said, as if reading her mind.

"Short for?"

"Wouldn't you like to know." His lips lifted into a wolfish grin.

"Not really. I was trying to be polite." The good thing

about being in a situation where you wanted to actively put people off was that you didn't have to bother with social niceties. *That* she could get used to.

"You're not trying to be polite." Theo's expression shifted, the grin turning to something sharper.

Like Dion and Nico, Theo was also of the tall, dark, and handsome fantasy. What the hell did they put in the water on this island that made all the men so hot? Although she had to say that this particular man had an edge about him that flipped red flags in Sophia's mind. He was powerful and seemed to lack the charm that Dion exuded like a pheromone. Aside from ticking the ultimate "hot Greek guy" fantasy checklist, there wasn't much comparison between the two men. Where Dion made her grudgingly respect him, Theo made her want to back away from the conversation.

"What's that supposed to mean?" she asked.

"You're up to something." He cocked his head. "The honored guest makes a spectacle of herself. Why?"

Sophia swallowed. "You tell me."

"You're making a statement." He narrowed his eyes. "And you're hiding behind that outfit."

The way he looked at her, like he could see every devious thought in her head, made her throat constrict. It felt like she was a bug trapped under his microscope. "Why do you care?"

"I thought we might be able to help each other." Theo pulled a business card out of his jacket pocket and handed it to her.

Theofanis Anastas: CEO Shine Corp. London.

"How do you think you can help me?" she asked.

"You're an American, right?" His dark gaze cut through her like a laser, and Sophia forced herself not to recoil. "Dion has been trying to get his hands on some American company for the last five years. Now, all of a sudden, you turn up looking like the last person he would *ever* have at his party. Not only that, you're his guest of honor."

Sophia's cheeks burned at his assessment. But she could hardly be angry; it was exactly her goal to look as though she didn't belong. So why did his words sting so much?

"He's calling you a family friend, but I suspect there's more to it than that. Marriage, perhaps? An arranged marriage?"

Sophia did her best to hide her surprised reaction. But Theo's laser-like scrutiny picked up even the slightest of movements, and his lips lifted into a smirk.

"Did I get it right?"

"I have no idea what you're talking about." She sniffed. "Now, if you'll excuse me…"

Theo planted a hand on the opposite wall of the hallway, blocking her exit. Bowing his head, he leaned forward. "If you want out of this situation, call me."

At that moment, Sophia's skin prickled as the feeling of being watched crawled over her like a swarm of beetles. At the end of the hallway, Dion rounded the corner. Now the charming smile was gone, replaced by a tight-jawed, crinkle-browed look that made her nervous. But he smothered it so quickly she had to wonder if she'd imagined it.

"Think about it," Theo said as he removed his hand from the wall. "I can help you."

"I don't need your help," Sophia said primly as she forced herself to smile so it looked to Dion like they were two people engaging in friendly small talk. "Enjoy the party."

She headed down the hallway, her heels making soft clicking noises against the tiled floor. Dion's charming mask returned.

Too late, Dion. I saw that look, so I know *there's something under that smile.*

"I thought we might have lost our guest of honor," he

said, holding out a hand.

"I'm still here."

Unfortunately.

She allowed him to lead her outside, where the party was still in full swing. People were clustered around the yard, and the party was louder than it had been before. The drinks seemed to be working their magic, loosening tongues and keeping the conversation flowing. Sophia spotted Nico and Marianna sharing a touching moment while the baby snoozed in her arms, and he leaned over to kiss the top of Katherine's downy head.

For some reason, the image tugged at her heart. Would she ever share that kind of moment with someone? A moment of tenderness and love, unencumbered by manipulation and power plays?

"What did Theo have to say?" Dion asked as he motioned to one of the waiters with a subtle gesture of his hand. A second later, they both had flutes of fizzing liquid.

Sophia took a sip of the ice-cold champagne. Damn, it was good—smooth and crisp. Much like the man of the hour. Dion's dark hair was loose and unstyled. It curled around his ears and kissed the collar of his white shirt at the back of his neck. Despite the very warm evening, he looked cool as a cucumber. His shirtsleeves were rolled up to expose strong forearms and a heavy watch hugging one wrist. He wore a small gold ring on his pinkie finger. It looked old...a family heirloom, perhaps.

"Not much," she said with a shrug. "He asked how I was enjoying Corfu so far."

Dion twisted the ring around his finger as if conscious of her scrutiny. "Anything else?"

She raised a brow. "Are you looking for a particular answer?"

He let out a short bark of a laugh and raked a hand

through his hair. "No, I'm not. I didn't mean to sound like I was giving you an inquisition."

"Who is he?" She'd sensed a tension between the men in the hallway. Theo's offer to help her indicated that there was some bad blood between them or, at the very least, a thread of distrust. Dion's interest now confirmed it.

"That's a complicated question."

Now she was even more intrigued. "Start with the simple answer."

"He's a business acquaintance."

"And the complicated answer?"

Dion looked out over the crowd like a beloved king surveying his people. It was hard not to notice how people flocked to him. Even as they stood deep in conversation, people drifted near, smiling and seeking him out. Power and influence. The man had it in excess. How had he acquired it? That was the important question. Had he bought it? Stolen it? Coerced someone into handing it over? Or maybe he was one of those rare kinds of men who'd earned it.

Even if he did, you've seen what power does to people. What money does to people.

She wanted no part of it.

"The complicated answer would take longer than the amount of time I'm willing to have you standing at the side of this party." Dion grinned and placed his hand at the small of her back.

Despite her thoughts, the soft gesture sent a ripple through her, disturbing her certainty of who he was. The touch made a gentle hum in her blood, a pulse of awareness that made her mind focus on that spot. Through the lightweight silk fabric of her blouse, his strong fingers laid a gentle pressure on her. It was all too easy to imagine how it would feel to have him slip that hand down farther, tracing the curve of her ass.

Sophia gulped, shoving the intrusive fantasy aside and

mentally chastising herself for letting it go that far. Dion was *not* someone she could afford to be attracted to, no matter how he looked or sounded or felt. He had to remain her opponent, or else she'd have no hope of avoiding this marriage.

"He's a dangerous character," Dion added, his voice rough-edged with emotion. "Not someone who has your best interests at heart."

There was a history there. A hurt. Had he invited Theo to save face in some way? It wouldn't surprise her. In the short amount of time she'd known Dion, one thing was clear: he had a Mr. Perfect image, and he wanted to keep it.

Which meant she needed to persist with her plans to be Little Miss *Imperfect.*

Chapter Five

Two days after the party, Dion decided to skip out of work early to visit his mentor. Being the boss meant he could leave whenever the hell he felt like it—though he was more often likely to leave at midnight than he was at 2 p.m. Running a company was hard work. Running a successful investing firm that was ranked in the top ten in all of Europe required sacrifice that most people couldn't even fathom.

Today, however, Dion had too much on his mind to concentrate. After he'd almost flubbed a deal with a wealthy expat from Germany because he hadn't read his preparation pack properly, he knew it was time to tackle the issues turning his brain to jelly. That meant first speaking with Elias. And then, secondly, going home to Sophia.

Dion walked through the foyer of Elias Anastas's home. The grand structure was like a museum with its high ceilings, gallery walls filled with paintings, and wide-open spaces. The sound of his dress shoes echoed through the building as he followed Elias's assistant, Dimi, to the back of the house. Even with a terminal prognosis and recent pneumonia, Elias was still working.

"At least I know he'll give himself some time to enjoy the afternoon if you're here," Dimi muttered as she escorted Dion to the large room where Elias liked to work by the windows that overlooked the Ionian Sea. "Maybe you could have a word with him. He really needs to let himself rest more."

"You think he'll listen to me?" Dion asked with a roll of his eyes. "You grossly overestimate my influence."

"And I think you underestimate it." Dimi pressed a palm to his shoulder and smiled. "He values your relationship very much."

Dion didn't respond. Too many years of masking the emotions that made him vulnerable had left him with a permanent deficiency in that area. He wasn't good at showing what he felt. And knowing that Elias didn't have much time left had Dion relying more than ever on his ability to quash his feelings. But the beasts that were grief and anger and sorrow were growing stronger with each passing day. He'd explode at one point. Nobody could put those things into a box forever.

But he would make sure it happened in a safe space. Alone.

"Dion." Elias looked up and smiled. He was in his wheelchair, one foot propped up in front of him on doctor's orders after twisting his ankle in the fall last week. How he hadn't broken something was a damned miracle. "They only make you work half days now? It's barely lunchtime. Why are you skipping out on work to see me?"

The sound of his voice—weaker than it used to be—made Dion's heart squeeze. Once upon a time, Elias had filled his room with that big, booming voice. Cigarettes had taken that away from him.

"I had a meeting close by," he lied with an easy smile. For

some reason, he couldn't admit that he'd driven over here in a mild state of panic over what he might find. Increasingly, he'd found himself asking whether the end would come today. "Thought I'd drop in on the way back."

"Dimi." Elias motioned for his assistant to come into the room. "Coffee. And bring some of those sticky honey things."

Dimi opened her mouth to argue. The doctor had told Elias to keep an eye on his blood sugar levels. But then she thought better of it and disappeared into the house.

"You can't use me as a way to get around your diet," Dion said.

Elias grinned. "She never argues when you're here."

"How's the ankle?"

He grunted. "Still swollen. Damn thing doesn't want to get better."

"And the breathing?"

"A bitch, as usual."

"And the—"

Elias silenced him with a hand. "If I wanted to be interrogated, I would have called my doctor. When you come, I expect you to make me feel young again, not to remind me that I'm withering away."

Fuck. How could time be so cruel to such a great man? It was too easy to remember Elias when he'd been younger. Not five years ago, he'd bounded up hills like a mountain goat. Now he couldn't even get himself out of his chair.

"How's business?" Dion asked.

"That's a better question." Elias nodded. "Good. Marcus is doing a fine job, although I still maintain that you would have made a better CEO."

"You know I wasn't ready to give up my company."

Dimi came back into the room with two small cups of strong coffee and a tiny plate of *loukoumades*. Dion passed one coffee to Elias and then grabbed the other for himself.

"I know. But you can't blame an old man for trying." Elias bit into one of the sweet honeyed dumplings and sighed. "I know they're bad, but they taste so good."

"That's what you used to say about the cigarettes," Dimi muttered as she fussed around her boss. They'd worked together for close to forty years, and she was more a family friend than an employee.

Elias rolled his eyes and motioned for Dion to hand him another. "Did you hear someone bought the land where the Afionas orphanage is?"

Dion's head snapped up. "Really?"

"Someone made them an offer. More money than it's worth, I heard. Three or four times as much, at least." He reached for his coffee and took a sip. "They're building a new facility."

"And what happens to the kids in the meantime? It could take years to build a new facility. Are they expecting them to live on the street until then?" He placed his coffee cup down a little harder than he intended, and some of the dark liquid sloshed up against the inside of the cup, leaving a drop to dribble over the edge. Cursing himself, he grabbed a tissue and wiped it up. "Is the new buyer providing interim accommodation?"

"They're relocating them for the time being," Elias said softly. "The kids won't be put out on the street."

"How much?" Dion asked, glossing over his slight outburst by moving the conversation along.

"I don't know exactly. Four million…maybe five."

"And the church grounds aren't protected? What would a company want with a place like that?"

"Property developers, apparently. They'll restore the church and other registered buildings on the grounds and then build their accommodation around it."

"Sounds like it will be good for the kids in the end." He

nodded. "Better than when I was there."

At the time, it had been a crumbling and lonely place, but still better than the alternative. Dion had only spent a few nights on the streets of Corfu. Which had been more than enough to instill in him a desire to never, *ever* be without a roof over his head and a meal in his belly. He'd worked damn hard to have security, and it would have to be pried out of his cold, dead hands.

He wanted to tell Elias about his plans to buy his father's business and burn it to ash, and the truth tap-danced on the tip of his tongue. For some reason, he couldn't bring himself to say it aloud—maybe it was because he knew what Elias would say.

The past is for fools and the dead.

If only Dion had been born to a man like Elias rather than his own father. Would Dion be so concerned with the past now? Not likely.

Elias moved the conversation on and, after not too long, his energy waned. Dion bid the older man goodbye with a firm hand on his shoulder—since a hug wasn't something they'd ever shared—and headed home. He tried not to worry about Elias's declining health, just like he did every time he visited. And like every time he visited, he failed to take his mind off it.

Dion was still pondering it when he pulled his car into its spot in the garage and walked into the house. It was the thought he was still pondering when he stalked into his bedroom and stripped off his suit and shirt, ready to head into the bathroom and wash the day—and worries—from his body. But all that came to a screeching halt when he walked through the bathroom door and smack-bang into a fox.

"What the *fuck*?"

• • •

Sophia clamped her hand over her mouth as Dion's surprised cry echoed through the quiet house. Baroness Sasha Foxington III was a fine specimen. She'd arrived earlier that day, thanks to express shipping that had cost a small fortune, wrapped carefully so that nothing had been damaged in transit.

The second she'd heard Dion's bedroom door close, Sophia had put aside her virtual-assistant work and crept out into the hallway, eagerly awaiting his response.

Since the party, he'd worked late and hadn't been around the house much. It had been good to have long stretches during the day to work on her business, since it was the only thing stopping her from spending each passing hour stressing about her future. Unfortunately, more time to work meant less time to convince Dion they were totally and utterly wrong for each other. The sooner she grossed him out enough that he pulled the pin on the whole thing, the better.

Mission Reverse Ugly Duckling was now in full effect.

Sophia had dressed in another one of her "high-fashion man-repeller" outfits, this time consisting of a highlighter-yellow dress. She had a pair of clogs on her feet, and while they weren't super ugly, they were the worst things she'd been able to find that she could actually walk around in.

She headed outside into the backyard, trying not to admire the view of the low sun bobbing at the horizon, where the water created a straight blue line of perfection. Dammit. Why did this place have to look like a freaking postcard?

"I assume this is yours?" Dion asked as he walked out of the house with the fox tucked under one arm.

Sophia had to hold back a snort. If *he* looked ridiculous holding the fox, then she was going to look ten times worse.

Perfect. Score one for the girls.

"Oh, you met Sasha." She manufactured a big smile. "Isn't she a specimen? I knew you would want to see her the *second* you got home. I had her shipped over because I feel quite bereft without my collection. The rest will come soon, but Sasha is my favorite."

Dion looked on with a bland expression. Sophia figured the less his expression showed, the more concerned he actually was…which was a good sign.

"Did you have a good day at work?" she asked sweetly as she set the fox down on the ground next to her.

"Yeah." He nodded.

Silence stretched between them for a moment, and Sophia resisted her natural urge to fill it with chatter. Ever since she was a young girl, she couldn't stand the sound of a long pause in conversation. Usually it represented something bad—like her father slowly blowing up inside because something hadn't gone his way. The silence was often followed by an explosion. Yelling or swearing. Sometimes a broken plate or glass. One time he'd yelled so loud he'd startled a little girl on the street outside their house.

"What about you?" he asked.

"Oh, good. I went for a walk on the beach during my lunch break. It's such a pretty place." It had been glorious to take the chance to wear something normal and get her feet wet in the ocean. Corfu was stunning, and it was a little too easy to imagine herself waking up to that view every morning.

In fact, it had that quiet, natural beauty that she loved so much. Whether it was a densely wooded forest or a pristine beach, Sophia loved being out in nature.

"It was nice to meet your friends at the party," she said, doing her best impersonation of small talk. "How did you and Nico meet? Did you go to school together?"

"Actually, we grew up together." He leaned back in his chair. From this angle, the early evening cast golden light over his skin, making him look even more tanned. His hair was a mess of waves and kinks, like he'd run his hands through it too many times. "At the orphanage."

"Oh." She blinked. Well, *that* was unexpected. Sure, she'd read something about him coming from humble origins to build an empire with his best friend, but she'd had no idea he was an orphan. "And you've been friends ever since?"

He bobbed his head. "Since the day he punched a bully in the face for me when I was four years old."

"So he was your protector?" She reached for a glass of wine that had materialized on the table while she'd been wrapped up in her discovery of Dion.

"We protected each other," he replied. There was something cryptic about the response that had her wanting to ask more, wanting to know him. Which was a very, very bad idea. "What about you? Do you still keep in touch with people from your childhood?"

The question was innocent enough, and she'd been asked it before. But the memories reared up like an ugly monster coming out from under her bed. She'd had a great group of friends in elementary school—a tight-knit gaggle of girls with important shared interests like posters of Zac Efron and shimmery lip gloss. The day she'd moved to middle school, it'd all changed, however, because her dad had plucked her out of her humble local school and stuck her into some elite place where nobody wanted to talk to her.

The other students seemed to know she didn't belong, and nobody invited her to their birthday parties or sleepovers. She'd been a social pariah.

"Not really," she replied noncommittally. "It took me a while to find my feet."

These days, she kept her friendship group small. The fewer people she let in, the less chance there was for her to be shunned. But now they were at an age where everyone was falling in love and getting married, meaning girlie hangouts were becoming less and less frequent. They were forgetting her. Moving on with their lives, while she continued to rebel against her father like she was stuck in her teenage years.

"Nothing wrong with that." Dion looked up as one of the kitchen staff brought out a platter of meats, cheese, and fruit, along with some smaller bite-sized food items. He eagerly reached for a meatball with a toothpick sticking out of it. "I was a late bloomer."

Sophia raised a brow. "I don't believe it."

"Believe it. I was that skinny beanpole of a kid with acne and patchy facial hair until well after it was fair." He grinned, and his endearing, full-lipped smile made her roll her eyes. The guy looked like he'd stepped off the cover of a movie poster. And if the smile was any more perfect, it would have been accompanied by a *ping* sound effect. "You could say I was an ugly duckling."

She smirked at his choice of words. "I *definitely* don't believe it."

"Girls wouldn't touch me."

"That's changed, hasn't it?" The quip came out before she could stop it.

Unfortunately for her, those four little words lit a fire of truth inside her. She was attracted to Dion.

How could she not be? The man was physical perfection. Even in a business shirt and dress pants—which had never been her thing—he looked at ease and comfortable in his own skin. The pale blue shirt sat open at the collar, revealing the tanned column of his neck. His jaw was strong and angled, highlighted by a slight shadow. But it was his mouth that got her. He had full lips, wickedly curved like the lines on a sports car, the kind of lips that were almost too sensual to belong on a man. But somehow, against the backdrop of unabashed masculinity, they were the cherry on top of a perfectly decorated sundae.

They were the kind of lips made for kissing…and she

didn't mean *only* the French kind.

Swallowing, Sophia clamped her legs together, shocked by the sudden pulsing there. This was so not the time to start indulging in fantasies.

Dion cocked his head. "You don't have to worry about that with me."

"Worry about what?"

"About me fooling around."

Sophia shook her head and held up a hand. "I wasn't worrying. I *don't* worry."

Suddenly, a flustered kind of heat washed over her. The absolute denial made her sound defensive, on the back foot. And that was never a place to be.

"I don't care who you sleep with."

Dion frowned. "I'm not sure what your father has communicated to you—"

"Nothing, other than to send me here." It came out more bitter than she'd wanted it to. The truth of her feelings was too close to the surface, too at risk of bubbling over. "He only told me that it was part of your deal."

Dion's frown deepened, creating a crease between his brows. "And you were happy to go along with it?"

God, she wanted to tell the truth so badly. She wanted to scream that she was only here because she was terrified her father would break her mother's fragile psyche if she wasn't there to intervene. That she was worn down by her father's ability to get exactly what he wanted. Frightened that she might not ever realize her dream of a peaceful, independent life.

But those fears were what kept her grip on the last vestige of control. She couldn't trust that Dion wouldn't report back anything she said. What if he called her father and repeated it back to him?

No. It was too risky.

"Of course," she said, wrestling her voice into a smooth, even tone. "My father is very traditional, and he wants nothing more than to see me married to someone with a high standing. And I want to do everything to keep my parents happy."

Her statement didn't appear to ease Dion's concerns. "So, you're on board with this?"

No. I will never be on board with this.

She opened her mouth and then snapped it shut again. The only way this would work was if *he* called off the wedding. Her father would be angry, but he'd have somewhere external to direct his anger. Somewhere *away* from Sophia and her mother.

No matter how much she wanted to answer Dion honestly, she…couldn't.

"Yes, I'm on board." She reached for a piece of melon, but it tasted of nothing. "Are you? You don't seem like the type of guy who needs someone to find him a wife."

"Truthfully?" He pushed the hair back from his forehead. "I never thought I would get married. It wasn't something I saw being part of my life."

"How come?" She shouldn't be interested, but dammit, she was.

"My mother never married," he said, his voice taking on a vague quality, as if he'd lost himself in his thoughts. "Because my father already had a wife. They were having an affair, and she got pregnant."

But he'd grown up in an orphanage. So how—?

"My mother died after I was born, and my father didn't want anything to do with me." The vague quality had taken on a razor edge. *This* was the man behind the charming smile. This was the real Dion. "He was fine screwing young girls on the side, but he didn't want to deal with the consequences. Apparently, he had an important reputation to uphold, or so the sisters at the orphanage told me one day. But I heard them whispering, it wasn't the first time he'd cheated on his wife."

He looked as though he wanted to say more, but he didn't continue.

"Have you ever met him?"

"Once, and I immediately regretted it." He cleared his throat. "But it's water under the bridge. He's dead now."

She waited for more information, but nothing came. This explained a lot—how he was fine with a marriage that meant nothing just to secure a business deal.

"So, there won't be any touching family moments at our wedding, I'm afraid." For a moment, he looked almost… regretful. "But at least you won't have any pesky in-laws to deal with."

"Fantastic," she whispered. A sick feeling settled in the pit of her stomach.

Dion's jaded view of marriage and family would be a hard thing to work against. If he had no expectation of a happy married life, then maybe he would do what was necessary to get his hands on her father's company without any care to what happened after the I dos.

"I, uh… I think I'm going to head to bed." Sophia pushed up from her chair so suddenly that the damn thing almost tipped over. But the need to get some space was clawing at her, panic settling into her muscles, making them twitchy. "Well, good night."

She grabbed the fox and tucked it under her arm before dashing back into the house, her stomach swishing. But then it hit her. The solution was crystal clear, and he'd handed it to her on a silver platter.

An affair.

A fake one, of course. There was no way Sophia would sleep with someone for any reason besides mutual attraction and genuine feelings. To her, sex was never a means to an end. Never a weapon or a tool. It should be an experience shared between two people who care for each other.

But if she *looked* like the kind of wife who'd be unfaithful, then maybe that would be enough for him to pull the pin. After all, it was clear he hated his father and the fact that he'd had an affair.

Guilt stabbed her in the gut. It was a shitty thing to do. A really, *really* shitty thing. But she reasoned that she wasn't actually going to be having an affair with Theo. And concocting a fake affair so Dion would pull the pin was doing them *both* a favor in the long run. Saving them from a marriage that wouldn't be good for either of them. Her father was pulling the strings so he could have what he wanted, and that wasn't fair. It wasn't right.

She was helping Dion as much as she was helping herself.

Sophia dug the cream-and-gold business card out of the drawer next to her bed and turned it over in her hands. Looked like it was time to give Theofanis Anastas a call.

Chapter Six

Dion had been making an effort to leave the office at a more reasonable hour than usual so he could try to spend time with Sophia—although he got the distinct impression she'd been avoiding him since their talk about his childhood. But time was ticking, and with his mentor being sick, he wanted to wrap things up as quickly as possible.

Would anything really change if he closed the deal and started dismantling his father's company before something happened to Elias? Probably not. But maybe there was some childhood logic lurking in there that told Dion if he got it all done in time, then maybe God would see that Elias was effectively Dion's father and spare him. At least for a little while longer.

Therefore, Dion couldn't treat Sophia like she was a ghost in his house, even if that's how she was acting.

He pulled his car into the driveway, the Corfu sun beating down relentlessly through the windshield. It was barely four p.m. and *unheard of* that he would leave the office at such an hour. But he wanted to catch Sophia off-guard in the hopes that he might convince her to come for a walk. Or perhaps a swim.

When he entered the house, it was quiet. No music or talking. No sounds of any kind. That was the very reason Dion's gasp felt like a gunshot. Stuck to the wall in his foyer—looking wholly and utterly out of place among the white marble tile and pale walls—was a picture of a turkey.

A stuffed one…and not the kind he knew Americans ate on Thanksgiving, either.

Oh no. This was a taxidermied turkey, and it came all the way up to Dion's thigh. Its eyes bored menacingly into his, tail fanned out majestically behind it. Dion gulped.

Above it, at eye-level, was another picture of a deer head. Walking as if in a stupor, he continued through the house toward the large, open-plan dining area, where he saw two more pictures taped to the wall with bright green painter's tape. A fox, similar in color to the one Sophia had taken to leaving all over the house, and a cat.

In his study was a picture of a squirrel standing upright on his desk. It had been taped to his desk lamp. The beady black eyes stared at him, as if challenging him to go one step farther into the room. A sinking feeling settled in the pit of Dion's stomach. He would bet all the money in his bank account that there were more animals lurking in his house. Well, print-outs of animals, anyway.

He could only hope these were "inspiration" pictures rather than planning pictures.

A few minutes later, Dion found Sophia in the room overlooking the garden, sitting on the floor and hunched over the coffee table. A jigsaw was spread out in front of her, and she worked, quiet as a mouse, tackling each piece as gently and methodically as an archaeologist might brush the dirt from a fossil.

"Are you turning my house into a menagerie?" he asked.

Sophia jumped, clapping a hand across her heart. "Dion! You frightened me."

"I could say the same for you."

Dion watched her from his vantage point, noting the tangle of dark hair sitting atop her head and the flowy pink dress with buttons all down the front. A pair of fuzzy bunny slippers capped her feet. She didn't have a scrap of makeup on, and her shoulders were tinted pink from the sun. Freckles that hadn't been there a few days ago had started to dust her nose like cinnamon powder, coaxed to life by hours reading and working beside the pool.

Attraction jolted him like a punch to the chest. Sure, the bunny slippers weren't the sexiest things he'd ever seen, but there was something raw and beautiful about her. It was like he'd caught her unaware, before she'd had time to slip a mask on.

"You're home early," she said, her voice a little wary. "I wasn't expecting you for a while."

"I thought a break might do me good," he said.

"And you normally sneak up on your guests?"

"I'm simply returning the favor, given your turkey startled me when I walked through the front door."

"He's majestic, right? I named him Tuttle." Her lips curved, and there was a glint of wickedness. "I've been trying to settle on the perfect home for each piece in my collection. We had our house redesigned a few years back, and the interior designer taped out the measurements of each piece of furniture so she could get an idea of how it would look in the space. I thought I could use that trick with my darlings to see which ones worked best in each room."

So they *were* planning pictures.

"How many do you have in your collection?" he asked, unsure if he actually wanted to know the answer.

"Twenty-three." She cocked her head, frowning. "Well,

maybe a few more than that. I count all the rodents as one, because…well, they're small."

"Rodents?" Dion blinked. "Plural?"

"Yes, I have a few rats and squirrels and a prairie dog. Oh, and a chinchilla." She nodded as though she might be talking about her collection of handbags or lipsticks or an extensive library of books, each of which would have been vastly preferable to a zoo of dead animals. "I'm trying to figure out the best way to have them all shipped over."

Whatever attraction he'd felt evaporated in a puff of smoke. The thought of all those eyes following him as he moved through his house gave him the creeps. He'd always hated the paintings in the orphanage where he'd grown up—it was bad enough being watched by all the nuns, but being watched by the paintings was worse.

"What are you working on?" he asked, nodding to the table, desperate to move the conversation on to something more palatable.

"A puzzle."

"Yes, I got that from all the scattered pieces." He walked into the room, looking over her progress. "What's it of?"

"I have no idea." She laughed when he looked at her strangely. "Seriously. I never really understood the point of a puzzle if I knew what the picture was going to be in the end. Where's the fun in that?"

"Isn't that *how* puzzles are supposed to be done?"

Sophia shrugged. "I was never very good at doing things the way they're supposed to be done."

Her list of quirky habits seemed bottomless. But at least this one wouldn't involve him having to explain to his friends why there was suddenly a turkey by the front door and a peacock in the bathroom.

Things you never thought you would have to say…

He could see she'd started to make progress on a few

sections of the puzzle's edge. The pieces looked to be green with hints of blue, but otherwise there was no real discernible image.

"Can I help?" he asked.

Sophia watched him for a moment, her eyes full of distrust. But in a flash, the expression was gone, and he wondered if he'd really seen anything at all. "Sure."

"What's the strategy?"

"It's easiest to start with the edges and corners. I've put all the edge pieces to one side of the table, and then I start grouping them by color." She indicated to one section of darker green pieces and one of lighter, along with a small pile of blue. "And then I try to fit them together."

Dion's hands drifted to two green pieces that looked like they would fit, and sure enough, they clicked together easily.

"Good job." She grinned, and it felt like the first time Dion had seen a genuine smile from Sophia.

Not a smile she felt like she should be giving or one that was a mask for something else. But a real, sparkling, warm smile. It lit up her whole face, and for a moment Dion was certain this was who Sophia *really* was: bunny slippers and bare skin and blind puzzles and pretty smiles.

On some deep level, his intuition tingled. She'd seemed *very* startled that he'd come home early—was it simply that he'd unintentionally snuck up on her? Or was it something more? Was she different when he wasn't around?

There'd been a hint of vulnerability during their dinner the other night. He sensed an intellect and earnestness lurking beneath her outlandish fashion and behind the taped-up pictures of stuffed turkeys and squirrels. Was it possible that it was all an act? She'd said she was on board with the idea of them being married, on board with her father's wishes...but something was definitely off.

And he was going to figure out what.

Later that evening, Dion sat in his office. The picture of the squirrel stared at him unnervingly, so he torn the photo down and crumpled it in his fist, suppressing a shudder. Then he grabbed his phone and dialled his assistant's number. Iva had worked for Precision Investments for the last five years as both his Executive Assistant and Chief of Staff. She was the person he trusted most in the world, aside from Nico.

"Hi, Dion," she said in a chirpy voice. "What can I do for you?"

"It's something you're not going to like." He leaned back in his desk chair. "And I don't want any questions."

"Well, when you put it like that…" She let out a breath. "At least tell me I'm not going to be committing a crime."

"I need you to follow Sophia while I'm in London."

He was going to be in the UK for two nights, just long enough to close a deal.

"At what point did you add private investigation to my job description?" Iva asked.

"Remember that line at the bottom that says *all other duties as required*?"

She huffed. "Yeah, like accompanying you on business trips and occasionally picking up your dry cleaning if you've been pulling all-nighters. It does *not* include following people around and spying on them."

"If I'm going to marry her, then I need to know what I'm getting into."

A pregnant paused stretched on for several heartbeats. "Excuse me?"

"I was going to think of a more delicate way to tell you, but delicate isn't really my style." He pushed out of his chair and walked over to the window. Outside, the garden glowed under a blanket of stars. "Yes, I'm marrying her. No, we're not in love."

"I wasn't going to ask," Iva replied. "Because I know you better than that."

"You know I'm a heartless bastard?" He laughed.

Nobody had ever called him that, because Dion could handle anyone. After he'd grown up and realized he'd be worth nothing unless he earned that worth himself, he'd gained a reputation for being charming…and disarming. Dion could put out a social fire with little more than a smile. Being on the outside as a child had meant lots of time to observe. And learn.

He learned how to read people, how to gain their trust, and how to peek behind the curtain that almost everyone hid their true selves behind. His intuitions were sharpened like a sword. Which was precisely why he *knew* something was up with Sophia. What that thing was, however, was another issue entirely.

"I know that you believe in the institution of marriage as much as you believe in unicorns."

"I'd say there's a case for unicorns," he quipped.

"Why are you marrying her?"

"Business reasons."

"Do you have any idea how hard it is to be married to someone you love, let alone someone you don't even know?"

Iva was divorced, so he wasn't about to argue that he knew more than her on the subject of marriage. "Marriage is hard work."

"I'm not afraid of hard work."

"And she wants this, too? A loveless marriage with a stranger?"

"She wants to please her father." He didn't quite understand it, but he wasn't going to argue if she was making that element easier for him. "And she'll have a comfortable life with me. Money will be no issue, she has a beautiful home to live in, and she can do whatever she pleases."

"*Whomever* she pleases?" Iva asked.

Dion's nostrils flared.

As far as he was concerned, marriage was still a vow. A promise. Just because they weren't in love—which was another thing he believed in as much as unicorns—didn't mean there weren't promises to be upheld. He wasn't going to be like his father, sleeping around on his wife and wreaking havoc on people's lives. It had felt a little too intense to jump into that discussion already with Sophia, but it would have to happen before they exchanged rings.

He'd put up with a lot of things…but not that.

"I want you to keep an eye on her while I'm gone. Report back. Oh, and I want to know what she's wearing."

"What she's wearing?"

"Yes. What she's wearing, where she goes, if she meets up with anyone. Everything."

"And how the hell am I supposed to do that?"

"She doesn't have a license here, so I've told her she can use one of the drivers. Make sure they call you the second she asks to go anywhere."

Iva sighed. "I'm going to be expecting a fat bonus this year, Dion. If anyone else were asking me…"

"I know. I know." He nodded. "I appreciate it."

Whatever was going on with Sophia Andreou, he was going to find out. If she had any plans of pulling a fast one on him, then he'd be right there to catch her out. He *would* figure out what her real plan was.

• • •

Sophia leaned against the back seat of the Audi and sighed. The weight on her shoulders was far lighter than it had been in weeks. Dion had left for London early that morning, and she'd been roused sometime around five a.m. by the rumble of an engine outside the house.

Now that it was a much more respectable hour, she'd awoken, showered, spent an hour doing website content updates for one of her virtual-assistant clients, and dressed for her trip into Corfu Town to meet with Theo. It was so nice to dress how she wanted. Sure, it probably would have been safer to throw on her scratchy cardigan and lime-green heels to maintain her character, but she was planning to slip out of the house before the staff could see her. And the driver on duty this week was a younger guy Sophia hadn't met previously. So nothing to worry about there.

The car raced along the coastal road, and Sophia had her window down, the breeze whipping her hair around as she enjoyed the view and the warmth on her bare arms. Stupid arranged marriage aside, it really was a beautiful place to be. Blue skies, bluer waters. Lush green trees and colorful buildings that looked like a rainbow selection of ice cream.

If Sophia was being totally honest with herself, it was exactly the kind of place she would want to live. She certainly didn't miss the hustle and bustle of Brooklyn, nor the clanking sound of garbage trucks, the constant rush of traffic and the intermittent wail of sirens that seemed to punctuate the hours there. It was all too easy to see herself in a crumbling little building overlooking the sea, with a huge sunny window for her mother to sit beside and a library heaving with books.

The driver pulled up and let Sophia out of the car. "Just call when you're ready to go home," he said. "I'll be close by."

"Thank you." She stepped out of the car and fished around in her purse for her sunglasses.

Theo had suggested they meet at a little tavern that was tucked away down a skinny alley, one of those out-of-the-way places that would afford them some privacy. Sophia trailed her hand along the building beside her, her shoulders almost bumping the smooth, white surface. On the other side was a courtyard with tables and chairs, and Theo sat with one ankle propped on his knee, the picture of confidence.

"I thought you might not come," he said as she took a seat across from him.

"Why's that?"

"You didn't look too impressed to be talking to me at your big party." His eyes were obscured behind a pair of mirrored sunglasses. But his intent to rile her up was still evident in the quirk at the corner of his lips.

"I wasn't."

"So why call me?"

Why, indeed. Because Theo had a tense relationship with Dion, which made him the perfect person to help her out of this situation. The only question mark hanging over her head was what he would want in return.

"I got the impression we might be able to help each other."

Theo looked like the cat who'd got the cream. He paused while two coffees were brought to the table. "I took the liberty of ordering you a drink. Now, how exactly can I help you?"

Sophia stared into the dark liquid, her stomach tied up in knots. Could she trust Theo? Her gut waved *huge* red flags, but what other option did she have? So far, Dion took all of her antics on the chin. Sure, he didn't exactly look thrilled when she'd walked into the middle of his party ready to draw eyes to her for all the wrong reasons, but he hadn't said a word about it. Nor had he mentioned her clothing, made any disparaging remarks about the fox, or said anything remotely indicative that he might be giving her father's demands a second thought.

She could keep up with her persona, but would it be enough? She wasn't convinced.

"You said that if I wanted out, you could help me." She

tilted her chin up, hoping she appeared a hell of a lot more confident in her decision than she felt.

"So I was right?" He sipped his coffee and leaned back in his chair. "You're a clause in a business deal?"

Acid burned the back of her throat. "Yes."

"I didn't think Mr. Perfect would need to stoop to that level to get a wife," Theo mused. "He must want whatever you're selling *really* badly."

"I'm not selling anything," she spat. "If I was the one doing the selling, then I wouldn't be in this position, would I?"

Theo raised a brow. "Message received. So, if you don't want to marry the guy, why not tell him that?"

"It's…complicated."

"I'm sure it's actually very simple."

Sophia sighed. "My father made this deal with him, and I didn't have a say in it. For the sake of my mother, I need Dion to decide not to go ahead."

"Otherwise your father will be angry?"

"If he only got angry, it wouldn't be such a big deal." Her chest tightened at the thought of what he might do. All of a sudden, emotion swirled inside her. Worries about her mother swam in her head. "He, uh…doesn't accept no for an answer."

Theo's expression shifted. A tightness overtook his jaw and lips, giving his face a hard edge. "I see."

"Can you help me?" she asked, her heart beating so hard it felt like the damn thing had traveled all the way up to her mouth.

"I can." He nodded. "But I'm also a businessman. I don't offer my services for free."

What on earth could he want from her? "And I don't offer myself in exchange for a favor."

"Relax, *asteri mou*. You're not my type." He pulled the

sunglasses from his face as the sun shifted behind a cloud. Now she could see all of him—and the bottomless black pits of his eyes were far more unnerving than not knowing what was behind the mirrored lenses.

"Then what do you want?"

"Something that belongs to me. Dion stole an item, and I want it back." He assessed her with a cool stare, possibly to see if she'd react. She didn't. "My father's ring."

"What does it look like?" She was certain she knew the answer already.

"It's a gold signet design. Square top." There seemed to be a fire in his eyes. Sophia would have bet her last dollar that this had nothing to do with a simple piece of jewelry. "His initials are engraved on it."

"I know the one." It was the only item of jewelry she'd seen on Dion, besides his watch. But it was strange that he'd so brazenly wear an item that he'd stolen.

"Get me the ring, and I'll get you out of your arrangement."

"How?" She shook her head when he didn't respond immediately. "I'm not sure if you're used to people taking you at your word, but I don't know you. I certainly don't trust you. I'd like to know *exactly* how you plan to get me out of this."

Theo cocked his head, those dark eyes running like a laser over her. "It's probably a good thing you're looking to get out of this. A woman like you can bring a man to his knees."

She wasn't sure what he meant by that.

"It's a compliment. You're smart, and he probably hasn't realized it yet." His smirk bloomed into a sharp-edged smile. "More fool him."

Sophia folded her arms across her chest. She wasn't looking to have Theo stroke her ego. "This is the point where you give me the plan."

"You're going to develop a bad habit."

"Another one?" If the taxidermy hadn't worked, then why would another strange habit be more effective?

"Theft. You can't *only* take the ring, or he'll be suspicious. So, you're going to take a lot of things and then I'll out you."

She blanched. "You want me to steal from him?"

"You didn't seem concerned about taking the ring."

"Yes, but," she spluttered. "You said he stole it from you, and, therefore, I'm simply returning it to its rightful owner. That's a totally different situation."

"You don't have to actually steal anything, Sophia. Just hide the items somewhere it'll take him a while to find." Theo sipped his drink. "If he questions you, blame one of the staff."

"No." She shook her head. "I'm not going to make anyone lose their job."

"Do you want out or not?"

She bit down on her lip. "Yes, of course I do. But not like that."

It was one thing to make Dion distrust her, but to ruin someone else's reputation… She would *never* do that.

"Then what did you have in mind? You don't strike me as the type to come to a meeting unprepared."

"I thought we could have an affair."

Theo's expression flickered, something stormy and visceral flashing for the briefest of seconds before he went back to looking perfectly calm again. But the change left Sophia ill at ease. He'd looked mad enough to spit fire. "And I thought you said you didn't trade your body for favors."

"Not a real affair, obviously. A pretend one. Text messages, not-so-secret meetings."

"There are few things in the world that a man hates more than an adulterous wife."

The dark statement sent an icy chill down Sophia's spine. Whatever happened to Theo was none of her business. The only thing she cared about was getting a plane ticket home, and if that meant doing something that skirted the boundaries of her ethics, then so be it. But she wouldn't pretend that one of his staff members had done something illegal. No way. A fake affair would only hurt *her* reputation.

"So, do we have a deal?" she asked.

"No." Theo stood. His eyes were like fire. "I've had enough trouble with one cheating wife. I certainly won't help to fabricate another."

Sophia's stomach sank as she watched him walk away. What on earth was she going to do now?

Chapter Seven

Dion sat in his home office, having a staring contest with his computer screen. The image had come through a good ten minutes ago, and he still didn't quite believe what he was seeing. At a distant glance, it could look like a first date. Cute girl, stylish guy, coffees in the sun. A little awkward.

To Dion, however, he saw it for what it really was: *deceit.*

It was hard to believe the woman in the picture was the same one living in his house. Outside his window, Sophia sat on the grass with a book in her hands. She wore a long dress patterned with swirls of hot pink and mustard, her hair in Princess Leia–style buns and bejeweled sandals on her feet. Music blared from a portable speaker—something called *K-pop*, apparently—and her feet bounced in time to the gratingly perky music.

In the picture, however, she was every bit the wholesome girl next door that her father had described. Dark, glossy hair in a bouncy ponytail, a slim figure enhanced by a yellow dress that floated down to her knees. Across from her was one of the only men in the world who could make Dion's mask dissolve faster than an ice cube dropped into boiling water.

Theo Anastas.

Dion's lip curled into a silent snarl. That bastard. What the hell was he doing with Sophia? His desk phone rang, and Dion snatched the receiver up.

"Iva?"

"You got the picture?" she asked. He could imagine the unimpressed expression on her face.

"Yes, I got it." His nostrils flared as he looked at the picture again. "What were they talking about?"

"I don't know. It was a small place, and you're lucky I got this shot without getting caught. What did you expect me to do, sidle up beside them wearing a bush as a disguise?" She huffed. "There were no free tables and nowhere for me to stand without it looking obvious."

"So you didn't hear anything?"

"No. But if you think she's cheating on you, then you're wrong. I didn't get that vibe at all."

Truthfully, he didn't get that vibe from the photo, either. Dion had become an expert in reading body language growing up. Being a lover rather than a fighter, he'd used his communication skills to get by. Nico was the one who could throw a punch, but Dion prided himself on managing a situation before it got to that point.

People had certain tells when they were attracted to someone. They would angle themselves toward the object of their affection, pointing with their feet, knees, or torso as if magnetically closing the distance. If a couple was trying to be subtle, there would still be something. Intense or frequent eye contact, touching of the hair or face.

But the picture showed Sophia sitting with her hands knotted in her lap, her legs tucked beneath her chair as her body twisted slightly away from the table. They were small signs indicating she didn't want to be there. Theo, on the other hand, appeared to be relaxed. But there wasn't a single thing that pointed to it being a meeting between lovers.

What on earth could they be conspiring about?

The only thing he knew for certain was that she was hiding something from him. Elias's greatest lesson had been to take notice of how people acted when they thought nobody was watching—because that was when the truest self was visible. Sophia was hiding behind her wacky wardrobe and her taxidermy hobby and her apparent acceptance of their arrangement.

But confronting her with questions wouldn't likely yield an honest answer, because he'd asked her multiple times if she was comfortable with the arrangement. To which she always said yes…but her actions indicated otherwise. He needed to engineer a situation where she tripped up.

"What are you going to do?" Iva asked.

"I'm going to act like nothing is wrong," he replied, shutting his computer down. "As far as I'm concerned, this marriage is going ahead."

"Is it worth it, Dion? You clearly don't know very much about this woman." The concern in Iva's voice was touching but misplaced. He didn't need her concern. He didn't need *anyone's* concern. "Something is going on."

"It doesn't matter. I need her father's company. End of story."

"I don't know where this is coming from. But do you really want—"

"You don't know what I want," he said calmly. Nobody knew.

"No, I clearly don't. Because I saw the paperwork for her father's company and I decided to do a little research. It's riddled with debt. I know it's not my place to question your business decisions, but—"

"This isn't a business decision. Precision Investments

isn't buying this company, *I* am."

"What is going on, Dion? This isn't like you to be skulking around, spying on people."

"It's nothing you need to worry about."

"But—"

"This isn't your business," he said firmly.

He valued Iva because she was by far one of the smartest, most hardworking assistants he'd ever come across. But his patience was hanging by a thread. Not because of Sophia's games. Not because she was acting like someone else behind his back. It had nothing to do with her...and everything to do with Theo.

"I have to go. Please have the papers couriered to my home office." He ended the call and pushed up from his leather office chair.

Right now, he had one thing—and one thing *only*—on his mind: making sure Sophia wasn't going to ruin his plans.

An hour later, Dion was leading Sophia through the streets in Corfu's city center. Her psychedelically colored dress swirled around her feet, and she had a huge floppy straw hat on her head—for sun protection, apparently.

"Where are we going?" she asked. Her dark eyes looked mysterious in the shadow of her hat—giving her an almost fifties-movie-starlet kind of vibe...if he didn't look at her dress, that was.

Today she'd left her face bare, and Dion found his eyes wandering to her full lips. On most people, the eyes were the most expressive part. But Sophia's lips could tell a story—they quirked whenever she was amused and flattened when she was annoyed and pouted ever so slightly when she was stuck in thought. They were beautiful lips, full and sensuous and so naturally pink one might think she was wearing lipstick.

She's a liar. Sexy lips don't change that.

"Don't you know the meaning of surprise?" Dion asked with a smooth smile. Artificial, of course, but they were trending more that way of late.

"I'm not sure I *like* surprises."

He chuckled. "You're good at giving them. I figured you'd be open to receiving them as well."

She pursed her lips but didn't say anything in response. Had his comment stirred some worries that she might have been caught out? Good. Let her stew.

"This way." He indicated for her to follow him down another street. They were almost there. When the opulent front of the luxury bridal store came into view, Sophia paled. "Surprise. We're going wedding-dress shopping."

"We haven't even announced the engagement yet." Her voice sounded a little off. Like something had constricted her lungs, giving her words a breathless quality. "Technically, you haven't even proposed."

"We can go ring shopping later."

His assurance seemed to do little to put her at ease. "I thought the groom wasn't supposed to see the dress. Isn't that bad luck?"

"You'll come to know this about me, Sophia." He placed his hand softly against her arm. This game of cat and mouse was going to draw to a close, and he was determined to be on the feline side of that equation. "I don't much care for tradition. We can make our own rules, don't you agree? Now, come on. I've arranged a private session with the owner."

He rang the doorbell, which was a fancy mother-of-pearl button laid into an ornate gold casing. No doubt that small detail was meant to reassure clients that every aspect of their experience would be carefully thought through, with no detail too small to warrant a luxurious touch.

A second later, while Sophia still eyed the shop with wariness, the owner, Annalisa, answered the door. As a former recipient of Precision Investments' "Young People in Business" award, she'd been quick to agree to Dion's request for a favor. As usual, her black hair was pulled up into a plump bun, and her signature red lipstick was artfully applied and matched the vibrant floral print on her black dress.

"Dion!" She leaned in and offered him a kiss on each cheek. Then she turned to Sophia. "And you must be Sophia. It's an absolute pleasure to meet you. Please, come in."

The inside of the bridal store was everything the doorbell promised—decadent, special. Rows and rows of frothy white gowns ringed the circular main room, broken only by a large section of mirrors surrounding a podium raised about a foot off the ground. Several cabinets dotted the space, filled with twinkling jewels and tiaras and gloves. He supposed many women wanted the true Disney Princess experience on their big day…some of them perhaps cared more about *that* element than what marriage actually meant.

"Now, Dion has given me *lots* of information about the kind of clothes you like." Annalisa's tone didn't hint at any shenanigans. "I understand you've got a really unique, quirky style, and we can absolutely make sure that's reflected in your wedding gown."

Sophia's face was as white as paper. "Really?"

"Of course. A woman's big day needs to reflect *who* she truly is. We want you to be yourself." Annalisa grinned. "Now, if you'll follow me this way, we can get you into a changing room and start trying on some dresses. I understand you're from America…"

Dion took a seat on one of the velvet couches facing the podium and leaned back against the plush material as he watched the two women disappear into the back of the boutique. He was going to get the truth out of Sophia, even if he had to make her try on every damn dress in this place. If something was up and she really didn't want to marry him, *this* should be the right button to push.

• • •

Maybe she was dreaming. It seemed the only logical explanation for this crazy-ass Twilight Zone she'd landed in. One where she was trying on wedding dresses and constantly talking about her love of stuffed animals while everybody acted as though it was a perfectly normal thing to do.

"Now, I always say that a bride knows the dress is 'the one' in much the same way they knew their fiancé was 'the one.'" Annalisa ran her hand over a small rack of gowns, pushing the hangers to one side as if looking for something. Each hanger made a slight sound as it was pushed aside. *Clink, clink, clink*. "You'll get a flutter in your tummy. A special feeling that tells you something special is about to happen."

Ugh, one ticket to vom town, please. Pass me a bucket.

This whole froufrou thing was so *not* Sophia's jam. She'd always envisaged a simple wedding day—close friends and family only. A simple dress, maybe in white. Maybe in something softer, like cream or eggshell. Perhaps even a pale gold. Certainly no ball gowns and diamanté and tulle. She could see herself skipping a veil altogether, holding a handful of flowers picked from someone's garden. Maybe she'd even stick one behind her ear.

But this…

Oh. Dear. Lord.

"Why don't we start with this one?" Annalisa beamed as she held up what looked to be a wedding gown that had consumed several smaller wedding gowns like some kind of grotesque satin-and-sequin-encrusted monster. "What do you think?"

It looked exactly like the kind of thing "Fake Sophia" would enjoy.

"It's very…artistic." Her voice almost gave out on the last word.

"Let's get you into it. There's no way to know how it's going to look until we put it on you." Annalisa motioned for her assistant to come over and help.

Sophia stripped down and climbed into the dress. It took the other two women to lift it up and get it over the shoulders. That's how much beading there was. A giant silk-and-organza flower sat on one shoulder, and another rested on her opposite hip. The enormous skirt was poufy and made of so many layers that Sophia had no idea how she wouldn't melt in such a dress. Not to mention the fact that it was so tight she could barely breathe. As the assistant did the buttons up her back, Sophia wanted to cry.

This wasn't a wedding dress. It was a torture device!

"How do you feel?" Annalisa beamed. "We chose this one for you to try on because Dion told us how you seem to love lots of details in your outfits."

Translation: you dress like a freak.

"It's a designer piece." She rolled off the name of the designer, though Sophia didn't recognize it. Why would she? Until two weeks ago, she had no idea she was supposed to be getting married. "Let's put on the matching headpiece, too, so we can get the full effect."

The assistant produced a large flower, which they clipped to the side of her head. It was so hideous that she was practically rendered speechless. "I don't even know what to say."

"It's definitely a statement piece."

Sophia was aware of that, but she was sure the statement it made to her wasn't quite what Annalisa or the designer intended.

"And don't worry," Annalisa continued. "If you don't completely love this one, I have fifteen more dresses picked out."

Fifteen. More. Dresses.

Kill me now.

If she was forced to try on every one, then it might simply be easier to let herself be eaten by the tulle monster. She could go peacefully into the night, surrounded by white satin and billowing fabrics. It would be dramatic, sure, but she could pretend she was in an eighties-power-ballad film clip. Maybe David Bowie would be waiting for her at the pearly gates of heaven?

"Ready to show your man?" Annalisa clapped her hands together. "This is always my favorite bit."

It was official. Sophia was going to die of mortification in the ugliest wedding dress in history. For some reason, the thought of Dion seeing her like this made her feel so much worse than all the outrageous outfits she'd picked for herself. At least those ones had come under her control. But the thought of having to go out in public looking like this…

Tears pricked the backs of her eyes. "I don't have words."

"That's a good sign." Annalisa clapped her hands together. "I always know my brides are falling in love when there's tears. Come on, let's show Dion."

"Oh, I don't think—"

"Don't be silly. He wants to do this for you." She laid a hand on Sophia's arm. "So many women would kill to have a guy be involved like he is. Let's not leave him out of the action."

Without giving her a chance to respond, Annalisa grabbed Sophia's hand and led her back out to the main area of the boutique. Her assistant followed behind, holding the train and making sure it didn't catch on anything. Suddenly, Sophia felt hot all over…and not in a good way. The tight dress and intense lighting of the store were making her head swim. Maybe she should have had something for breakfast after all.

"Okay, dress number one!" Annalisa made a grand gesture to Sophia and helped her step up to the podium. All the while, she rattled off the details of the dress—hand-sewn Swarovski crystals, couture beading, specially designed boning in the bodice and the one-of-a-kind design.

No wonder it was one of a kind—finding one person who truly loved this monstrosity would be difficult enough.

"Wow." Dion raked a hand through his hair. The silence was thick, like an oppressively muggy day.

"Wow, good or wow, bad?" Sophia asked. She pressed her hands to her stomach.

"It matters more what you think." He offered her a smile, but it didn't seem to reach his eyes. "Do you love it?"

"I..." She swung her head to the bay of mirrors in front of the podium. It reflected the hideous design from almost every angle. She'd never, ever felt so...not like herself. "How much is it?"

"Twenty thousand euro." Annalisa smiled as though she'd said a number that was vaguely normal.

Dion nodded. "The price doesn't matter, Sophia. I want you to find a dress that makes you feel good."

Twenty thousand euro. Her mind couldn't compute the figure, and her breathing became shallower and shallower.

"It's very tight."

"Oh, that's fine. We can get it adjusted, no problem." Annalisa tapped a red lacquered finger to her chin. "I think maybe the flower headpiece is a bit much."

No shit, Sherlock.

Annalisa unclipped it and placed it carefully onto one of the empty couches. She held up a finger, indicating for them to wait while she went to one of the cupboards and pulled out a tiara. And it wasn't just any tiara. This one was made up of hearts studded with twinkling pink stones. It looked like the grown-up version of something a little girl might dig out of a cereal box.

In her real life, Sophia hated all this over-the-top wedding stuff. So much money for one day—like the total of a couple's bill was an indication of how well the wedding would last. One of her friends who had gotten married had been forced to invite three hundred people on the day—half of whom she didn't even know personally. But her parents were convinced that the wedding was a reflection of the family's position. The next friend to get married had invited three-fifty.

Sophia had promised herself she would never engage in that kind of gross excess. Nor that icky "keeping up with the Joneses" that obsessed her father. And yet, she was standing in a twenty-thousand-euro wedding dress, feeling smaller than a dormouse and uglier than a cave troll.

When Annalisa placed the tiara on her head, she had to fight the urge to rip the damn thing off and hurl it across the room. This wasn't her! Why was she finding this so tough now? She'd been playing this role since she arrived almost a week and a half ago.

She knew the reason.

It's because her mother would see her like this. Dion had somehow—against all odds—accepted her quirks, manufactured as they were. Which meant that there was a strong chance she might not get out of this.

Yes, you will. You'll find a way.

But her current plan wasn't working, and Theo had refused to help her. Well, they'd refused each other, really. But she certainly wasn't going to steal from Dion and blame his staff.

What if she had to walk down the aisle wearing this ugly dress, handing over her freedom and ensuring she was no better than her mother?

She glanced at Dion. Sure, he was handsome, and apparently he was generous enough to want to spend an inordinate amount of money on a dress he thought she'd like. But that was nothing more than him dressing up a doll. He didn't know her…the *real* her.

But one thing was abundantly clear: the fake Sophia had failed. Her scratchy-cardigan-wearing, taxidermy-loving, classless persona had failed to repulse Dion. She'd lost. The game was over. And that meant it was time to get out of this damn dress.

"I hate it," she said, and it was like a weight lifted off her shoulders. "This dress should be burned in a fire."

Annalisa blinked at her, but Dion didn't show an ounce of shock. The corner of his lip lifted a hair…but that was all Sophia needed to know that she'd walked straight into the spider's web.

Chapter Eight

"I hate it." She repeated the words while twisting on the spot, desperately trying to reach the buttons behind her. "I hate it, I hate it, I hate it."

Dion watched for a moment, his eyes flicking to Annalisa in a silent request for her not to intervene. Did it make him cruel that he wanted to see Sophia squirm? It seemed only fair, given she'd been lying to him ever since she came to Corfu.

Huffing a piece of hair out of her eyes, Sophia continued to twist and turn to no avail. When she eventually stopped and looked at him for help, Dion rose off the couch. "Could you give us a minute?" he said to Annalisa, who nodded and motioned for her assistant to follow her out of the room.

There was a standoff between them. Sophia's big, brown eyes were like lasers cutting away the layers of his skin, stripping him down to nothing. But Dion wasn't the kind of guy who would shy away from confrontation. Sure, he was a lover. Sure, he could talk his way out of anything. But the fact was, if it came down to it, he had zero issue standing his ground. His "fiancée" was about to learn that.

"Do you want me to help you out of the dress?" he asked.

"Unless you want to pay twenty thousand euros to watch me rip this monstrosity off my body, yeah." Her cheeks were scarlet, and her chest heaved against the confining dress. Each breath made her breasts push against the neckline.

Calmly, to show he was the one in control, he walked up to the podium. Even without stepping onto it, he matched her height. Sophia was petite all over, but the dress looked as though it had been made to fit the lanky, long-limbed frame of a runway model. It swamped her, drowned out the curves that suited her so well. His fingers started work on the fiddly buttons, popping each one through the fabric loop holding the dress securely shut. There was an angry red mark on her skin where the bodice had cut in.

He frowned. A deep urge made him want to kiss that line, to soothe the mark as he continued to undress her.

No way. You don't know what you're up against yet. Always know where you stand before you cross a line.

"Better?" he asked when he got to the last button.

"Yes." She nodded. "I was feeling panicky."

"No wonder. That thing had you like a vice."

She cupped her hands over the bodice to keep the dress up. He could tell from her naked back that she wasn't wearing a bra. Hanging on a hook nearby was a collection of silky pink robes. He handed her one and turned while she slipped it over her shoulders, then he helped her to step out of the dress. Even without a body to hold it upright, the dress didn't completely fall down. The bodice sat up straight in a large pile of fabric, almost as if the person wearing it had melted away.

For some reason it made him think of the Wicked Witch of the West.

"Has this been fun for you?" she asked, swallowing. Her

arms were wrapped around herself as though she needed a layer of protection. The pale pink silk brought out the flush in her skin, giving her face life and making her dark eyes look even more arresting.

"I can't say wedding-dress shopping is one of my personal hobbies," he said drily. "But isn't that what a good fiancé should do? Be supportive of his bride?"

Her nostrils flared. "Don't act like this is a genuine gesture. You brought me here for a reason."

"To pick a dress."

She rolled her eyes and looked around the store. "Right."

"If anyone is going to admit to having ulterior motives, it should be you." He shoved his hands into his pockets.

"What on earth do you mean?" Her tone was saccharine sweet, but he didn't miss the angry glint in her eyes.

"Where to start? Firstly, there was the incident at the airport." He ticked the item off his index finger.

"Where *you* thought I was begging for money."

"Then there was the cocktail party." He ticked the second item off his middle finger. "The clown pants were an interesting touch. Then the taxidermy hobby and that damned fox. But none of that was enough to make me think you had something up your sleeve. In fact, you were so good I totally bought the 'quirky girl' act hook, line, and sinker. Well done."

She averted her eyes for a second, as if guilt had dragged her gaze away. Then she drew her bottom lip between her teeth and gnawed on it.

"But you made a critical error." He stepped onto the podium, causing her to take an instinctive step back. Now his height was on full display, and Sophia had to tilt her head up to make eye contact. "You assume I don't know what my staff are up to at all times of the day."

Dion could tell she was wracking her brain, trying to

figure out what he was referring to. He could let her stew in the uncertainty a while longer, but he was done with the game. He wanted everything out in the open.

"My driver."

She sucked in a breath.

"He dropped you off at a quaint little street yesterday, right near a nice tavern. Good place for a coffee with friends. I was interested to hear what you were wearing." He narrowed his eyes. "Which would have been puzzling but not concerning if I hadn't found out *who* you were meeting."

"You had me followed?" She bobbed her head. "Now I don't feel so guilty for assuming you were a controlling asshole like my father."

"Ah, so the truth finally comes out." The victory was hollow. "It's about time."

"Why do you care what the truth is so long as you get me down the aisle? All you give a shit about is getting your greedy hands on my father's company."

"*Your* father was the one who demanded the marriage, not me. So your ire is misplaced."

"And yet you're happy to marry a stranger for the sake of a business deal? You could make a hundred deals just like it without the wedding contract." Her eyes glittered now, like angry stars. "Why say yes?"

Perhaps this whole "poor damsel" thing was an act. Dion didn't trust easily, and Sophia had pushed all his buttons in the last twenty-four hours. But her reaction now seemed genuine. Her resentment was palpable.

Did he even want to marry someone who was so clearly against the idea?

Dion swallowed. The truth was, no. He didn't. But the thought of letting his father's name live on in the company Cyrus now owned... It made him feel sick. Just as sick as the time he tracked his father down, hoping for a reunion befitting people who were connected by blood, only to be rejected in the cruellest of ways. His father's harsh reaction had swiftly ended any fantasies Dion had that they might one day become a family. That one day he might be loved by the man who created him.

As far as he was concerned, his father didn't deserve a legacy.

Not that he could confess his real reason for wanting Cyrus's newly acquired business—she might have been fond of her dad's old boss. Maybe she knew him like a kind uncle. Maybe he was like family to her. And Dion didn't want to hear a good word spoken about his father. Not to mention that if she knew, she'd probably call the whole thing off. Or clue her father in. And he couldn't have that.

So he'd have to walk the gray area of his morals by doing something good—giving Sophia a comfortable life of freedom that could cater to her every whim—to offset the bad—marrying her with an ulterior motive. It wasn't perfect. But for a boy who'd grown up with nothing and nobody, he'd never had the luxury of letting perfect be the enemy of progress.

"It will be better to show you than tell you," he said. "If you give me the afternoon, I'll show you exactly why I said yes."

Sophia regarded him with bottomless chocolate eyes that revealed nothing. "Why should I hear you out?"

"You don't have to." He was taking a risk now, calling her bluff. "If you really want out of this arrangement, then I'll call your father right now and tell him that I won't marry someone who isn't a willing party. I can have you home by tomorrow morning."

Her face paled, the pink draining out of her cheeks in a way that told him a lot more than any words that might have left her mouth. Clearly the "happy family" image he'd been sold by both Cyrus and Sophia was a fabrication. Or, at the very least, an embellishment. Which explained why Sophia had lied when he'd asked if she agreed to their arrangement.

Was Cyrus involved with Theo? Had they set this whole thing up? He wouldn't put it past either man.

"We don't have to do that," Sophia said, shaking her head.

"Why don't we get you back into your clothes and go for a drive? We can start over, be more honest with each other."

Swallowing, she nodded stiffly. "Sure."

If Sophia or her father or Theo had any plans to screw him over, then he was going to do everything in his power to stop them. Dion had his plans, and he was going to see them through.

• • •

After a quick stop at home so she could change, Sophia sat beside Dion in his car as they curved around Corfu's eastern coast. They were approaching the top of the island, around the point at which Greece gave way to Albania on the mainland. Over the Ionian Sea, there were shadowy hills and crests in shades of dusky blue and green. It had become hazy today, giving the view a mystical appearance.

They rounded a corner and started up a steep driveway shrouded by dense trees and shrubberies. Eventually, they came to the front of a house that was so magnificent Sophia had to force herself not to gasp. Everything was covered in bright, white stone, offsetting the color of the sky and trees perfectly. The huge sweeping driveway ringed a fountain, where blue water glittered. A man came over to open the car door when Dion killed the engine. What kind of a house had its own valet?

"*Kalos irthate*," the man said with a friendly smile. He

waited while Sophia exited the car and shut the door behind her, all the while chatting in Greek.

Dion returned the conversation as the three of them headed into the house. On the inside, the building was even more opulent. White marble, exotic plants, and gold frames housing artwork so stunning Sophia wanted to stop and stare at every single piece.

"Are you going to tell me what we're doing here at some point?" she asked.

"Soon."

Ever since they'd left the bridal shop, her mind had been whirring. He'd certainly stopped her in her tracks by offering to call her father and send her home. Tempting as it was to fly off this island, the consequences killed that fantasy dead in the water. If Dion told her father she wasn't a "willing party" then this would all be for nothing. Her father would make sure there was hell to pay. But hope was slipping through her fingers like grains of sand. And the tighter she tried to clutch them, the faster they fell.

A woman with a severe bun and inquisitive eyes led them to a room at the back of the house. When she opened the doors, Sophia's heart clenched. A man sat in a wheelchair by a window, a blanket draped over his lap. His white hair was thick and shiny, but his pallor didn't look healthy. Sunlight bounced all around him as his head lay back, his mouth open slightly as he dozed.

He still had a pen and paper in his hands.

"Should I wake him?" the older woman asked, looking at Dion.

He shook his head. "It's fine. We'll wait."

He took a seat in a richly upholstered chair outside the room. Today, he'd worn jeans and a linen shirt, which had rumpled slightly during the drive. Instead of making him look messy and unkempt, it added an air of attainability to what was otherwise wholly unattainable.

Unless you happen to be up for grabs in a business deal.

Sophia swallowed down the sour thought. She took the seat next to Dion and watched the sickly old man. The woman had left the door open so they would know when he woke up.

"I'm guessing he's not a relative," Sophia said, wincing as the man coughed in his sleep. She knew the sound—the rattling, hollow sound of someone whose lungs weren't working the way they were supposed to. She'd heard it too many times in the hospital from patients who had breathing disorders.

Dion shook his head. "No, but he's the closest I'll ever get."

Despite her feelings about Dion and the deal he'd struck with her father, his statement reached into her chest and grabbed hold of empathy that shouldn't have been there. How lonely the world must feel without any family at all? Sophia had no idea what she would do without her mother, broken as their relationship was. Because the memory of what her life had been before her father's chosen career intruded on their lives kept her going.

"This is Elias Anastas."

Sophia frowned. She instantly recognized the surname. Surely that wasn't a coincidence.

"Yes, he's Theo's father." Dion leaned forward and braced his forearms on his thighs, his head bowed slightly. "They've been estranged for years."

A sinking feeling settled in the pit of Sophia's stomach. Her intuition that something had been fundamentally off between Dion and Theo was clearly on the money.

"Elias has been my mentor for over a decade. He was doing a guest lecture at the university in London where I had a scholarship, and he inspired me so much that I went up to him after the class and told him I would do *anything* if he would take me under his wing." Dion raked a hand through his hair. His voice was softer than she'd ever heard it, less polished and more…raw. "I started working for him after I graduated, and he taught me everything I know. He helped me set up my business, and even now I go to him when I need someone to bounce ideas around with. Our relationship was…*is* very important to me."

Was. He was already speaking like the man had already gone. Probably preparing himself for the inevitable. As if to support that theory, one of the machines attached to the old man beeped softly. He stirred and shifted in the wheelchair but didn't wake.

"Elias looked at me like a son, and I looked at him like a father," Dion continued. "Theo and Elias's relationship has always been strained. There was an incident some years back where a lot of money went missing, and he found out it was his son stealing from him. Theo moved overseas, and they haven't spoken since."

"They're *still* not speaking?"

"I don't think so. Theo has been skulking around since it became apparent that Elias's diagnosis was more severe than we first thought, but I don't think it's because he cares that his father could die soon." Dion made a noise of disgust. "He was the son of a marriage much later in Elias's life. His wife was nothing but a gold digger, and when it became apparent she wasn't going to get anything out of him, even with a child, she started shopping around for another husband. Eventually Elias kicked her out, and Theo went with her."

Such a tangled family history. Maybe her own family wasn't so unusual after all.

Dion toyed with his ring as he spoke, his lithe fingers twisting it over and over. So, he was the son Elias wished he'd had, and Theo was the thieving son cast aside…at least if Dion's story could be believed.

"What has this got to do with you acquiring my father's

company?" she asked.

"Elias was going to buy the company before your father took possession of it, but then he got sick. I want to finalize the sale before..." His jaw ticked.

Dion's gaze was full of fire, turning his dark eyes molten. Passion oozed from his every pore, and instead of making Sophia want to run, it had her enraptured and rooted to the spot. *This* was the man behind the charming, slick persona. Behind the bespoke suits and the fancy cars and the successful image. And she couldn't look away.

"I want him to know he's the only father I ever needed."

The words didn't totally make sense to Sophia, but the meaning was clear enough: he wanted to make Elias proud. His father figure, since he'd never had a father of his own, was dying, and he wanted to give him the gift of seeing his success.

"You don't think he'll get better?" she asked softly.

"The prognosis isn't good." A line deepened between his heavy brows.

"How long?"

"Not long enough." For a second it looked like there might be a tear glittering in his eye, but he blinked, and it was gone. Perhaps it was a trick of the light. "Six months, maybe. If we're lucky. More likely less."

A lump formed in the back of her throat. "I'm so sorry."

She shouldn't feel his pain. Hell, he probably brought her here to manipulate her into doing what he wanted. But unless the man had missed his calling as an Oscar-worthy actor, his grief was real. Because the love he had for Elias Anastas was undeniable. Unmistakable.

It was the kind of love that caused someone to do things they normally wouldn't. Things they possibly didn't *want* to do. She recognized it because it was the exact same love she had for her mother.

In a way, she and Dion were the same.

"Why was Theo at your party, then? If he's estranged from his father and you're the…" She bit down on her lip.

"The replacement?" His laugh was hollow.

"I didn't mean it like that."

"It's true, I guess. And I invited Theo because I wanted to see what he'd do. I don't trust him, so I figured it was better to keep him close." He shrugged. "I hate him for what he did to Elias. I know it broke his heart. So forgive me if I sound like a bastard, but the fact that you snuck off with him… I was incensed."

"I don't know what you don't tell me," she replied quietly. "I'm not clairvoyant."

"And I can't tell you anything if I don't know *who* I'm dealing with." His gaze flicked to hers. "So can we cut the persona now? Can I please talk to the real Sophia Andreou?"

She bobbed her head. "You're talking to her now."

"Why did you meet with him?"

She dug her nails into her palms, making crescent-shaped indentations. "He gave me his card at your party. I called him, and we had coffee. End of story."

Just because she wasn't going to hide behind ridiculous outfits and an outlandish fake personality didn't mean that she'd open herself up to Dion. *Or* let on what Theo had asked her to do. If Elias was sick and there was tension between the men, she was hardly going to pour gasoline on an already-burning fire. She knew how unbearable angry men were—her father was a prime example. She'd refused Theo's offer, anyway.

And he'd refused hers.

Learning Dion's motives for wanting her father's company—understandable as they now were—didn't change a thing. She still wanted out of this marriage in a way that wouldn't cause her family to implode.

For her to have what she wanted, he would need to give up his dream. And vice versa.

Chapter Nine

The meeting between Elias and Sophia had left him with a funny feeling in his gut all afternoon long. His mentor had been well and truly charmed by the bubbly American, her tinkling laughter punctuating all Elias's jokes and her hand coming to rest on his shoulder as they talked animatedly about their shared love of Alfred Hitchcock movies.

The worst thing was, however, that Dion had been utterly charmed, too.

It seemed the real Sophia was frighteningly close to the kind of woman he gravitated to—warm, well-rounded, a good conversationalist, interested in creative mediums such as music and art. The fact that she shared his passion for old movies was an unusual check mark.

But he remained silent through the entirety of the meeting, his brain whirring at this turn of events. Perhaps he'd been looking at this all wrong. Rather than trying to give Sophia space to come around to the idea of being married to him, he needed to tempt her toward it.

Seduction.

It wasn't a strategy he generally used. He preferred to rely on a charming presentation of the facts over selling a dream. But it wouldn't exactly be a stretch to seduce Miss Sophia Andreou.

As she exited the car in front of his house, the wind kicked up the edge of her dress and sent it flapping around her slim thighs. Without her retina-searing costumes distracting his eyes, it was easy to see how beautiful she was. How attracted he would have been on first sight if they'd met under the usual circumstances. Her dark hair gleamed as it fell down her back in gentle waves, and her fair skin was starting to tan under the persistent Greek sun.

But to Dion, physical attraction was only one part of the equation. One part that, alone, didn't satisfy him. Corfu had more than its share of beautiful women, so if that was all that was required, then he could have taken his pick. But he wasn't the kind of man to sell himself short. And so it wasn't until he'd seen Sophia come out of her shell with Elias that he'd truly been struck with desire…and the thought of how he could best deal with this situation.

By getting close to Sophia, he might be able to show her the potential their marriage could yield, and he might gain her trust enough that she would admit the real reason for her meeting with Theo. Because he *wasn't* buying the noncommittal story of a coffee and chat.

"Do you have a bathing suit?" he asked as they walked toward the front of his house.

Her hair danced around her shoulders, disturbed by the breeze. "I do."

"Then I'll meet you by the pool in five minutes. I have a surprise for you."

Dion was already in the water by the time Sophia pushed the sliding glass door to one side and came out into the evening air. The sun had set while they'd driven back from

Elias's house—and the sky had shifted through shades of orange and red and lilac to settle on a dark, inky blue. Perfect for what he had planned.

He tracked her every movement, sucking in the details of her like an eager student poring over a textbook. He wanted to learn every little piece of her. Sophia padded barefoot to the covered area where the banana chairs faced the water, lined up perfectly like chess pieces on a board. As if unsure of herself, she slowly unwound the towel from her body and dropped it onto one of the chairs.

"Come in," he said. "It's very pleasant."

Thank god Dion had already submerged himself. The vision of her lithe figure encased in a classic black swimsuit that fit her body like a fantasy had filled him with desire. Black fabric clung to her small but pert breasts and the gentle curve at her hips. It highlighted the delightful dip at her waist and cupped the sweet space between her legs.

She tugged at the strap curving over her shoulder. He devoured her with his eyes, hungrily observing her shapely legs and the shadow of her cleavage. The woman was luminous, and it had been so very long since he'd taken anyone to bed. Not since there had been a whiff of their arranged marriage.

If he was being honest with himself, not since *quite* a bit before that.

He could pinpoint the moment he'd shut off that part of himself. An older woman—beautiful and glamorous, an English professor with an accent that had made his pulse race. He'd pursued her relentlessly, and eventually she'd given in. The moment she'd started talking about her husband, Dion had been filled with rage. He wanted no part of her adultery. No part of her betrayal of her husband. And when he'd demanded to know why she hadn't told him she was married, she'd laughed as though *he* were the fool. It had been another nail in the coffin for his views on marriage. The final nail in the coffin for his belief that there was even a shred of merit to love…if it even existed at all.

It was enough to kill his libido dead in the water. That was, until Sophia Andreou had arrived in Corfu and tried to tip his life upside down.

"What's the surprise you have planned?" she asked, a nervous smile twitching on her lips as she walked cautiously down the steps leading into the pool.

"Patience." He treaded water lazily, his hands moving back and forth in the water. "You'll see it in a moment."

Sophia came closer, slowly sinking down in the dark depths that glittered with the reflection of the stars adorning the night sky. As her loose hair hit the water, it fanned out, making her look like some kind of nymph or sprite. Dion swallowed and found his muscles coiled.

"You certainly know how to create drama." She tipped her head back and floated for a second, her hands causing ripples around her.

"What's life without anticipation?" He swam closer to her.

She eyed him with caution. "Personally, I prefer life to have as little anticipation as possible. Easier not to be disappointed that way."

"Doesn't that make for a dull life?"

"It makes for a predictable life, which isn't a bad thing. I like being prepared."

She certainly had been when she came to Corfu. Armed with a plan that included hiding her true self, deceiving him, and possibly building alliances with the man he hated most in the world, she had been most *absolutely* been prepared.

"If you're too prepared, you might miss out on something amazing," he replied.

She made a derisive snorting sound. "I'll take the certainty of knowing what's to come over the vague chance of amazing, thank you very much."

He was going to have his work cut out for him. That much was clear.

"You never did answer Elias's question today." He changed tactics, bringing her back to something comfortable.

"Which one?" She cocked her head.

"Your favorite Hitchcock movie."

"I *did* answer that question." Her feet kicked beneath the rippling surface of the water, keeping her upright. "I don't like choosing a favorite child."

He laughed. "Could you narrow it down to a top five?"

"Possibly."

"I'd like to know if we'd pick the same ones."

Her brow shot up. "You're a fan?"

"The biggest."

"You didn't say anything today." She peered at him.

"I don't need to dominate the conversation all the time."

"Just *most* of the time?" she teased.

Good. Her barriers had softened, even if only a fraction. "Elias doesn't get many visitors who don't want something from him. I didn't want to take away from him enjoying a conversation about something he loves."

"That's sweet," she said. "He's lucky to have you."

"I'm lucky to have him." The automatic response was far too true and too real. It socked him in the chest, like it did every time he thought of his history with Elias lately. Swallowing down the pain, he covered the rawness up with a smile. "And you're *still* dodging the question."

Sophia made a drawn-out *hmm* sound. "I feel like I have to say *Psycho* because it's so iconic. I had to sneak into the living room in the middle of the night to watch it because my father didn't want me to see it."

"Agreed. Not my number one, but *definitely* top five."

"*To Catch a Thief*, because Cary Grant. *Rear Window*,

because I could never look at my neighbors the same ever again." She counted the names with one hand, tapping each finger to her thumb as she named them. "*The Birds*, obviously. It's the most terrifying thing I've ever seen. Oh, now I only have one left." She bit down on her lip. "It could be *North by Northwest*."

"Because Cary Grant?"

She grinned. "The most perfect reason to ever watch a movie. But then I haven't said *Vertigo*, which was brilliant. I also love *Strangers on a Train*. Oh, and *The Man Who Knew Too Much*."

"The remake?"

"God, no." She looked appalled. "The original, obviously. Even Hitchcock himself couldn't beat it."

"You still won't choose a favorite?" He swam a little closer. Now he could see the droplets of water clinging to her chest and shoulders and the way her hair darkened in the water.

"I refuse." She tilted her chin up at him playfully.

"Then you leave fate in my hands." He tapped at a screen protected with a waterproof case set into a mount beside the pool. Over the shaded section of the outdoor area, a large screen silently descended.

"You have a movie screen in your backyard." She laughed. "I don't know why I'm surprised."

"You might find it more comfortable here." He inclined his head toward the hot tub neatly tucked away into one corner.

The water had been set to the perfect temperature, warm enough to ward off the slight coolness in the air as the night progressed without being too hot. And the kitchen staff had set out a small platter of fruit, pastries, *saganaki*, and calamari, along with a bottle of champagne on ice and two glasses.

They waded over to the hot tub as the iconic and recognizable theme music accompanying the Universal Studios logo moved onscreen, followed by the opening credits for *Rear Window*. By the time they settled into the warm, bubbling water, the screen was showing a slow pan of the movie's one and only setting: the backs of several New York apartment buildings that surrounded a shared courtyard and the apartment where the protagonist lived.

"I haven't watched this one for a while." Sophia couldn't hide her glee as she leaned back against the spa and reached over to the platter to grab a piece of apricot. "It's been at least a year."

"That's not too long."

"It's my mom's favorite. We had this tradition where we used to watch a Hitchcock movie every Thursday night. My dad was always out doing business stuff, and we'd get into our pajamas and make popcorn and curl up on the couch together." A wistful expression flittered over her face. "We'd always race to point out the cameo, even though now I have them all memorized."

What it must be like to have a family and traditions and routines that involved movie nights and popcorn. As much as he valued his relationship with Elias, it was—first and foremost—a business relationship. "You used to do that but don't anymore?"

"Mom got sick a little while ago." Her gaze shifted back to the screen—though whether it was due to interest in the movie or because she wanted to hide something from him, he had no idea.

...

Sophia reached for the champagne flute containing golden liquid and downed half of it in one go. Talking about her mother always summoned that instinctive desire to drown out her emotions. The last twelve months had been hard. Her mother's "moods" had gotten worse; her periods of self-imposed isolation had gotten longer and more frequent. No amount of begging would convince Dorothy to see a therapist. To get the professional help she needed. Probably because Sophia's mother knew her husband would put a stop to it, lest she accidentally let some unflattering information slip about their marriage or family.

Her father thought seeing a therapist was no better than "airing dirty laundry."

So Dorothy had turned in on herself, become more of a shell and less of the vibrant woman Sophia remembered from her younger years. She lived with the fear that one day the memories might fade completely if not reinvigorated by her mother's return to her former self. But Sophia's pleas continued to fall on deaf ears.

"I'm sorry to hear that."

The opening scene of *Rear Window* played on as James Stewart's character watched the people in the buildings around him. The ballerina in the pink bikini top and shorts pranced around her apartment, kicking her leg back into an arabesque as she pottered around her kitchen.

"It's my father's fault," she said bitterly. "He controls her like she's a marionette on the end of his strings. Just one more person to bend to his whim. She used to be so…everything."

She had no idea why she was even telling him this. Maybe it was the movie stirring up all the memories she was so afraid to lose. Maybe it was the way James Stewart watched his neighbors, making assumptions about them the way she knew *everyone* back in their Brooklyn neighborhood made assumptions about her family. Maybe it was being here with Dion as herself for the very first time, against everything she wanted and believed in, purely for the sake of her mother.

"I shouldn't have said that." She shook her head, wishing she could snatch the words back and tuck them safely away. She could *not* afford to give Dion any more leverage against her.

When she chanced a sidelong glance, his eyes were smolderingly dark. In the starlight and the glow of the giant movie screen, his eyes were a shifting view deep inside him. Anger simmered, along with something else. Understanding? Compassion? She turned away. She was only seeing what she wanted to see.

Dion was not her friend or her confidant.

"Are you worried I'll be like him?" he said eventually.

He asked the question so quietly, so honestly, that it grabbed her heart in a vice-like grip. "Yes."

He nodded as if a piece of the puzzle had slipped into place. For a long beat, he didn't respond. His eyes were focused on the hot tub's bubbling water in the way a fortune teller might look at a palm or a crystal ball.

There are no answers to be found. Trust me, I've looked everywhere.

"I don't want someone to control," he replied.

Sophia snorted. "The current arrangement doesn't exactly support your statement."

"You'll be free to do whatever you please. If you want to study or continue running your own business, or if you want to sit by the beach every day, then you can do it here."

The insult stung like a whip across her skin. "I don't aspire to be a lady of leisure living on someone else's dime. Ever."

"I didn't mean it like that." He reached out and grabbed her hand. "But I don't know you yet. I don't know what you want or what you need because you haven't given me the chance to get past the 'Sophia Andreou' you've been putting on display."

"Is this the point where you tell me you *want* to get to know me?" she scoffed. "Please, we both know why I'm here."

"Look, I know this isn't what you wanted. Truthfully, it's not what I wanted, either. I never planned to get married." He raked a hand through his hair, and the water kept it in place. "I think the whole marriage thing is a sham. But I want your father's company, and apparently that means getting married to you. I won't give up this opportunity, but I am fully committed to making it work."

"Gee, a fake marriage that neither party wants where I can be a trophy who sits on the beach all day. How could I possibly refuse?"

"Give me a week," he said.

"A week for what?"

"A week where you'll pretend to be open to the idea of marrying me so we can get to know each other. If you're still appalled by the idea at the end of the week, then we can make a plan to figure out an alternative solution. I can tell your father that you're not happy—"

"No." She shook her head. "That's not an option."

"I've talked a lot of people into a lot of things, Sophia. Perhaps he'll reconsider." His dark gaze slid over her bare shoulders and arms, over where the curve of her breasts emerged from the bubbling water. "I can be very persuasive."

"You're not *that* persuasive." She looked at him with a dark expression. "Trust me."

"Give me a chance. It'll give me time to come up with a proposal for your father."

"You can't tell him I've been…" She swallowed.

He quirked a brow. "Creative?"

"Difficult."

"I won't tell him that, I promise." He shook his head. "Just give me a week. No preconceived notions, no disguises."

"No foxes?" Her lip quirked upward, as much as she

hated herself for it. It was hard to say no to Dion, especially when he looked at her like he meant every word of what he was saying.

You're not dumb enough to actually fall for his lines, are you?

"Definitely no foxes." He held his champagne flute up to hers. "Give me a chance to win you over."

Never. Going. To. Happen.

"Fine," she said, touching her glass to his. The chime rang in her ears. "One week, and I'll try to forget what brought me here. But you have to promise not to out me."

"I promise." He sipped his champagne, and her eyes were drawn to the muscles working in his throat. To the slide of a water droplet down his neck. To the sharp cut of his jaw and the way the full lips wrapped around the edge of the crystal flute.

Dion had a lot of moves, she'd give him that. The whole "one week" thing was a clever attempt to get her to relax and to trust him. Too bad for Dion he didn't realize that Sophia wasn't good at trust.

Just another thing she could thank her father for.

Chapter Ten

Sophia seemed to have agreed to most aspects of his request for the week…except one. Dion lay in his bed, his heart hammering in his chest as he looked into the lifeless eyes of Baroness Sasha Foxington III.

Now you're calling the damn thing by its name?

How the hell had she snuck into his room and planted the fox there without him waking up? Again?

"You know what this means, Sasha?" He propped himself up onto his forearms. "War."

He got out of bed and stashed the fox in the corner of his room. Later, he'd figure out how to get her back. But hopefully this little game she'd started was a sign that she would trust him…for seven days, at least.

For the time being, he needed to engage in full seduction mode. Sophia wasn't going to know what hit her. For some reason, the anticipation and challenge she'd presented had his heart pumping a little harder than usual. Everything was on the line. Because if what Sophia had told him last night about her father was true—and not simply another story she'd spun since arriving in Corfu—then he couldn't tell her father she'd refused to marry him.

He *wouldn't* send her back in a way that might put her at risk. Which meant that this week needed to work…because how else would he convince Cyrus to go ahead with their deal if marriage was off the table?

It was time to pull out the big guns. Sophia Andreou was about to get wined and dined on an epic level.

Dion strode through the house and found her sitting on the island in his kitchen, her legs swinging back and forth so that her heels bumped lightly against the cabinets beneath her. Today she looked like a vision. She was wearing the same dress from yesterday, which managed to look even more enticing being somewhat rumpled and creased. Her hair was piled on top of her head in a messy bun with a few wisps falling down to frame her face. A simple gold necklace hung around her neck, catching the light and winking at him as if it held the secrets of the universe.

"Good morning," she said with a sly smile. "Did you sleep well?"

"I did." He jammed his hands into the back pockets of his jeans. "I woke with a bit of a start, however."

She toyed with the hem of her dress, her lips twisted as if she was suppressing a laugh. "Oh? Bad dream?"

"Yeah. I had a feeling I was being watched."

"Strange. I wonder what caused that."

He stalked over and placed a hand on either side of her thighs, hemming her in. She continued to look smug as hell. "Do you usually sneak into people's rooms at night?"

"Technically, it was the morning." She cocked her head. "You snore like a chainsaw, you know. Might want to get that checked out."

She was lying, the little minx. He could see it in her eyes. "The next time you decide to sneak in there, it won't be to plant a fox."

"No? Do you think I'm suddenly going to be so overcome with desire that I can't stop myself from coming to you in the middle of the night?"

"I would say 'coming with,' but yeah, close enough." He was being totally cocky and not at all serious, but it didn't stop a surge of something primal through him. Okay, so maybe it was a little serious. Sophia was gorgeous and it had been a *long* time since he had anyone in his bed. Something told him they would be very compatible.

One step at a time.

Her cheeks flushed a delightful shade of rosy pink. "You've got a dirty mind, Mr. Kourakis."

"And a dirtier mouth." He grinned when her nostrils flared, a flash of something a hell of a lot like excitement lighting up her eyes for a moment. "No fox given."

She threw her head back and laughed. "Oh, now we're starting with the fox puns, are we? I don't think I'll be able to take that for a whole week."

He stepped back and held out a hand, helping her down from the counter. Her flat sandals made a slight slapping sound when she landed. Damn. She was impossibly pretty.

Pretty enough to hide a multitude of lies. Remember that.

Okay, so he couldn't trust her. But then again, she didn't trust him...so at least they were on an even playing field.

"Ready to start the day?" he asked, grabbing an apple from the bowl sitting atop his counter and biting into it. The sweet flesh hit his tongue, bursting with flavor.

"Sure. Do I need to bring anything?"

"Just your passport."

She blinked. "My passport?"

"Uh-huh. It's a requirement when one leaves a country," he teased.

"Where exactly are you taking me?"

"Surprise." He dabbed at a dribble of juice with the back of his hand. The entire time he'd been eating, her eyes were trained on his mouth.

"But I haven't packed."

"Are you really going to bring clown pants on vacation?" He raised a brow.

"Well, no. But…" She had the decency to look a little sheepish. "The only normal outfit I brought with me was this dress that I wore on the plane on the way over."

"It's no problem. Taken care of." He turned to head out of the kitchen before she could protest. "Just grab your passport. And hurry up—the plane's waiting."

Within the hour, they were in the air. Sophia had walked onto the plane, clutching her bag to her chest and looking more than a little awestruck. The Precision Investments private jet was a Gulfstream G150, which seated eight at maximum capacity, meaning the executive team could fit comfortably for flights to their annual strategy-planning retreat. Dion believed that at some point in life, a man's success should reward him with the ability to avoid flying with the general public.

Once the plane leveled at cruising altitude, two members of the on-call cabin crew came through with refreshments.

"Are you going to tell me where we're going yet?" she asked, accepting a cup of coffee from the crew member. "I've never flown private before."

"You could have flown private on the way over," he reminded her. Outside the plane, blue skies were decorated with puffs of wispy white cloud that whipped past as they sliced through the air. "I *did* offer."

"Wasn't really fitting of my image." She lifted a shoulder. "Besides, the last thing I needed was your staff telling you that I dressed normally on the flight."

He snorted. "You thought of everything, didn't you?"

"Not everything. Otherwise I wouldn't be on this plane now."

He didn't detect any malice in her voice. Did that mean she *was* actually giving him a chance this week? "You really want to ruin my surprise?"

"I told you, I don't like anticipation." Her eyes skated over him, and something told him that Sophia needed a lesson in how anticipation could be the most incredible thing in the world.

She looked at him differently now. Before, as her alter ego, her gaze had either been furtive or intentionally forceful. Both approaches meant to hide the real her. Now, when she looked at him, there was curiosity. Interest. Perhaps even a hint of attraction, though he imagined she would be doing her best to suppress it.

"Paris."

Her eyes lit up. "Really?"

"I worried it was a bit cliché, but I got the impression you hadn't seen much of Europe before, and really, Europe is nothing without Paris."

"I'd only left America once before I came to meet you. I accompanied my father on a trip to Niagara Falls, and we crossed the border into Canada." Her eyes darkened a moment. "I only got to see the inside of a casino."

"You went to Niagara Falls and didn't see the falls?" He raised a brow.

"It wasn't a vacation." Her lips pressed into a rigid line.

"Well, this *is* a vacation. In fact…" He reached into his pocket and pulled out his smartphone to switch it off. "It's a vacation for both of us."

That wasn't totally the truth. Running his own company meant there was no such thing as true time off. Invariably, something would require his attention. But he'd left everything in Nico's capable hands, and he would simply log on in the middle of the night while Sophia slept. During her waking hours, he was hers.

"I get the impression that doesn't happen very often," she said.

"It doesn't."

"Your business means a lot to you."

The statement took him by surprise. "It's everything to me. To build what I have in such a short space of time takes incredible sacrifice. I know people see me as the charming guy, always hosting cocktail parties and working a room, but that's work. All the dinners and the introductions and the conversations… It's work."

That was the truth of it. Everything in his life—even, to some degree, his relationship with Elias—was work. He didn't regret it at all. But it struck him then that if work suddenly vanished, he would have nothing, which was a far more sobering thought than he was prepared for.

"When you grow up with no family, you tend to crave something to be part of." He had no idea why he was telling her this. But it was like she'd yanked a stopper out of him, and the words flowed out before he could think about the consequences. "I never had control over my life growing up. I was at the mercy of the orphanage's schedule and rules. I woke when they said to, I ate when they said to, and I went to bed when they said to."

"Doesn't sound all that different from my life," Sophia said softly. "I've never had control over anything."

And Dion was contributing to her feeling of helplessness. Guilt slashed through him, but he tamped the feeling down. Sophia would be able to do whatever she liked if they were married. He had no interest in tracking her every move or telling her what she could and couldn't do.

"Well, we have a week in Paris ahead of us. The itinerary is wide open. What do you want to do?"

"Oh, I…well…*everything*." The smile lit up her face better than if she'd been wrapped in fairy lights.

"Then everything is what we will do."

• • •

It was hard not to be swept up in the glamour of it all. Private plane. Skipping lines. A limo waiting at the front of Charles de Gaulle. They rounded the corner at Rue de Vaugirard and coasted by the Luxembourg Gardens. Sophia held her breath, palms pressed to the window as the buildings rolled slowly past. It was like everything she'd ever imagined—white buildings with quaint Juliet balconies and windows that poked out of the roof in a neat little row like tin soldiers. Was she really here? Or would she wake up when the sharp sting of her thumb and forefinger proved her imagination was, indeed, too active?

The car pulled up in front of an apartment building overlooking the garden. "Welcome," the driver said. "I will have your things taken up to the apartment. Your guest coordinator is upstairs, and we have a light afternoon snack prepared for you."

Sophia shook her head in wonderment. Unlike when she'd flown in the past, the private jet hadn't left her feeling disheveled and tired. Probably because there'd been no snaking check-in lines and arduous security processes. No trudging along, trying to dodge other bustling travelers.

Dion got out of the car and held the door for Sophia. Feeling every bit like the heroine of a romantic movie, she stepped out onto the street. It was way too easy to see herself strolling along the sidewalk, coffee in hand and a baguette sticking out of her bag, a handsome man on her arm.

A handsome man, not this *handsome man.*

"Shall we?" He held out his hand, and she took it, shutting

down the disparaging voice in her head so for once in her damn life she could enjoy herself.

The princess-related feelings only grew stronger. The building was pretty in that spectacular French way, but the apartment itself was something else. Modern and sleek, the white walls were broken by pieces of colorful artwork—paintings in shades of poppy red and lilac and soft blue. Another wall had a gallery of black-and-white photos in thin, brushed-gold frames. And the furniture was just as divine—two black leather Herman Miller Eames chairs faced the windows overlooking the garden. The only reason she even recognized the chairs was because her father had an imitation one that he told everybody was real.

"Welcome to the sixth arrondissement." A woman wearing a charcoal shift dress and black heels smiled warmly. Sophia adored her smooth French accent.

"We're very pleased to be here," Dion said graciously.

"Let me give you a quick tour. Outside through these windows are the Luxembourg Gardens. Unfortunately, the Notre Dame will not likely be open while you're here due to the recent fire. But we're walking distance from some other beautiful churches, such as Saint-Séverin and Saint-Étienne-du-Mont, as well as the Odéon-Théâtre, many museums, restaurants, and shops. We have a list of recommended dining locations personally selected for you." The woman walked through the open-plan living area, past a chic black and silver galley-style kitchen to a small alcove with several sets of doors. "You have all three bedrooms at your disposal in case you would like to have any guests stay with you."

"It will only be the two of us," Dion corrected her.

The way he said it, his voice calm as a lake on a breezeless day, sent a ripple through her. It was almost like he'd been thinking about getting her alone. Having her alone…for an entire week. She swallowed and found her hand toying with the neckline of her dress. Had the room shot up several hundred degrees all of a sudden? It sure felt like it.

"We have the master bedroom set up for you." The woman led them into a large room with a huge king-size bed framed by shelves and shelves of books against an exposed-brick wall. Dion's travel suitcase was sitting in the corner of the room. "We received your email yesterday, Mr. Kourakis. A selection of items in Ms. Andreou's size have been placed into the main closet, along with matching accessories."

Rows of floaty dresses in a rainbow of shades hung neatly from thin gold hangers. One dress glittered with thousands of tiny champagne-colored beads and was trimmed with a layer of netting so fine it looked like a wisp of smoke. Beneath the dresses was a three-tiered shelf with an assortment of strappy sandals and elegant pumps.

They were beautiful…but something about the dresses reminded her of home. Of her father's insistence that she look the part at every turn. That she play a role for him.

Sophia brushed her hands along the dresses, her breath catching in her throat.

"If you have any questions at all, we have a concierge line for this apartment which is available at all hours." The guest coordinator continued, "All the details are in the book on the coffee table. If you need any reservations made, transport, meals…anything, please don't hesitate to call."

"Thank you." Dion nodded.

When they were left alone, Sophia found her mind swirling. Mixed emotions clattered around in her head—the thought of being here, alone, with Dion filled her with bristling energy and anticipation. But on the other hand, she didn't want to keep being a doll to be dressed up by whatever man she was meant to be pleasing. Absently, she rubbed the hem of a vibrant cobalt blue silk dress between her finger and thumb. It caught the light, looking more like liquid than fabric.

An illusion, just like her.

"Surprise." Dion leaned against the doorframe of the bedroom, watching her with a stance that appeared relaxed and eyes that were anything but.

"I don't even know what to say."

He chuckled. "You can say anything you like."

"A full wardrobe isn't going to change my mind," she said, looking over at him. "My father makes sure I have one of those at home."

His long legs were encased in a pair of dark denim jeans. The hem pulled up slightly to reveal a pair of striped socks beneath tan dress shoes, which matched the leather belt highlighting his trim waist. Further up, a white cotton shirt encased his muscular torso, which—thanks to their night in the pool—she knew to be perfectly sculpted. Perfectly hard and ridged and…

Sophia swallowed.

Don't be fooled by good looks. You're smarter than that.

But knowing they would be here alone—no staff, no one to interrupt them—had sent off some kind of response in her body, a building sensation like the mounting of an idea that had her very, *very* excited. Too excited, considering nothing was going to happen. She would agree to Dion hospitality, and she would stick to her guns.

Her fingers released the silk dress.

"Why don't we take a walk in the gardens?" he suggested. "I saw an ice cream cart out front."

Now *that* she could get on board with.

"Give me a moment to get changed?"

"Of course." He nodded and backed out of the room. "No clown pants this time?"

She laughed. "No clown pants, I promise."

As Dion winked and shut the door behind him, Sophia's

gaze rested on the expansive bed dominating the room. Both of their suitcases were here. Clearly the guest coordinator assumed they'd be sleeping together.

Her body temperature shot up a few hundred *more* degrees at the mental image of tangled limbs and hard pressing lips and hands fisted in hair. Would it be *so* bad to indulge a little? What happens in Paris stays in Paris and all that.

She immediately cast the thought out of her head. No, the only way she'd get out of this situation with her freedom intact was to make it clear to Dion Kourakis that while he might be good at persuading the rest of the world, he would *not* persuade her.

At the end of the week, she'd remain strong in her desire to go back home unwed.

Chapter Eleven

The first two days of their trip had been a whirlwind—vising the Eiffel Tower, the Louvre, Le Cinq, Sacré-Cœur. Champagne and pastries and baguettes and people watching. Dion couldn't remember the last time he'd behaved like a tourist. In fact, he'd been to Paris four times in the last year, and not once had he set foot in a museum or a church or a gallery.

Experiencing it all with Sophia was like opening his eyes to a new world. Seeing the joy and wonder that she saw. Feeling the excitement that she felt.

They'd decided to take it slower on day three and had sat in a café for almost three hours over breakfast—drinking strong coffee, eating buttery croissants, and watching the world go by. On the way back to the apartment, they'd passed a quaint gift shop, and Sophia's eyes had lit up at the stack of puzzles in the window. So he'd gone inside and bought her one, laughing at the strange look the cashier had given him when he'd asked the man to stick a piece of paper over the picture on the cover.

"You know, I thought the mystery-puzzle hobby was part of your act," he said as they walked into the apartment and settled in at the large glass table. Sophia eagerly pulled the box out of the bag and opened it up. "Granted, it wasn't quite as disturbing as the whole taxidermy thing."

"Relieved that you won't have to go to the bathroom with a bird watching you?" Her eyes glinted mischievously.

"You have *no* idea," he said drily. "I much prefer the puzzles."

"My grandmother actually got me my first 'mystery' jigsaw," she said, tipping the pieces all over the table. Dion stooped down to pick up one that had raced over the edge. "I would get bored during the summer break, and she wanted something to occupy me for a few hours that wasn't television or video games. So she bought me a jigsaw, taped a piece of paper over the image on the front, and bet me that I couldn't solve it."

Dion laughed. "Quickest way to fire up a bored kid is to give them a challenge."

"Well, it certainly worked. I was quiet all afternoon and evening, determined to prove her wrong." Sophia's dark eyes twinkled. "Then it became a routine. Every school break when I stayed with her, a new box would appear."

An automatic twinge of jealousy ricocheted through Dion. All he'd wanted as a boy was someone to do those things for him. Small acts of kindness that became tradition, something that could be carved out as a special memory and passed on as a way of preserving it forever.

"What else did you learn from her?"

"She taught me a lot of things, actually. I love baking because of her—not sweets, but bread. To me there's nothing better than a fresh, crusty loaf of bread right out of the oven," Sophia said. "And she taught me how to garden. She used to have a vegetable patch in her backyard, even though it was very small. There was barely any place to put your feet that wasn't soil with vegetables growing in it. I grew up with dirt under my fingernails and bits of twig stuck in my hair and the juice of homegrown strawberries running down my chin."

She sounded so…happy.

It was intoxicating, this reverence she had for simple things. Real things.

"Would you have a vegetable patch one day?"

"Absolutely!" She nodded enthusiastically. "I'd love to grow all the things she taught me about—chard and beans and lemons from a huge tree."

"She sounds like a very special woman."

"She was my savior, at times." Sophia didn't look at him as she spoke. Instead her eyes were focused on the fragmented picture in front of her, her fingers drifting in the air until she plucked another edge piece from the fray. "My father was very strict, and I found it…stifling at home. Going to my grandmother's place was like being given a small piece of freedom. We baked cookies and watched movies and went for walks in the park."

"You miss her?"

Sophia nodded. "She passed away ten years ago."

"I'm so sorry."

"Don't be. She lived a great life. She was one of those people who understood what was really important, you know?" Sophia looked up, spearing him with a look so full of sincerity Dion wasn't sure how to process it. "A good life isn't about fine clothes and fancy artwork and having people envy you. It's the relationships that you cultivate and the quality of the work you do. It's the kindness you pay other people."

"I've always believed that." It was something Elias had instilled in him—relationships were what made a man successful. And while suits and cars might be needed to uphold an image, thinking they were the end goal was a grievous mistake.

"I, uh..." She paused, worrying her bottom lip between her teeth. "I haven't shown you much kindness at all. You've had me in your home and treated me well, and I..."

"Covered my house with pictures of dead animals and wore clown pants to a cocktail party," he deadpanned.

"It was pretty funny to watch your reaction." Her lip twitched for a second, but it didn't materialize into a full smile. "I'm sorry. I've probably given you nightmares about turkeys and foxes."

"As much as I'm glad the charade is over, I respect that you were doing what you felt was necessary to protect yourself," he admitted. "I've been in that situation a lot over the course of my life. I know what it means to get creative with a solution. To have to find a way out."

Sophia stared, the puzzle forgotten. It was like having someone pry open your chest and look right into your soul. Her eyes were dark, the warm Paris light giving them an almost golden tone. Her dark hair tumbled over one shoulder, wild and unrestrained. She'd worn nothing but jeans and a tank top the whole time they'd been here, eschewing the pretty dresses because she'd wanted to be comfortable. To be herself.

And the more time they spent together, the more Dion realized that he and Sophia had *a lot* in common.

"Finding a way out seems to consume my life," she replied.

"What would you do if you got out? What's your big dream?"

She blinked, as if surprised by the question. But it only took a second before her eyes took on a soft-focus quality that made her beautiful face even more luminous. That moment right there—that switch from reality to dream—socked Dion right in the chest. Because he knew what dreams could do to a person, how they could save a person.

Without a dream of having a secure life, a secure home, Dion might not ever have picked himself up out of that filthy city gutter as an angry eighteen-year-old.

"My big dream is a cabin in the woods," she said, holding up a hand as if warding off an interjection. "I want a property that's secluded, perhaps by a lake or a stream. I want it to be surrounded by beautiful nature, to be quiet and peaceful. I'm going to buy it on my own, with no help from my family, and I'm going to move there with my mother. I even have a Pinterest board with *exactly* how I'm going to decorate every inch of it. It'll be my oasis."

She looked like a new person as she spoke, like she'd come truly alive. She was more beautiful now than she would be wearing any couture dress hanging in the bedroom closet. She was more beautiful now than she would be with high heels or the right lipstick or hairstyle. Because this was *real*.

And Dion had always craved real things. Meaningful things. It was the balm to his soul—an antidote to all the real things he never had growing up.

"Then I'm going to keep running my virtual-assistant business so I have money to pay the bills—but also because I love the idea of being my own boss. I keep my own hours and take the clients *I* want to take. I've never had that kind of control with anything." She shook her head. "My dad has no idea I'm even doing it. He just assumes that I'm going to follow his orders, but I've been working toward this for almost a year now. And I'm sure it seems silly to you that my 'big dream' is nothing but a cabin in the woods, but it's what I want."

"I don't think it's silly at all, Sophia. It's a symbol of everything you want out of life—privacy, security, beauty, peace." He smiled. "It seems like the perfect dream for you."

• • •

There were a lot of things Sophia had never really felt in her life, and one of them was understood. But right now, sitting next to Dion, the fancy backdrop of the apartment shimmering in the late morning light, she finally felt it.

Maybe it was because he was the first person who'd listened to her. Maybe it was because he was the first person interested enough in her to even ask what she wanted.

He's interested because he needs something from you.

But even as her cynical inner voice tried to downplay his actions, she couldn't quite cast them aside. Because she got the feeling they were two misfits who'd worked so hard to find their place in the world. Because they'd always been at the mercy of people who thought they knew better. Or worse, who didn't care enough about what they wanted to guide them toward those dreams.

"I really hope this isn't a ploy," she said quietly. "I'm trying to remind myself I'm only here because of my father's company."

"Can't it be that and *also* something else?" He was so close, his body turned toward hers. Today an even coating of stubble enhanced his sharp jawline. He'd thrown on a soft white shirt and left the top button open, sleeves rolled back to his elbows. Faded jeans hugged his thighs, and the whole look was so perfectly touchable. So perfectly appealing.

He's handsome. That's nothing but a fact.

Only it wasn't about his looks, mouthwatering as they were. It was the way he looked *at* her, giving her his undivided attention in such a way that it made her think, if only for a second, that he really *did* care about what she had to say. That he found her interesting, intriguing.

And the only things people seemed to have ever found intriguing about her before were surface stuff. Her looks, her body. Her father's reputation.

Nothing to do with who she was underneath it all.

"What's the something else?" she asked.

"I'm…fascinated by you."

Sophia laughed, suddenly self-conscious. Like she'd shown too much. Said too much. "I'm not sure that's a compliment."

"It is. I think there's part of you that calls to me, in some weird way. Like calls for like, don't they say? We're both fighters, and I think we understand that about each other."

A warm feeling started low in her belly and seeped through the rest of her, like a glow being carried through her bloodstream. "But our goals are opposed."

"They don't have to be. You want a beautiful cabin in the woods, and I can give that to you. You want to be your own boss and do puzzles in your spare time and dictate the way you live your life. You want space to be yourself."

"And you can give that to me?" she asked. Sophia was a woman at war with herself, and her eyes flicked over his face as she weighed the pros and cons.

"I can." He nodded. "I will."

Her fingertips drifted up to touch the edge of his jaw, catching the prickly hairs that he battled every day with his razor but had grown a little unruly while they holidayed. It was like she was exploring him the way his gaze explored her. Unpacking. Assessing. Letting curiosity run riot.

Energy snapped between them, building with a crackling force *far* beyond anything she'd ever experienced before. A fleeting thought zipped through her mind: what if this was meant to happen? He was the first man to ever really get her. Understand her.

And the more layers she peeled back, the more she liked what he saw. The more she liked *him.* He was thoughtful, sweet, and loyal, which she'd always thought was a good sign of someone's values.

"You're very tempting, Dion Kourakis." Her fingers toyed with the collar of his shirt. "You know exactly what to say. But I've grown up surrounded by men who could talk a big game."

"That's where you misunderstand me," he said, capturing her wrist and rubbing the pad of his thumb over the delicate inner portion. "I don't talk a big game. I *act* on what I say. When I make a promise, I deliver."

Her breath stuttered as he stood, still holding her wrist. Holding her close to him. The scent of his cologne—something warm and woodsy—wrapped around her like a blanket, and his dark gaze held her. She felt ensnared in the best way possible.

"If my father's company wasn't part of the deal, would you even look twice at me?" she asked.

Dion's lips curved into a sinful smile. "Would you be wearing clown pants and your scratchy cardigan?"

She shot him a look, but the seriousness was broken with a twitch in her lips. "Maybe."

"I find you beautiful, yes. And I am a man who enjoys beauty, so I would look." He brushed her hair back from her face, and it sent a shiver through her. "But I am much more interested in people with substance. So I might look, but it would be once I spoke to you that my attention would be captured. I want to hear what you have to say. I want to know all about your cabin in the woods and your grandmother's vegetable patch and why you do puzzles without knowing what picture you're putting together."

"Wow." She looked at him, almost with new eyes. "That's a hell of an answer."

"People interest me."

"And *I* interest you?"

"Very much. You're like a puzzle with no box," he replied.

"A mystery."

"And you want to solve me?" she asked.

He traced the edge of her jaw, the shell of her ear, and his touch was like a balm and a flame all at the same time—soothing and stoking and so utterly intoxicating it took everything not to melt against him.

"I want to see you without all the pretence."

"Well…here I am." Her gaze was smoldering, smoking. "Get your fill."

• • •

Dion didn't want to stop at looking; he wanted to taste, consume. He wanted to see how she would morph under his kiss—would she melt against him? Or would her fists curl into his shirt?

She was strong, this woman. Not wavering in her stare, not retreating with her words.

He lowered his head down, just to see what she would do. Just to test her.

But she didn't budge, not an inch. Sophia met him, her lips parting in anticipation as if inviting him in. Accepting his challenge.

The first kiss was so brief it was barely more than a graze of the lips. But he felt her reaction instantly, the soft little gasp. The way her hands slid up to curl over his shoulders. The way she angled to him.

Yes.

This time, when he kissed her, it was an invitation to explore. He coaxed her mouth open, and her tongue darted out to meet his. He tasted the remnants of pastry on her lips, the sweetness of orange. But there was nothing saccharine about this kiss—no. Sophia was hot and willing, pressing into him in a way that made his body roar to life with a force he hadn't experienced since his younger, wilder days.

He turned them around and wedged her against the table, the movement so sudden that the sound of puzzle pieces skittering to the floor barely registered in his brain. His hands wound into her hair, and hers in his. The kiss was deep, a combustion of passion that had lain dormant for too long, as though they'd both unlocked something in each other that had been waiting. Wanting. Desperate.

His body pulsed, and Dion's cock hardened against her thigh. He pressed into her, delighted in the needy moan that came from way back in her throat. There was a natural connection here—something that was bigger than both of them. Something he hadn't expected.

He kissed along her jaw, down her neck, his palm skating up over her breast. Her nipple was beaded beneath the soft cotton of her T-shirt and whatever scrap of fabric was masquerading—unsuccessfully—as a bra beneath it.

"Wait." Sophia pressed her hands against his chest, breathless, and Dion stilled immediately. "This isn't what I should…what I…"

"What?"

"I'm not supposed to be attracted to you." She wriggled off the table, her eyes wide and black. She'd been into the kiss—he could feel it.

And frankly, he was *also* reeling from the connection between them. It wasn't what he'd expected, either.

"I'm sorry. I need a minute." She pushed her hands through her hair. Her skin had started to glow, the sun's subtle gold tinting her. "God, if this were any other situation, I wouldn't hesitate."

He wouldn't push Sophia—but it wasn't lost on him that this attraction would help his cause. It would help him get what he wanted. Hopefully, what they both wanted. If Sophia could break free of her father with his help, then she *could* have the cottage and her own business and freedom. Of course he needed a wife who would attend events with him and charm his guests, but Sophia could do that with her eyes closed.

Even at the cocktail party, where she'd been trying to put him off, everyone *still* loved her. In fact, Nico had commented to him the very next day how taken his wife, Marianna, had been with her. That she hoped they could be good friends.

"Why don't we get some air?" Dion suggested. "You said that coffee spot by the gardens looked nice."

Sophia nodded, looking at him while she bit down on her lip. He sensed a change between them—a bond of sorts, even if she was skittish. But that kiss didn't lie—there was *real* attraction between them. Sizzling attraction.

And he would use that to his advantage.

Chapter Twelve

Halfway through the Parisian escapade, Dion came to the conclusion that it was time to pull out the big guns. He'd been sleeping in one of the spare bedrooms so Sophia could experience the luxury apartment in full by having the king suite to herself. But their kiss had been playing on his mind in a loop.

Not to mention that watching her day after day, blossoming from the guarded woman who hid behind false quirks to a woman who was as beautiful as she was fun to be around, had him thinking a hell of a lot about what it would be like to crawl into that big bed beside her.

He'd caught her staring at him a number of times as he'd padded from the bathroom to his bedroom with only a towel around his waist. He knew the unmistakable signals of lust, and she was sending them loud and clear. But she was holding back, as was he. Sophia was skittish. Moving too fast would scare her away, but slowly he'd been drawing her into his orbit. Tempting her with the possibility of them.

And in the process, he'd totally and utterly tempted

himself.

"You're staring." Sophia looked up at him. Even in towering silver stilettoes with fine platforms under the balls of her feet, she was a good several inches shorter than him.

But her petite stature didn't seem to affect the length of her legs, which were given the illusion of endlessness thanks to the heels and the racy hemline. They walked along the Parisian street, and Sophia was getting attention from almost everyone—men and women—who passed them. How could he blame them? The woman was a knockout.

Each day she'd ventured into the closet of designer items. Each day she grew a little bolder in her choices, bypassing the pretty dresses he'd seen her wear in pictures from events with her parents to more daring, artistic outfits. Perhaps the *real* Sophia was somewhere between cocktail dresses and clown pants after all.

It was like watching her be born—watching her true self come alive under the warmth of freedom. Without her father and without the pressure of maintaining a false identity, she'd become the best version of herself. Not simply beautiful because of her looks, but because of fact that she laughed more readily, spoke more confidently, and revealed more of herself and her past.

"How could I not? You're a vision."

She slipped her hand into his as they came to the edge of the sidewalk, relying on him to make sure she stepped down carefully so they could cross the road. Afterward, she didn't remove her hand.

"You don't look so bad yourself."

"Was that an actual compliment?" He pressed his free hand to his chest. "Wait. Say it again so I can record you."

She rolled her eyes. "You act like it's the first time you're hearing it, and I *know* that's not the case. In fact, I'm pretty sure that waitress at dinner propositioned you when you were paying the check."

"She did, but that's entirely beside the point."

"It's kind of rude, if you ask me," she grumbled. "I was standing right there."

"Jealous?"

She shot him a dirty look. "I was simply pointing out that for anyone else, it wouldn't be a stretch to assume we were together, and so that kind of behavior is in poor taste."

"So that's a *yes* to the jealousy thing?"

"You wish."

"I wish a lot of things, Sophia." Still holding her hand, he led her to the entrance of a nightclub.

"We're going dancing?" Her face lit up, and any residual annoyance over his teasing—or the waitress's flirtations—was instantly dissolved. "You didn't mention that. I thought we were just going for a walk."

"I'm full of surprises this week."

"It's because I said my dad never let me go out at night, isn't it?" Her deep brown eyes pierced him. "You've been listening to every word I've been saying."

The fact that she'd noticed filled his chest with an unwelcome warmth. For the last three days, he'd been cataloguing the little bits of information she gave away, like a child hunting out Easter eggs and stashing them in a basket for safekeeping. There was so much he didn't know about Sophia, but against everything he knew to be true about relationships…he *wanted* to know.

He'd also gotten a much clearer understanding of the way she lived at home…or didn't live, as the case most certainly was. So if he could give her this week to catch up on a fraction of what she'd missed out on while being stifled by her parents, then he would give it to her.

It's not about that. It's about winning her over and securing this deal.

But the line had gotten blurred along the way, when Dion found himself wanting to spend time with her. Wanting to do the things that a real married couple might do, like exploring a city together or talking about their goals and aspirations. Wanting to do mystery puzzles and talk about Hitchcock.

"Dion…" They paused outside the nightclub. It was dark now, and the streets of Paris were alive. It had started to rain, barely a fine mist, but it covered everything with a glossy sheen. He pulled her close to him, shielding her. "Thank you."

The sincerity made his throat constrict. "For what?"

"For giving me an experience that I probably would never have had otherwise." She sucked on her lower lip, worrying it back and forth between her teeth. "I know that the reason we're here is kind of messed up and that we want different things—opposing things—but…"

"But?"

Her eyes shone. "I don't regret coming here with you."

It was like a punch to his chest. Bringing her to Paris had been about furthering his own agenda, getting what he wanted—such was the backbone of every action he took. But it was hard to remember that with the way she looked at him.

"Let's go inside." He pressed his hand to her back, letting his fingers rub against the beading on her dress, taunting himself with a gentle touch when what he really wanted was so much more…primal. "I don't want you to get soaked."

The nightclub was a members-only place, highly exclusive. Invite only. The lighting was low and intimate, the club itself decked out in moody shades of claret and black. There was a hint of burlesque to it, but tastefully so. As they walked into the main room, a woman in an elegant black dress swanned past them.

"Was that…" Sophia blinked. "Princess Maria-Olympia?"

"I think so." Dion pulled Sophia close to him as they wove through the crowd. "I hear they get quite a few of the young royals here."

"Wow." Sophia's eyes were wide as saucers. "I'm used to fancy parties back home, but this is…next-level."

They were guided to a small booth in the back of the club, away from the dance floor, where it was possible to carry on a conversation. The server unhooked a thick black rope and motioned for them to take a seat. A bottle of champagne was brought to the table immediately, without either of them asking for it.

He reached for his glass and held it up to hers in silent challenge. She'd been resisting the wine all night, determined to keep her head. Determined to maintain her control. After their kiss, she'd gone to bed alone, casting a longing look over her shoulder but never extending an invitation to join him. And Dion would never cross that threshold without her explicit word. Which meant he had a case of blue balls—the worst he'd experienced in all his life.

Sophia eyed the glasses, her fingers flexing at the edge of the table. It was like an internal battle waged inside her, desire and sensibility duking it out. "You know, I think Princess Maria-Olympia might appreciate my clown pants."

"Who knows, maybe you'll spark an international trend." Dion smirked. "Sophia Andreou, pushing the boundaries of fashion."

"We'll call it the Circus Chic movement." She laughed. "In complete honesty, as fun as it has been to dress up, I'm much more comfortable being barefoot, wearing jeans and a T-shirt and doing puzzles with you."

"I like you like that, too." And he meant it—as incredible as she looked tonight, he hadn't been able to get that image out of his head. Loose, messy hair, bare face, simple clothes. She'd shone more then than any other time he'd seen her, because when she was like that, she wasn't hiding anymore.

Her hand crept forward, her forefinger reaching out and stroking the stem of the champagne flute. "Do you think I'm going to fall for you just because you've whisked me away to a romantic city and made me feel like a princess?"

"It would certainly make my life easier."

Instead of becoming annoyed, she lifted her lips in a wry smile. "You're honest. I'll give you that."

"I want your father's company for my own gain. I'm prepared to pay handsomely for it…more than it's worth, I might add." His glass still hovered in the air. "And I know this isn't the fairy tale you wanted, but I really think we can make it work. It's a practical solution to a problem we both have."

"How is this a solution to my problem?"

Dion placed his glass back down without taking a sip. "Your father is a bit of a tyrant."

"That's putting it mildly."

"By marrying me, you'll have more freedom than you'd ever have at home. I'm not looking to control you or manipulate you. Hell, you can bring your mother over here as well, get her out of the situation."

"You'd want my mother to live with us?" Her expression softened.

"I don't know if any man *wants* his mother-in-law to live with him," he teased. "But of course she could stay with us. If it's important to you, it's important to me."

She narrowed her eyes. "You really want my father's business that much?"

"Yes. And my guess is that if this falls through, your father will look for another avenue to save his business." Dion thought for a moment, unsure how much he should reveal. "I've done my research. The company is free-falling, thanks to all the bad debt your dad's old boss racked up. And I don't mean bank loans."

Her gaze shifted. He'd hit the nail on the head—gambling debt, he'd wager. Dogs, ponies, cards…something.

"Not many people will want to buy him out," Dion continued. "Not the kind of people who want the company for any legitimate reasons, anyway. What happens if we call things off and you go home without a ring?"

"I don't know." For the first time since they'd met, he saw genuine fear on her face. It seemed he'd earned enough trust with her that she would allow him to see her true reaction. But he almost wished he hadn't—because the thought of her father doing anything to hurt her…

It curdled in his stomach like off milk.

"I honestly don't know what he'd do." She stroked the champagne glass, making lines in the condensation. "I just… I'm sick of being his puppet, you know? I'm a grown woman, for crying out loud. I should be able to live my own life, make my own decisions."

Tears shimmered in her eyes but she blinked them away, giving her head a frustrated shake. She was sad and beautiful and angry and sensual and raw. And fucking hell did it fill him with fire. He could only imagine the kind of life she'd led with a father like that.

"All I want is a place of my own, where I can live with my mother. I've been putting money into a secret bank account." She looked at him suddenly, as if she'd said too much. But then she sighed, defeated. "I want the chance to live my own life… Is that so much to ask?"

"No, it's not." Dion raked a hand through his hair. He was utterly torn—not willing to give up on getting his father back for abandoning and rejecting him. But yet, equally, he didn't want to hurt Sophia.

The biggest problem, however, was that if Cyrus didn't sell to Dion, he'd find another buyer eventually. Or the debt collectors would come knocking and he'd need something to bargain with. Who knew how that might end up? Sophia needed a way out from under her father's thumb, and Dion was her best option.

"But you're right." She swiped at her eyes with the back of her hand, smudging her mascara a little. "He's never going to let me leave unless it benefits him somehow. He's never going to stop dangling my mother's welfare in front of me."

• • •

The realization came down on Sophia like an avalanche. Dion was absolutely right—if she ruined this deal for her father, did she really think that she'd be able to weasel her way out of his grip the next time? Would she ever be free?

Suddenly, her borrowed dress felt too tight, like a hand crushing her ribs in a death grip. This was the truth she'd been ignoring ever since her plane touched down in Corfu. If she could just get out of this arranged marriage, then she could go home and make a plan.

A plan to what? Run away and let her mother bear the brunt of Cyrus's anger? Or would she bide her time and hope that her father would give up on the idea of trying to save his company? That he'd suddenly realize the arranged marriage was a dumb idea? Yeah, right. This cage had a lock and no key. No way out.

She stared at Dion across the table. Ebony hair, still damp from the rain, curled around his ears. His dark gaze bore into her, like he could see all her secrets and fears and the blood pumping through her veins. Maybe this was the only way out. Marriage to a handsome stranger. She had no idea if she could trust him. But she knew one thing for certain—she *couldn't* trust her father.

"I want my mother to come and live with us," she said.

Her tongue felt heavy and thick in her mouth, like it resisted what was about to happen. "And I want a stipend for her."

He folded his hands into a neat parcel on the table. "Done."

"I mean forever. While she's alive, you'll pay her. I don't care if you have me sign a prenup so I don't get a cent from you myself if we divorce, but I need to know she'll be taken care of forever."

He nodded. "I understand what you're asking, and I agree."

"I want a place I can go if I need quiet. Somewhere beautiful and small and peaceful." She swallowed. "And I want to keep working for myself so I can have my own money in my own bank account."

He sat statue-like for a moment. "Done."

"I don't ever want you to tell me what I can wear, who I can talk to, or how I need to behave." The fire roared up within her like the demon ghost of hurts past. "You are buying the company, but you are *not* buying me."

Something flickered in Dion's eyes. Respect. "I will never treat you the way your father has treated you."

"And I want people to think we're in love." Her voice caught, emotion so close to the surface she could almost see it bubbling under her skin. "Because I don't want people to know that I let myself be forced into this. I couldn't bear the humiliation."

That's when Dion's eyes went flat. As if at the very mention of the word love he shut down on a cellular level. "I'm not husband material. My work will always come first."

"I know. In fact, that's a good thing."

He raised a brow. "Really?"

"Yes. I don't plan on actually loving you. Just looking like I do." The relief that streaked across his face told her everything she needed to know. "Eventually, I'll want to leave."

He nodded. "A marriage in name only."

"We'll need to stay together long enough that I can set my mother up and long enough that my father has moved on to something else." Surely, he would...right? Eventually he'd turn his attention to another get-rich-quick scheme.

It was the only way she could see clear of this situation. Marry Dion, get her mother out of Brooklyn, save every damn penny until she could be independent and have her idyllic, peaceful house away from everyone. Then, once she was divorced and had enough money to take care of herself and her mother—along with the stipend, of course—then she could be free.

If she was never able to marry again because she'd still be tied to Dion, then so be it. She didn't want a husband. She didn't want marriage. But if that was her ticket out, then she would make it work.

Dion cocked his head. "Anything else?"

"You have to let me know you. I've told you more about my family than I've ever shared with anyone." Fear and shame had always kept her quiet. Her friends simply thought her father was strict... They had no idea of her reality. "You have to tell me something intimate and true. Because even with all this, we're on even footing, and I am *so* tired of giving other people the upper hand."

"Done."

Sucking in a long breath, she reached for her glass and held it up. "Then we're going to get married."

Something darkly victorious lit his eyes, and it set off a chain reaction inside Sophia. All the negotiating, watching him say "done" over and over, had filled her with a power unlike anything she'd ever known. Her entire life had been a series of concessions, of sacrifices, with each one chipping away another little piece of her soul until it felt like she had nothing left.

And yes, this marriage would be another concession. Another sacrifice. But this would be for the greater good, for her future. For her mom's future.

Dion lifted his glass toward hers, and the chiming sound rang through her entire body. She was really going to do this. She was really going to marry this man.

"Promise me you're not going to fill my house with stuffed animals."

"You have my word." She brought the champagne to her lips and savored the fizzing sensation for a second before tipping her head back and downing the entire thing in one go. "Should we have our first dance?"

"That usually happens *after* the ceremony," he said.

"I need practice." She poured herself another glass and this time took it slower. Tonight would be about letting go. About releasing the old Sophia. The new Sophia would do whatever it took to have the life she deserved, to have the freedom she deserved. To have everything.

Dion stood and held his hand out to her, looking every bit like the love child of Prince Charming and something darker. Not a villain, but not quite a hero, either.

"Then let's make that dance floor ours," he said.

With the champagne flowing through her body and the warm grip of Dion's fingers around her hand, Sophia was finally feeling like herself again. She let him lead her through the crowded outskirts of the club's main room and onto the dance floor. Loud, pulsing music pumped through the club's speakers, and lights glittered and flashed above them. The crowd was illuminated in flashes, the decadence of the rich and famous revealed to her in staccato bursts. A woman drank straight from a bottle of Dom Pérignon, and a man in a tuxedo kissed the flavor from her lips. Everyone here was obscenely beautiful, like an army of peacocks parading and preening for one another. The beautiful people…and tonight, she would be one of them.

But when Dion settled his hands on her hips, pulling her tight against him, it was like the rest of the room evaporated. She wound her arms around his neck and let her head fall back, feeling the music with her body.

Their situation wasn't perfect. But she had her way out, her plan. And her husband-to-be was going to give it to her.

Chapter Thirteen

This victory was sweeter than any other thing Dion had tasted. Better than sex, better than the finest scotch, better than the zeros in his bank account. Because his childhood had been a world of failure. Unwanted from the second that he exited his mother's womb, he'd grown up too skinny and too gentle-natured to defend himself. So he'd wallowed on the bottom rung of the social ladder at his orphanage, never to be accepted or adopted—a reject among rejects.

Therefore, it wasn't money that motivated him. It wasn't even the growth of his company, necessarily. It was having someone say "yes" to him. It was fronting up to a challenge and coming out on top, because he'd spent too many years being on the losing side of every battle.

But now, with one of the most important company acquisitions finally within his grasp, it wasn't victory he felt.

Her breath hitched as he pulled her closer, his hand snaking around her lower back. Under the lights, her eyes were almost black, like a portal to another world. They glittered—the full breadth of her emotional range on display for him to see. Sophia was nothing like the woman she'd presented, and it had little to do with her change of outfit.

"Don't look at me like that," she said. Her smile was almost like a baring of teeth.

"Like what?"

"Like you want to eat me alive."

The words were like sparks, like the fine blade of a knife running along metal so that bursts of orange and red threatened to burn them all down to the ground. People pressed into them from all sides, forcing the distance between them to evaporate like smoke. He moved easily, as though conducting the music, and she followed his lead, her movements mirroring his. It was sexy as hell, and when he pulled her against him, his hips brushing against hers, he felt a tremor ran through her.

The pulsing flicker of strobe lights made her eyes gleam and her hair look like silk. He took the wispy strands between his thumb and forefinger, turning them so they caught the light. Maybe it was due to the shelter of the dim lighting, the champagne, or the fact that he'd finally gotten what he wanted…but Dion felt like he could take on the world.

"So we're going to have a celibate marriage, are we?" He brushed his thumb along her jawline and down the center of her throat. The touch was so soft. It was all about the anticipation. He was going to teach her to love it, to crave it. To dwell in the buildup.

"Not necessarily. But I don't want you to get the wrong impression about me."

He cocked a brow. "Which is?"

She leaned forward, her lips brushing his ear. "That I'm weak. I'm not. I'm stronger than you or anyone else could possibly imagine, and if anyone is going to do the devouring, it's going to be me."

"I'm happy to go to battle." His lips curved into a wicked

smile.

"I'll make sure I bring my sword." Her eyes were alight, power radiating from her like a magnetic field that gripped him by the balls. She was majestic. "I'm making a vow to myself that I am done being a puppet. I'm done being a pawn. From now on, I'm going to take care of myself."

He dipped his head, forehead pressing against hers as he sucked it all in. Perfume on her skin, champagne on her breath, the fierce set of her lips. She fisted her hands in his shirt. Was this what it was like to fall for someone? Because no other woman had ever captivated him like this.

He was inches from the edge of the cliff, ready to tumble into the deep abyss below.

The bass from the low, sensual dance music created a rhythm in his blood. There was nothing tangible left, only sensation. The flicker of lights, the tightening grip of her hands at his shirt, the pulse of his cock as she rubbed against him. The club was warm, the scent of booze permeating the air, intoxicating them. While she was languid, liquid softness, he was hard. Everywhere. His teeth scraped her neck, stubble roughing up her skin. His hands were full of her, roaming the curve of her ass and the slope of her hips. Dion's seduction had come to fruition.

Watching Sophia's transformation tonight had been truly fascinating. Now, with her eyes turning slowly black with excitement and her body softening under his touch, this was raw, uninhibited Sophia. The real Sophia. The woman she'd tried so damn hard to hide away from him. *That* was the woman he wanted. And he was certain with every cell in his body that she wanted him, too.

Her face tipped up to his, eyes fluttering shut as her lips parted. Her body was perfectly soft and gently shaped with a sexy yet subtle dent at her waist followed by the sweet swell of her small breasts. Touching her was like lowering himself into a bath—heat crept through him, slowly swallowing him whole.

It wasn't enough. Nothing would be enough until he dragged her to some dark corner and got what he needed.

"You're so fucking sexy like this. So powerful," he growled into her ear. "Why have you been hiding from me all this time?"

She rested her cheek against his, her lips brushing his skin. "I needed to figure out who I was."

They moved together, hips swaying and hands roaming. Her dress had ridden up her legs, tempting him to brush his hand along the inside of her thigh. Everything about her was a trip for his senses—all that smooth skin and silky hair. She was a goddess.

"Don't screw me over, okay?" she said, her hands driving into his hair. "I don't want to have to take you down."

He chuckled. "Easy. I'm not your enemy."

"I guess you're not, *fiancé*."

"I have to get you the ring first. Get down on one knee."

Something flickered across her face—an emotion so fleeting it was gone before he could identify it. The shifting lights made it hard to read her. "I guess we should start acting like we're in love, then."

"With pleasure."

He brought his mouth down to hers, coaxing her lips open so he could taste her. His free hand pressed into her lower back, and she arched into him. God, it was like heaven and hell—sweet as candy and fiery hot. Her tongue swiped along his lip, leaving the taste of champagne in its wake.

Sophia held him tight, her fingers gripping his hair as she kissed him back with brute force. This was no chaste kiss—it was raw and desperate. A battle for supremacy. Her breath quickened, and her lips devoured his.

Yes.

Victory again. The sweet fuel set his blood boiling, his cock impossibly hard, and the voice in his head screamed at him to push her up against a wall. The DJ shouted something over the music, and a whooping cheer rose from the dance floor. The sound swelled, getting louder and louder, drowning out Sophia's voice. When the crush surged, he took her hand and pulled her along. They found a dark corridor, slipped behind the barricade that said "staff only," and tucked themselves around a corner. The wall vibrated with the thump of bass from a speaker on the other side. They were right near the DJ booth.

She grabbed his head, bringing his mouth down to hers with a determination that made his whole body throb. A thought flickered at the periphery of his mind, a concern about professionalism and having the paparazzi see them like this. Because this kiss was about to ignite them both. He traced the curve of her shoulders, the smooth length of her thigh from her knee to where the hem of her dress finished.

She sighed, dropping her head back as he kissed his way up her neck and winding her arms around him. The way she clung to him, trusting and willing, was everything. It set him alight. He lifted her, her legs coming up around his waist. Pressing. Wanting. His cock found the sweet spot between her thighs and nestled there, her warmth penetrating the thin layers of fabric that kept them from total satisfaction.

One hand cupped her breast, thumbing the hard nipple beneath the beaded fabric. A sharp bite of pain flared within him as her nails dug into his shoulders, but the sensation blossomed into an electric heat that burned through him.

"I want you." He could barely hear the words as she shouted into his ear, the vibrating thump of the bass rattling through his body.

He shook his head. "Not here."

He let her down and pulled her farther into the bowels

of the club, following the winding corridor until they exited out of a small door. They came out into an alley and headed toward the street.

"Do you not..." She was still holding his hand, still following him. "Am I not what you like?"

He speared her with a look. "Let me make something clear, Sophia. We might be getting married to further our own futures, but that doesn't mean I'm not attracted to you."

"Then why are we leaving?"

He paused in the street and bent his head to hers, capturing the surprised "O" on her lips and forcing her mouth into submission. There was no hesitation in her return kiss.

"Because when you scream my name, I want to be able to hear it." He tucked a strand of hair behind her ear.

Her lips quirked. "That's presumptuous."

"Confident," he corrected. "And accurate."

• • •

The second they got back to the apartment, they tumbled through the front door and all the composure they'd maintained on the street—walking hand in hand like two well-behaved adults—was gone. Dion had her up against the wall, the sharp intake of her breath cutting through the quiet air when he shoved her skirt up and pressed the heel of his palm between her legs.

"That's what I was talking about," he said. "That sound. I wouldn't have heard it in the club, and what a fucking crime that would be."

He captured her mouth, and the soft glide of his tongue against hers left her weak at the knees. He tasted of heaven. One hand ground slowly against the tender, throbbing space between her legs while the other was at her waist, then her rib cage, then her breast. Kneading. Squeezing. Flicking.

"Oh!" Her head jerked back as he thumbed her nipple through her dress. It was like a volt of electricity had shot straight through her.

"And I wouldn't have heard that." He chuckled against the side of her neck as he nipped at the sensitive skin there. Each bite was soothed with a swipe of his tongue in a maddening pattern.

Shamelessly, she rubbed against his hand. It had been so long since she'd felt this good, strung tighter than a wire and ready to snap. But she wanted more. Skin-to-skin more.

"My dress," she gasped. "Help me out of it."

He pressed his lips to her neck. "Turn around."

Feeling suddenly shaky on her heels, she turned to face the wall. They were still only just inside the doorway to the apartment, having not even wasted a step or two coming farther into the living room. She planted her hands against the wall. Deft fingers swept her hair away from the back of her dress, and a sharp sound pierced the air as he drew the zipper down. She pulled her arms out, and the fabric slid down her body to puddle at her feet.

Sophia resisted the urge to cover herself. Any time she was naked with a man—which had occurred on precisely three other occasions, with two other men—she heard the words of her first boyfriend taunting her flat chest. Fried eggs, he'd called them. Needless to say, he hadn't seen anything else after that.

"Maybe we could turn the lights off," she said, breathless. It was a strange sensation to be so utterly turned on and yet so incredibly self-conscious at the same time.

"But then I won't be able to see your beautiful face." His voice was like nails pinning her to a wall. "Or your beautiful body."

He curled his hand into a loose fist and ran the backs of his knuckles down her spine, causing her breathing to become shallow. Sophia bit down onto her lip as he traced the subtle curve of her ass and back again.

"You're not…disappointed?" God, did she have to sound so pathetic? She was going to ruin this incredible night with her inferiority issues.

"Nothing about you is disappointing," Dion said. "Not on the outside or on the inside. Now that I know the real you, I am even more attracted to you."

For a moment, there was nothing. No touch, no sound. Just a great, stretching absence of sensation that made her body vibrate like a tuning fork. How could she feel something so strong when there was so little to warrant it?

"Do you feel that?" he asked eventually.

"What?" She turned to look over her shoulder, palms still planted against the wall.

"Anticipation." He looked like the devil himself—with his dark stare and black suit. With the shadow along his jaw and those wicked, wicked lips. "Buildup. You feel as though I'm touching you when I'm not."

She did feel it. A tightness gathered at her sex, a strange pulsing sensation that made her want to press her thighs together.

"Why wait?" she asked. Her voice did not sound like it belonged to her anymore—she was detached with lust. Unhinged with the need to have him.

"Because the waiting is the best bit." He planted his hands on the wall, next to hers, caging her body with his. But there was no contact—he held himself in such a way that no part of them touched. Yet she trembled, and the lacy panties she'd bought on a whim the day previous were growing damp.

"Please touch me. I…"

"Yes, Sophia *mou*?"

She knew that word. *Mine.*

"I need it." It was like her body had suddenly realized

how much she'd deprived it of affection. After the boy who'd claimed her virginity had turned out to be a master manipulator, a carbon copy of her father, she'd shut herself away. One more man, and he'd been as disappointing as the first. She'd become afraid to get tricked again. Sex had slid way down the list of her priorities. Even touching herself had felt pointless.

But now all those years of disappointment and loneliness and unfulfilled need came roaring back like a monster out of the darkness.

"Please." She wanted to weep. "Please touch me."

"Almost." The whisper of warm breath on the back of her neck was as strong as a Taser, and her body jolted. "I'm going to teach you to crave this part. To know that I'm so desperate to have you that I'm punishing myself by holding back until the very moment I can't bear it any longer."

She had no idea what voodoo he'd woven on her, what spell he'd cast. But for all her reservations and games and resistance—tonight, she was his.

"Dion." His name was a keening moan of desperation on her lips, and the returning growl set her soul on fire.

He reached around her body, his fingers finding her center, rubbing a series of slow, intense circles against her sex. Her clit ached, desperate for release.

"Yes," she gasped, her fingers curling against the white wall. There was nothing for her to grab onto, but that didn't stop her from trying.

His mouth came to the back of her neck, a finger breaching the edge of her panties to softly stroke the seam of her sex. He'd be able to feel how wet she was, how insanely aroused and excited. But she didn't care—couldn't care. Not while he was pushing her so close to an orgasm she knew would shatter her completely.

"Please." The word dissolved on her tongue as he kissed

her shoulders and spine, the tip of his finger pressing against her entrance.

"Are you ready?" His words were rough, sharp. Like gravel. "Are you ready to feel my fingers inside you?"

"Please, please." She couldn't string any more words together. "Yes."

The second he slid a finger inside her, she thought she'd break. Her internal muscles clenched around him immediately, trying to draw him all the way in. But he held on to his control, sliding in and out slowly. Easing her into it. Stretching her.

She ground her ass back against him, feeling the hard length of his cock digging into her. So big. Hard as a goddamn rock. Then he shifted, slipping another finger inside her, rubbing against the little bundle of nerves with each stroke. That was it. Game over.

"Oh. My. God." Her body shook, and she tumbled, wave after wave of pleasure crashing over her. Filling her. Drowning her.

He held her there until it subsided. Until her heart slowed and her breath came in longer beats. Until she was able to stand on her own. She twisted her body, turning her head to look at him as best she could while still braced against the wall. Only then did he withdraw his hand and kiss her trembling lips.

"See. It's so much better when you wait," he said.

Almost immediately, her hunger resurfaced, and she turned. "I don't want to wait now."

Her fingertips grazed him, feeling the strength of him through his suit pants. She wasn't done yet, not by a long shot. Finding the tab on his zipper, she pulled it down, and she snaked her hand in so she could wrap her fingers around his cock. He was hot against her palm, thick and heavy. *Very* thick. She squeezed tentatively and was rewarded with a low, ragged groan.

"We need a condom," he said, swearing in Greek when she slid her hand along his length. "Bedroom. Now."

He practically dragged her through the fancy apartment, his pants only hanging on to his hips because she hadn't undone the hook at his waist. It was undeniable how good his attraction made her feel. It smoothed over her, filling in the cracks and dents and chips in her confidence. Working against the erosion that had happened over many years. It restored her. Made her believe that she was a powerful woman who could start over.

Be someone better. Someone stronger.

Her calves hit the edge of the big king bed as he backed her up. The duvet was perfectly smooth from where she'd made it this morning, having absolutely no idea that they would be here now. Together. He left her only for a moment, returning with a foil packet. Then he tossed it onto the bed.

"Take everything off," he said. His voice was ragged and low, his accent more pronounced, as though lust were slowly turning him into a base version of himself.

She stuck her thumbs under the elastic of the lace underwear and slid it down her hips, peeling the fabric from her body. But the towering stilettos were going to stay, she'd decided. The extra height gave her confidence and a wiggle in her step that she liked very much. She tipped forward from her waist so that her hands landed on the bed and her ass waved high in the air. A guttural groan came from Dion's throat.

"You're incredible." He stalked closer. "Stay there and let me look."

Her whole body clenched as cool air drifted across her sex. She'd never done anything like this before. Let herself be scrutinized in the most basic, primal way possible. She wanted to cover herself, her hand drifting over where dark, curled hair covered her sex, but Dion's hand shot out and stopped her.

"It's beautiful."

"You need to strip down, too," she said. "Even this up a little."

She turned and watched intently, heart in her throat, as he did what she said. He ripped his shirt out of the waistband of his pants and popped only enough buttons so he could tear the damn thing over his head. Then came shoes, socks, his pants. All that was left was a pair of black boxer briefs, and soon they were gone, too.

He was all bronzed muscle and sharp lines. His erection curved up toward his belly, strong and hard. She'd never really looked closely at one before, her only experience with sex done under the cover of bedsheets and a blanket. It had always been quick, over before she'd really begun to enjoy herself. There'd been no… anticipation.

There was that word again.

She could feel it winding through her, like a creeping vine slowly consuming her. Breaking her down. And while she perhaps should have been nervous, there wasn't even a hint of it anywhere. She wanted this. Wanted him. Wanted the pleasure she'd been denied for far too long.

"Talk to me," he said, cupping her face. "You've gone quiet."

"Isn't that part of the anticipation?"

His cock pressed against her inner thigh as he kissed her. "Fast learner."

A second later, the sound of foil tearing broke through their heavy breathing, and Sophia watched him roll the condom down his length.

"We'll go slow, okay?" His palm cupped her face, and she kissed his hand.

"No." She reached out to touch him, her fingers skating

over the swollen head of his cock. "I don't want you to hold back."

"What *do* you want, Sophia? Tell me."

His eyes were like black holes, sucking her down. Hypnotizing her. "I want you to treat me like a wife."

Groaning, he eased her back against the bed and used his strong thighs to part her softer ones. The contrast of his warm, bronzed skin against her pale skin tinted pink from the sun sucked the breath out of her lungs. He was so beautiful. So confident and capable and strong.

Yet there was a gentleness to him, a level of care that she wasn't used to.

Closing her eyes, she breathed in the surroundings. The scent of sex, the unique male aroma mingling with cologne and rain. She wanted to absorb it all.

"You still with me, Sophia?" His lips brushed over her jaw and down her neck.

"Yes." Her fingers raked down his back as he shifted forward, the head of his cock pressing against her opening. "No more waiting. Please. I want this."

His hand cupped her breast, and he rolled a nipple between his thumb and forefinger. "So impatient."

"Now, Dion." The words dissolved into a cry as he pushed inside her, filling her. Taking her.

She sucked in a breath and let it out slowly, willing her body to relax into it. As he started moving, all of her melted against him, turning pliant in his hands. Each stroke pushed her higher and higher, toward an apex of something she hadn't even known existed.

He rained kisses down over her, and her eyes fluttered, pleasure filtering through her as she lifted her hips, anchoring her legs around his waist. Urging him to go deeper. Drawing him in. The rhythm became frantic as they chased pleasure. Together. As a team.

The muscles in his arms corded as he thrust, and she gripped him, digging her nails into his skin. Marking him as hers. And when his name fell from her lips, he shuddered inside her, thrusting long and hard one last time.

The silence washed over her as they lay there, tangled in one another, and a deep calm claimed her.

Maybe Dion was exactly the person she needed to help turn her life around.

Chapter Fourteen

In the lazy glow of late morning, Dion quietly slipped out of bed and out of the apartment, into the pale Parisian sunshine. When he returned, Sophia lay in the center of the large mattress, where she'd invaded his space in the middle of the night, her hand reaching for his. The sweet gesture, regardless of the fact that it was made unconsciously, had warmed him to the depths of his soul.

Which was precisely why he needed to make Sophia learn her lesson.

Walking slowly so that each footstep fell as soundlessly as possible, Dion crept out of the room. He paused at the doorway, turning back to admire her languid form, the sheet pulled up to her waist and her dark hair fanned out like a halo on her pillow. She had one arm flung over her eyes, leaving her breasts free to the morning air. The apartment air-conditioning kept a cool breeze running through the rooms, which made her nipples stiff and peaked. He had half a mind to abandon his plans and go back to bed so he could wake her with his mouth.

But they were about to enter a marriage, which would leave plenty of time for the carnal delights of such things. Now, he needed her to know something important.

Dion Kourakis was not a man to be trifled with.

He snuck into the spare room where he'd been sleeping up until last night and located Baroness Sasha Foxington III. Sophia had no idea that he'd brought the fox with him. It had required a little planning, like finding a suitcase that would easily fit the damn thing and having it loaded onto the plane after they'd already boarded and distracting Sophia while the driver brought it up the afternoon they arrived.

Initially, he'd planned to let Sophia pick her own engagement ring. After all, a marriage for a business arrangement didn't really require such romantic notions as getting down on one knee. He would have been more than happy to buy her whatever sparkly rock took her fancy and call it a day.

But somehow that didn't feel quite right, now. Last night had shown him what kind of person she was—strong, fierce, determined. Qualities he held in the highest regard because he'd spent his own life cultivating those very things. The more he learned of her father's tyranny and controlling nature, the more his respect for Sophia deepened.

And while the plan was not for the marriage to last forever, Dion had grown to enjoy Sophia's company. And hell, he'd even grown to enjoy her antics. They'd come at an important time, helping to distract him from his growing concerns about Elias's health.

Dion twisted the signet ring around his little finger. It wasn't at all his style, with the flat top and engraved initials that were so well-worn they could barely be read. But Elias had owned that ring since receiving it on his twenty-first birthday, and Dion had never seen him without it, right up until the day that he got diagnosed with lung cancer and slipped it into Dion's palm.

You're the closest thing I have to a son.

Dion knew the sentimental value of a ring, and so he'd decided to take the old-fashioned route. A small velvet box was burning a hole in his pocket. He'd visited a jewelry store he'd noticed several times on their walks through Paris because their designs were beautiful, unique, and a little unconventional. Much like Sophia.

The ring he'd chosen was simple in its beauty—almost antique-looking. It was engraved with a pretty vine design that twisted all the way around the band, small emeralds punctuating each leaf. In the center of the ring was a larger square-cut emerald. It reminded him of the descriptions of her dream cottage and how she wanted to be surrounded by nature.

He slipped the ring onto a ribbon that he'd found adorning a box of fancy toiletries in the bathroom and tied it around the fox's neck. Then he snuck back into the bedroom, silent as a dream, and placed the fox on the end of the bed. Since Sophia was all of five feet nothing, there was plenty of space at the foot of the bed for the fox to sit undisturbed by her feet.

As if sensing his presence in the room, Sophia stirred. Her arm flopped down by her side, and she shifted, eyelids fluttering and an adorable *hmm* sound emanating from her lips. She blinked once, twice, and sat bolt upright, clutching the bedsheet to her chest, a shriek on her lips.

"Dion!" The shriek turned to laughter, and she placed a hand to her mouth. "Oh my god, you scared the shit out of me."

"Not a great way to wake up, is it?" He stood on the other side of the room, arms folded as he leaned against the wall.

"What's this?" She crawled forward to inspect the ribbon around the fox's neck.

Her eyes were like saucers, staring up at him in this wide,

guileless way that made his heart thump. She fingered the ring, rubbing it between her thumb and forefinger.

"I thought we should make it official." He stalked forward, suddenly hungry. He loosened the bow from behind the fox's neck and placed the animal on the ground. "I know a lot of women want a big white diamond for their wedding day, but something told me your tastes run a little more unique."

A smile lifted her lips. "Something told you, huh?"

He reached for her hand and pushed the ring onto her finger. For some reason, seeing it on her hand filled him with pride. "I know this marriage isn't what you wanted. It's not going to be traditional or even normal. But out of all the women I could have married, I'm glad it's someone with your wild spirit. You keep me on my toes, and that's not an easy thing to do."

"Thank you." She reached out to touch his face, her fingers rubbing against the bristles coating his jaw. "For giving me a way out."

"I'll have the paperwork drawn up as soon as we get back. Everything you wanted—it's done."

"And what about what I want right now?" Her gaze turned sultry, her touch turning from soft and gentle to hard and demanding as she raked her nails against his scalp.

"What's that?" He sank down to his knees on the bed, one hand bringing her palm to his lips.

"You. Me. A morning in this bed?"

"Only a morning?"

She grinned. "For starters."

He eased her back, settling his hips between her legs as his lips came down on hers. As well as this had worked out, their marriage would never be about love. The clock would count down their time together, and then they would part ways with what they wanted—him with closure, and her with her freedom. And when it happened, he would welcome it.

Love could never be part of the equation.

• • •

Sophia had no idea it was possible to organize a wedding in a month, but it seemed that Dion's influence and power opened more doors than she could ever have imagined. Venues were chomping at the bit to host them, and Sophia's second visit to the bridal store had been a lot more successful than the first.

In that time, Sophia and Dion had fallen into a rhythm. She'd started accompanying him to work two days a week, running her virtual-assistant business out of one of the offices in his building. On her off days, Sophia visited the children's ward of the Corfu hospital. She volunteered weekly to read stories and keep the kids amused. Life wasn't anything like what she'd thought it would be here—it was busy, fulfilling, and she found herself settling into her new home. Today would be the day it all became official.

Her mother had tears glimmering in her eyes. "You look wonderful."

Sophia stood in the middle of the dressing room, the simple vanilla silk dress caressing her skin. The fine straps accentuated her shoulders, the pale color amplifying the warmth that Corfu had given her skin. She had pink in her cheeks and the shiniest ember glint to her hair and freckles dusting her arms and chest. The island had been kind to her; it had breathed life into her in a way no other place had.

She stared at herself in the mirror, assessing the stranger looking back. The stranger who'd finally found her power and confidence thanks to one imperfect man.

"I know this can't have been easy for you," Dorothy said, coming up behind her daughter. In the mirror, their relation was apparent. Sophia had her mother's fine, wispy hair and wide eyes with inky lashes. She had the same little bump on her nose and the same heart-shaped face.

But all the similarities were on the outside. Because inside, Sophia was *nothing* like her mother.

"Yes, knowing I have to marry a stranger to keep my father happy *is* difficult." Bitterness coated her tongue like a poison. Despite growing to really enjoy Dion's company—in *every* way—this situation still made her blood boil.

Dorothy cringed. "Do you think I've been a terrible mother?"

She hadn't wanted to get into this today. A wedding was supposed to be a joyous occasion, but it had been impossible not to think about why she was here. What she was required to sacrifice. Knowing this wasn't her choice would always mean there was an uneven footing between her and Dion. They would never be equal, because she had not been party to the arrangement from the outset.

"No, I don't think you've been a terrible mother." She turned to face the woman whose weakness had made Sophia become stronger. "But I don't understand why you're still with Dad."

"I love him," she replied simply.

"How?" Sophia shook her head, the delicate chandelier earrings tinkling like tiny windchimes. "How can you possibly love someone who treats you like that?"

"Your father saved me, Soph. I was starving and doing awful things to keep food on my family's table when I met him. He came into my life and things finally started to look up—he saved me. He even gave my brother a job and helped my sister pay for her schooling. He was my white knight."

"He's a manipulator."

"You don't know him like I do. You haven't seen what he's done."

"It doesn't matter what he's done, Mom. It matters what he's *doing*. Today. Now." She couldn't understand why her mother didn't get this. "I'm going to fix everything. After Dion and I are married, we've already discussed how you can move here. We have plenty of space and—"

"I'm not leaving Brooklyn, Sophia." It was the first time she'd ever heard any strength in her mother's words. "I'm not leaving your father."

"But you can be here with me." She enclosed her mother's hands between hers. "It's all part of the plan. We'll move you here and—"

"No."

Sophia blinked. She wasn't sure her mother had ever said that word before—she'd certainly never *heard* it come out of her mouth. Especially not when her family requested something. So Sophia hadn't assumed, even for a second, that her mother would refuse the offer. Why *wouldn't* she want a way out, like her daughter did?

"Why not?"

"I know you don't understand it, Soph. But he's my world. I've been with him since I was sixteen years old, and he knows me inside and out. And I know him. I see the good in him that others don't."

There is no good in him.

Tears of frustration pricked at her eyes. Was her mother really so blind to how controlling her husband was?

"I love him more than anything in my life, aside from you." Dorothy cupped her daughter's face. "You're going to be married now, so you'll understand it someday. The bond between a husband and wife is something blessed and worth protecting. When you work on a marriage together for so many years, you develop a closeness that is totally unique. These days, people don't have the same views on marriage, I know, but it's worth the bumps in the road. It's worth the tears and the nights when you lay awake wondering what to do. Without your father, I might have ended up on the streets for good. I can't ever forget that."

Sophia's heart sank. Nothing she could say would change her mother's mind. Which meant her father would get his money, and he'd still have her mother to dangle, ensuring his daughter's compliance. Just. Like. Always.

Sophia wanted to shake her mother, to try and rattle some sense into her. But it was hopeless. So instead she swallowed her pride and enveloped her mother into a hug. Maybe there was some truth in Dorothy's words—because Sophia *did* still love her mother, despite how her weakness had held Sophia easily within her father's spiderweb for her entire life.

Maybe it would be better for Sophia to run. Pack her bags and get the hell out of dodge in the hopes that her father would forget about her.

But what about your mother? Do you think you can vanish and leave her to fend for herself?

"One day you'll understand," Dorothy whispered. But Sophia seriously doubted that would ever be the case.

Chapter Fifteen

Dion hadn't been able to stop staring at Sophia all day. At *his wife*. The second she'd stepped into the church, all breath and brain function had flown out of his body. Her father had insisted on walking her down the aisle, which he knew she would hate. But the second Cyrus had left her, the world had become theirs.

She'd looked up at him with those luminous chocolate eyes, lifted her own veil because she liked the idea of presenting herself to the world instead of having a man do it for her, and when she'd said "I do," he felt the intensity of it right down to the marrow of his bones.

Dion hadn't anticipated being so affected by the day. And while his views on marriage and relationships still hadn't changed—they made you weak, if you let them, and he would avoid that at all costs—he would rather have Sophia by his side in this arrangement than anyone else. They were partners. And together they would bring down her father. And his.

"I'm glad Elias was able to make it today," she said as

they walked through the back garden of the wedding venue. It was dark now, with fairy lights wrapped around all the trees and lanterns in shades of blue, lilac, and gold bobbing in the breeze. The night would soon draw to a close. "I was worried he might be too sick."

He didn't have the heart to tell Sophia that her fears were almost confirmed. Elias had been unwell earlier that day, and the nurses had protested his attendance, but nobody stopped him from doing a damn thing if he wanted to do it. They'd pumped him full of drugs and monitored his every move. He'd only stayed for the ceremony, but it had given Dion a feeling of belonging that filled a hole in his heart.

"You look really amazing today," he said.

"You're just saying that because I set a low bar to begin with." She laughed.

"I mean it. When I saw you walking up the aisle toward me, I wanted to tell everyone to get out and leave us alone." He paused as another couple came toward them, hands outstretched, offering well-wishes and kisses. "You're a vision."

For some reason, the return smile didn't seem to reach her eyes.

"What's wrong?"

She shook her head, her eyes suddenly sparkling, and not in a way that spoke of wedded bliss. "Nothing."

"It's not nothing."

"I didn't want to talk about it until we got home." She brushed the back of her hand over her cheek, where a tear had fallen.

"Then we'll go home." He grabbed her hands and squeezed them. "That's it. Wedding over."

She looked around the garden. "But there are still so many more people—"

"If I can't prioritize my wife on our wedding day, then

that doesn't bode well for us, does it?"

"How is it possible that you treat me better than the two people who are supposed to be my family?" She shook her head, her throat working as she swallowed.

"Come on." He tucked her under one arm. "Let's get out of here."

He pulled her through the garden, his long-legged strides telling everyone around them that now would be a bad time to interrupt. As far as he was concerned, it was his wedding and he could exit whenever the hell he pleased. Iva could handle the guests.

They rounded a corner into the back section of the building, which had been a working farm for many years but now was used almost exclusively for events where people wanted privacy along with amazing views. Dion found his driver sitting around and chatting with some of the venue staff, but he jumped to attention the second his boss approached. In under five minutes, Dion and Sophia were in the back of the limo, with the farmhouse fading rapidly in the rearview mirror.

Dion tapped the button to close the privacy screen between them and the driver. "Tell me," he said simply.

"It's my mom." She leaned back against the limo seat and looked up at the ceiling. "I told her that I wanted her to move in with us, to get away from Dad…"

He could feel her pain as if it were his own. "She wasn't interested?"

"No. She says she loves him, but I have no idea how." Her voice was tight with stress. "He treats her horribly. He treats *me* horribly, and I'm her child. Doesn't that mean something to her?"

It had taken all of Dion's strength not to land a fist right in Cyrus's face when he'd approached them with well-wishes. The man was practically glowing with self-satisfaction, and every smug smile had only made Dion hate him even more.

And yet you still agreed to his terms, didn't you? You still allowed her to end up in this position.

"I think you and I aren't much different," she said, resting her head against the glass window of the limo. "You never had a family, and neither did I. Not a *real* family."

He wanted to reassure her. But the fact was, she was right. She was alone because her father alienated her from people. Dion was alone because he didn't have anything but his work. His two most important relationships in all the world—Elias and Nico—revolved entirely around Precision Investments.

"Elias told me something important once: 'We cannot learn without pain.'" The quote came to him easily. He remembered the first time Elias had said it to him, after he'd invested his meager wages into a project that had gone belly-up so quickly he'd gotten whiplash watching the money disappear. At the time, he'd wanted to scream at the older man. But it was the backbone of his life. Take the pain, transform. Shield against further pain. "And yes, I'm a Greek man quoting Aristotle, which makes me a walking cliché."

"Sitting cliché." She turned to face him. Her earrings twinkled and winked, catching the passing streetlights and reflecting the light back at him with tiny rainbows. He'd never seen a more beautiful woman in all his life.

"You can't change her."

She twisted the emerald ring around her finger. After they'd returned home from Paris, he'd offered to have a wedding band made to go with it, but she'd refused. She wanted to keep things simple, but in the back of the limo, it felt anything but.

"I know." She nodded. "I just don't understand why she feels that way."

"Love makes people do stupid things. It seems to override self-preservation and logic and every other skill we've developed with evolution. It turns people into idiots."

"What's the story?" she asked.

"Remember how I told you I met my father and I regretted it?"

"Yeah?"

He shifted his gaze out to the window as the coast blurred past in the dark. The moon was fat and full. "I had always been under the impression that my mother died in a car accident. At least, that's what the sisters at the orphanage had told me."

"Right." Her eyes softened as if she could feel the gaping hole in his chest.

"Well, she didn't. He, uh…had a letter from her." The moment he'd read it, his heart breaking into a million tiny little pieces, he made himself a promise. He'd never love anyone. Ever. "She left me on his doorstep and took a bunch of pills. The cops were called, but they got to her apartment too late."

"Oh my god." Sophia pressed a hand to her mouth. "I'm so sorry."

"Her letter said that she couldn't imagine a life without him loving her." His lips twisted into a cruel imitation of a smile. "Apparently she got pregnant on purpose because she thought a baby would make him leave his wife. Then, when that didn't work, she pulled the rip cord. I was her act of desperation, and I failed."

"Her plan failed, not you. You were only a baby." Her eyes shone with fire and passion. "God. How can our parents be *so* fucked up?"

"I don't know." He reached out and cupped her face. "But let's take that pain and learn from it, okay? Let's take the pain and let it fuel us. You can be free, and so can I."

"We'll take the pain," she echoed. "Turn it into something good."

"That's right."

She leaned forward, coming up onto her knees on the seat. The heat in her eyes had turned molten, like lava fields and liquid fire. "No love."

"Never love."

• • •

Sophia slipped one leg over Dion's lap and settled down against him, her dress bunching around her hips. He was hard as stone, his grip strong and sure in a way that made her feel like he would take care of her. That he wouldn't let her fall. He was exactly what she needed right now, a force to help her turn her anger into something productive.

Sacrifice now for success later. Turn the pain into lessons.

Dion's hands smoothed up and down her arms. The memory of his kiss lingered on her lips, making them tingle and throb. Her mind flitted between Paris and today. Between the moments she'd continued to give in to him. It would be okay; it had to be okay.

In the reflection of the car's window, they looked like darkness and light. His skin was deep and olive, his suit dark as midnight. And she was his opposite.

His hands continued the soothing up-and-down motion along her arms, and she allowed him to touch her, because for some stupid, stupid reason it made her feel better. She wanted to make *herself* feel better, but the fact was, she needed Dion. He was the only one who'd helped her break away from her father, who'd given her an actual road out.

But now she was Dion's wife. She'd made the ultimate sacrifice for her mother, a woman who would probably never acknowledge it.

Vicious words swelled in her head, voices telling her that she was weak and an idiot and digging her own grave.

Because as much as she hated being in this position—being beholden to Dion and to her father—she *wanted* to be here now. In this limo. With him.

He was a different man than her father. He was a good man.

She saw how he cared for his friends, for his employees, for his town. He was proud, loyal, hard-working. Smart. And that was what made it hard. Because she could see herself falling for him, she could see herself wanting to be his wife in every sense of the word: physical, emotional. Everything. Because he made her burn from the tips of her toes to the top of her skull; he made her feel things that nobody else had. And if she was being truly honest with herself, she'd already started that descent. She'd already started to fall.

"Did you ever think about trying to trick me?" She shifted against him, and he let out a strangled groan. It was taking all her willpower not to lean in and take his mouth with hers. "Trying to make me think you loved me so I'd agree to the marriage?"

"I don't want to give you false promises," he said, his hands flexing against her hips, encouraging her to rub against him. "I want us to be on the same page about what this is and what it isn't, because that's the only way I can see it working."

"This is my wedding night," she said, tilting her face up to his. From this angle, his face was full of shadows, making his cheekbones sharper and his jawline harder and his lips fuller. She curled her hands into his suit, holding him tight. "This might be the only wedding night I have."

"Might?" The corner of his lips lifted in that oh-so-subtle way that she'd come to find devastatingly attractive. "Are you thinking about the potential husband already?"

"I should be." She swallowed, finding her mouth dry and her blood pulsing hard. Against everything she knew, against any bit of logic that was left, she wanted him.

"But you're not?"

"No, I'm not." She closed her eyes and let herself dwell in the rolling tornado of feeling currently eating her up inside. The smart thing to do would be to walk away now. To start acting the way she should: like this marriage was a complete and utter sham. But her stubborn hands wouldn't let him go.

"What do you want, Sophia?" His fingertips brushed the hair from her forehead, the gentle gesture searing a path over her skin. "Do you really want me to lie to you? To say whatever it takes to get you to stay, even if I don't mean a word of it? I thought I was doing the right thing by being honest."

"I don't want you to lie." Her eyes were still shuttered, keeping him out. But it only served to amplify her other senses, so she could hear the subtle ragged edge to his breath, smell the faded cologne on his skin, and feel the intensity radiating from him and penetrating her down to the very core of her. Slaying her. "I'm sick of people lying to me."

"Then what?"

The silence felt like it would drown her. She imagined this was how the ocean sounded when it sucked you down, filling your nose and ears and lungs. But Sophia wasn't the kind of woman to go down without a fight. She wanted this… and she would have it.

"Am I who you thought I would be?"

He laughed. "No. You're nothing like what I thought you'd be."

A dark shadow of a beard had started to show through his olive skin, making him look rougher around the edges. Personally, she preferred him that way, even though the man shaved religiously, always trying to maintain his perfect image.

But today had been a very long, very exhausting day.

"You're nothing like what I thought, either."

"And what did you think? That I was a heartless bastard you could tame?" He shook his head. "You can't change me, Sophia."

"You're not half as bad as you think you are," she whispered.

"And you're not half as helpless."

A sound of agreement caught in the back of her throat. "I've been at the mercy of my family ever since I was a little girl, doing literally anything and everything I was asked. I've never made my own decisions, never done anything simply because it was what *I* wanted to do. Is that not the definition of helpless?"

"I find it hard to view a woman who tortured me with a taxidermy fox helpless." He chuckled, and the sound seeped into her chest and clutched her heart. "You're possibly the truest, boldest woman I know."

Her breath caught. Nobody had ever viewed her like that before—not like she was a pawn or a princess in a tower. Not like she was passive in her own life. Dion saw the person she wanted so desperately to be.

"Then let me be bold, dear husband." She parted her lips and looked at him through the thick fringe of her eyelashes. "I don't want to go to sleep until tomorrow has begun."

He looked at her with wild hunger. The car had come to a stop in the driveway of Dion's house. They'd forgone getting a hotel for the night, since his place was better than most hotels on the island anyway. Shoving the door open, Dion stepped out of the limo, still holding her. She shrieked and wrapped her legs around his waist as he strode toward the house, carrying her as though she weighed no more than a bag of sugar. Sophia laughed as the driver stared after them, bewilderment etched into his features. Obvious this was the first time Dion had carried a woman up the driveway.

"Poor Silas."

"He'll figure it out," Dion said as he punched the code into the pad beside the door. A second later, the door burst open, and they were heading through the dark toward the bedroom.

"Kiss me." She curled her fingers against his scalp.

His lips were hard and firm, tasting of the strong traditional alcohol they'd had in small glasses at the wedding. He smelled like cologne and the ocean, salty and refreshing and something she wanted to drown in.

He entered the bedroom and kicked the door shut behind them. Now that they were alone, everything suddenly felt real. Terrifying. She wanted Dion, and she had no idea how far that want went. She was in deep, and she hadn't even known it until now. When he set her down on the bed, it was with a reverence that shook her. A gentleness and appreciation that she'd never expected to see.

Dion lowered his head, pressing his lips to the edge of her jaw and making his way down her neck. His fingers toyed with the strap of her dress before gently sliding it down. Underneath, she wore very little. No bra, since she barely had breasts to worry about, and only the tiniest little scrap of lace covering her sex.

Knowing it would not take him long to uncover all of her sent a shiver rampaging down her spine.

"You taste like dessert," he murmured against her skin. "Like honey and strawberries and pastry."

Sophia tipped her head back as he started the slow seduction she'd been trying her damnedest not to think about all day. There'd been a moment when perhaps she thought it would be possible to draw the line—to define her boundaries. That she might have the willpower to go to bed alone. But that notion evaporated like smoke on a breeze as he palmed her breast through the silk.

Her nipples tightened immediately under his touch. They

ached, begged. But the slow, maddening circle of his palm only served to stir her arousal further, without fulfilment.

"Please," she gasped, arching into his touch and having no idea what she was really asking for. She simply wanted more…of everything.

"It's a wedding *night*, Sophia *mou*. Not a wedding hour. You'll get what you want…" His lips curved into a wicked smile. "Eventually."

He pushed the other strap from her shoulder, and the silk slipped down her body, revealing her breasts and pooling at her hips. His hands snaked behind her, curving over her ass as he pulled her tight against him. The hard length of his erection couldn't be mistaken. It dug into her belly, skyrocketing her body temperature and filling her with a strange squirming, pulsing feeling that she'd never experienced before. Instinctively, she rubbed against him, feeling a delicious twitch in return.

"What do you want to do to me?" Sophia no longer recognized her own voice. It was the voice of a seductress, a temptress. The voice of a woman who knew her sexual power and wielded it to maximum damage.

"Everything." His pupils were so big and so dark it was like staring into an abyss. "I want to take you to bed, keep you up all night, and wake you up with my lips against your skin."

Her hands ran up and down his chest, settling on the button closest to his throat. She pushed it open and gently pressed the fabric back to expose an inch more of his tanned olive skin.

"I want to learn everything you like. I want to watch you touch yourself, showing me how you like it." He was lost now, his eyes black and smoky. Sophia relished the squeeze of his hands on her ass. "I want to get you nice and wet, so I have something to taste when I put my head between your legs."

She trembled as she continued to unbutton his shirt. Dear lord, the man knew exactly what to say to get her going.

"What happens next?" she asked, yanking the shirt out from where it was neatly tucked into his pants. Only three more buttons to go. *Pop. Pop…*

Pop.

"My head will be between your legs for quite a while." The lamplight played over his cheeky smirk.

"I've noticed you enjoy doing that," she said, pushing the shirt from his shoulders and watching it flutter to the floor. His black tuxedo pants were secured with a black belt, making the most of his trim waist. She traced a fingertip over his abs and followed the lines of his muscles until they disappeared right where she wanted to touch him.

"I like making you feel good."

"Then we'd better get started. Morning will be here too soon." Her eyes met his, and she reached for his hand, drawing it down her body and between her legs, just as he'd described. "I don't want to waste a second of tonight."

Dion swore under his breath. "And you call yourself powerless. You should see yourself now."

He turned her back around to face the mirror. When she looked at her reflection, she didn't see the uncertainty from earlier today. She didn't see a possession. She didn't see a bargaining chip or a piece of paper. She saw a woman unleashed, a woman finding her own power for the very first time.

Dion cupped her breast with one hand, his olive skin and the dark smattering of hair on his arm darkly contrasting against her skin. He shoved the dress over her hips, and it fell to the floor with a whisper. The white lacy thong she'd purchased from the bridal boutique seemed almost obscene now. The scant triangle barely covered her.

"You're a vision." He toyed with the edge of the thong.

"You're my every fantasy."

Her feet were still in the delicate, strappy sandals she'd worn to the wedding, and the dress sat in a puddle around them. The chandelier earrings Dion had given her that morning shimmered in the light, showing off with each subtle movement of her head. Her left hand was heavier than usual, the weight of her ring feeling more like a boulder than a gemstone.

"Touch me," she commanded softly, forcing her brain to concentrate on the physical rather than the mental. Tomorrow, she could worry about her future. For now, she wanted only to indulge in the present.

Chapter Sixteen

Dion cradled Sophia in his arms, watching every thought and emotion shift over her face like clouds on the wind. Watching her walk down the aisle with flowers in her hands had created a war inside him. Sophia deserved a husband who was with her *for* her and not for what she could give him. And yet, he felt an unshakable rightness as she took that last step to be next to him.

Dion's biggest mistake had been in looking over to Elias, however, who sat in the front row of the church, his nurse next to him and tube after tube connecting him to all kinds of apparatuses to stop him from dying in the middle of the ceremony. The old man's face hadn't shown such pride and joy since before he'd been hospitalized. He wanted to do everything he could for Elias before time clutched its greedy hands around the man's throat for good. Dion would take control of Cyrus Andreou's business and crush his father's memory, he would be a loyal husband to Sophia, and he would try to make Elias as proud as possible.

He would be all things to all people.

"Touch me," Sophia said again, her fingertips dancing over the back of his hand, tracing patterns he couldn't see.

"You want to watch?" He pressed his face to her hair and inhaled the scent of the perfume that had been wafting up from her body all day. *This* was where he could show Sophia that she was wanted. Desired. This was where he knew how to make her happy. "I want to see that beautiful face when you come."

Her chest rose and fell with quickened breaths as he slid his hand down the flat plane of her stomach, his fingers diving beneath the waistband of her thong. "Yes. I want to come."

"I bet you do, Sophia *mou*." He teased the folds of her sex, finding her wet and ready. She made a slow, sexy *hmm* sound as she circled her hips against his hand. Beneath the fly of his suit pants, Dion was hard, and he ached for her. "I bet you'll be ready to go again the second the first one is over."

She let out a throaty chuckle. "I get more than one?"

"One is a warm-up." He used his free hand to brush her hair away from her ears so he could tug on her earlobe with his teeth. "Two is for practice. And three…"

She raised a brow. "Three?"

"Three is when the fun starts."

"Well, *husband*, I guess I should stop talking and let you get to work."

He loved this playful side of her, the side that let go and embraced uncertainty. Even more, he loved how open she was. How responsive and communicative. As he moved his hand against her sex, curling his fingers at just the right angle, she dropped her head back to his shoulder and let out a long, breathy *yes*.

"You're going to make me embarrass myself, Sophia." He growled when he slipped a finger inside her, fighting the urge to come on the spot at how tight she was.

Her body trembled as he pushed her close to climax,

switching between sliding a finger inside her and withdrawing to rub against her clit. He worked her body perfectly, watching her reflection for cues so he didn't push her over the edge too quickly. The crease deepened between her brows, and her lips were glossy and open as she panted, incoherent pleas and demands falling from her mouth.

"Almost there," he whispered into her ear, never taking his eyes off the mirror. A slight sheen covered her skin—the room was air-conditioned, but they were making fire. Preparing to burn each other alive. "Almost…"

"Please, Dion. Please, I want it so bad."

He made her wait a fraction of a second more, and then he took her clit and squeezed it ever so gently between his thumb and forefinger, giving her the extra pressure she needed to tip over. Moisture coated his hand as he worked her through the orgasm, her cries bouncing around in his head while he did everything in his power to preserve the moment forever.

He never wanted to forget this.

She sagged back against him, so he scooped her up in his arms, disentangling the dress from her feet, and carried her to the bed. The staff had scattered rose petals on the covers—a gesture they must have decided on themselves, since he hadn't asked—and he brushed them to the floor before laying Sophia down. The sexy, pencil-thin heels glinted in the light. A row of stones ran over the tops of her feet, highlighting her fine bones and her delicate ankles.

"You're a goddess, Sophia. That's why you belong in Greece."

She smiled and looked up at him, her makeup slightly smudged. Hell, it looked even better like that than how it had at the start of the day. By the end of the night, her eyes would be dark and sooty with the stuff.

"Does that make you Zeus?" She grinned. "Can I see your thunderbolt now?"

Dion rolled his eyes. "Here I am, trying to be romantic, and you're only interested in getting me naked."

A rosy flush filled her cheeks, but he kissed her before she could say anything defensive back to him. Her hands went immediately to the belt at his waist, tugging and pulling until the *chink* of metal on metal sounded, and she pulled it open. Then her hands were on his zip…feeling inside his fly… wrapping around his cock.

He cursed.

"Good?" She worked her hand up and down, squeezing just the right amount to make his balls feel tight and achy.

"Too good." He pulled back and toed off his shoes before ditching his pants and underwear.

"Zeus, indeed," she whispered, propping herself up on her forearms.

He felt like a god, that was for damn sure. A god who had everything he could possibly want—power, success, a beautiful woman who looked up at him like he was her world.

Stop that right fucking now. You are not her world. You're her husband, and that's the best it will ever be.

He reached down and wrapped his hand around his cock, stroking himself while she watched, mesmerized. Then he reached into the bedside table and pulled out a condom. Love wasn't part of the deal, and that meant kids weren't, either.

After he'd worked the protection down his length, he came over her, lips eagerly seeking her out. Her body was warm and pliable beneath him, her gentle curves fitting against him like their bodies had been made with each other in mind.

"You still want this?" he asked, nipping at her jaw.

She shivered and wound her hands around his neck. A smile played on her lips, her eyes glittering in the lamplight. "Do I want my sexy husband to fuck me senseless on our wedding night after he's promised me at least three orgasms?"

"Minimum."

"Hmm, let me think about that..." She dragged his head down and pressed the sweetest, most gentle kiss to his lips. "Uh, yeah, I still want this." Her voice was tinted with darkness. It was raw and sensual, and it lit a flame inside him. "I want it so badly I think I might burst."

Dion slid an arm underneath Sophia's back and drew her up to him, enough that he could tear the covers back. She clung to him, face pressed to his neck and arms like a vice. If this was only pretend, then she was doing a hell of a job making it feel real. Because he'd had sex before. A reasonable amount of it for a man in his thirties.

And nothing had ever made him feel like this.

He guided them under the cover, against the cool thousand-thread-count sheets, and delighted in the her body beneath his. Words clogged the back of his throat—he wanted to say something meaningful, something to show her that even though this might not be what she always wanted, it still could be good. That, on some level where it felt safe, he cared.

But his brain wouldn't produce the right words.

"Now," she said, her thick lashes fluttering.

When he pushed inside her, a feeling of rightness rocketed through him. His ears rang with her pleasured gasps; his skin burned where her nails dug in. Bracing himself on his forearms, denting the pillow on either side of her head, he watched her.

"I could watch you make that face forever," he said. He pumped his hips in long, steady strokes, giving her time to adjust to him.

Sophia locked her legs around his waist, urging him on. Taking what she wanted. Good. Let her take. He wanted to give her this pleasure. When the slow rhythm didn't satisfy anymore, he pushed harder. Faster. Her fingers bit into his ass, and he drove his fingers through her hair, plundering her mouth with his tongue.

Claiming her.

"Yes." Her moan was lost in another kiss, one that seemed to stretch on endlessly.

He couldn't get enough of her. When her thighs started to tremble, he slipped a hand between them to help her along. One climax rolled into another, and eventually he let himself chase her over the edge.

Afterward, when the moonlight spilled through the slats of his blinds, creating glowing bands across the bed, he listened to the sound of her breath—even and relaxed. He had no idea what tomorrow would bring or how long it would be before their passion stopped masking what brought them here. He had no idea how she would feel when he dismantled the company on which their marriage had been a condition. Would she want to leave? Would she be happy? He had no idea.

• • •

Married life proved to be more pleasant than Sophia had ever anticipated, at least based on the poor example her parents had set. After the initial unpleasantness of having her father come around to the house to sign the paperwork for Dion to buy the company out—with all Cyrus's many terms and conditions—Sophia fell into an easy routine. Each night, she went to bed with Dion, wondering if that would be the night he grew tired of her—or her of him—but that was yet to be the case.

In fact, the more she spent time with Dion, the more she found herself craving their routine. He'd go to work early, and she'd go along with him, spending the days growing her business and loving how she could help her clients organize themselves. Then they'd come home and eat dinner on the couch—steadily working their way through the entire Hitchcock catalogue.

Sometimes they'd only make it halfway through before his hands would find the inside of her thigh, drifting up higher and higher until he found her pulsing and wet. Then they'd have to attempt that movie all over again the next night.

One morning, two weeks after the wedding, Sophia woke. Not even bothering to fight the smile growing on her lips, she looked over at Dion. Her *husband.* She'd never woken up beside a man before him, and now she knew why it seemed to be such a big deal in the movies. He looked like an angel who'd gotten lost and ended up in bed with her. Shaggy, dark hair was scattered across his face, a lock resting on his forehead. A delicious shadow coated his jaw, and his bare chest showed flat, bronzed nipples and a dusting of hair.

It was funny—she'd never thought of a chest with hair as being something sexy before. But on Dion, it worked. She especially loved the trail from his belly button down to where the crisp white sheets failed to cover the outline of his impressive erection.

Smirking, she leaned over and placed a featherlight kiss on his cheek. Dion slept like the dead, apparently. At least, that was, after a night of endless exploration…which was every night with them.

Just as she was about to doze back off to sleep, a sharp vibrating noise startled her.

"Dion?" She was already so close to him, having curled into his side in the middle of the night. "Your phone is ringing."

"Hmmrph." He sat up and pushed the mop of dark hair from his eyes.

True to his promise on their wedding night, he enjoyed keeping her awake until the wee hours of the morning, until she demanded rest. Last night, she'd collapsed into his side and had fallen asleep with her face pressed to his chest, his arm cradling her shoulders.

Would the honeymoon period be over soon? She sure hoped not.

"Hello?" Dion's voice was sexy as hell in the morning. Usually it was smooth and deep, like dark chocolate and fine wine. But in the mornings, it had this unpolished edge to it, a slight growl that did incredible things to her insides.

She watched as he got out of bed, totally naked and not the least bit shy. The man had an ass that deserved placement in a museum. His back was long and lean, the muscles honed through his daily runs on the beach.

"When?" Suddenly, those muscles turned rigid. His shoulders tensed, and he spun around, brows knitted and his mouth set into a grim line as he yanked the drawer next to the bed open. "I'll leave now."

Sophia was almost afraid to speak as he hung up the phone. "What's going on?"

Dion swallowed, his Adam's apple working as he pulled on a fresh pair of underwear and yanked a T-shirt over his head. It was creased from being on the floor overnight.

"He's dead."

Sophia sucked in a breath. She didn't even need to ask who—the crack in Dion's voice was enough. But his face remained impassive. There were no tears in his eyes, no quiver in his lips. Just hard nothingness all over.

"I'm so sorry," she whispered.

He stormed around the room, getting ready with all the grace of a robot. "I need to go to the hospital."

"I'll come." She got out of bed and quickly located something appropriate to wear.

"You don't have to do that." Dion tucked his wallet into the back pocket of his jeans and grabbed his phone and keys from the bedside table.

"I know." She pulled the dress up over her hips and fastened the buttons at the front. It, too, was a little wrinkled, but she didn't have time to go digging through the closet. He needed to be at the hospital now, and she needed to be by his side.

"You barely know him." Dion had stopped in the middle of the room as if reality were catching up with him. "*Knew* him."

She had no idea if he would explode or shut down. This was the first time she'd seen him in a situation that really tested him. And it was the worst possible kind of test.

"I'm not going for Elias." Sophia leaned forward and slipped her sandals onto her feet. "I'm going for you."

He looked at her long and hard. This was a moment that would be trying for a real marriage, let alone for two people who'd been pushed together for the sake of a business deal. They had amazing chemistry, sure, and Sophia could admit that she liked Dion as a person. But they didn't have the bonds that a real husband and wife had. They didn't have the history or the emotional reservoir to draw on.

But she'd be damned if she let him down in this dark moment.

"Come on. We don't want to keep them waiting." She grabbed her bag and slung it over one shoulder, choosing to act like this was totally normal behavior instead of encouraging either one of them to wonder about what it meant.

He barely said a word all the way to the hospital. The second they walked into the ICU, they were greeted by a doctor, and Sophia gave her husband space. She had no idea what she was supposed to do, and she couldn't understand a word since everyone around her was speaking Greek. But her gut told her that being here was enough. Dion hadn't broken yet, but he would. This man might not have been his biological father, but his influence and love had been real. They'd seen

Elias only two days before, to check on him. He'd seemed fine—tired, as usual, but fine.

Sophia blinked back the tears welling in her eyes. Why was she even crying? Dion was right, she *didn't* know Elias that well. But she felt Dion's pain as if it were her own. The more composed he appeared to be, the more torn up she felt inside. Her mind raced, wishing that she could do something to give Dion some comfort.

When he finished talking to the doctor, he came over to where she sat on a hard plastic chair against a wall. He dropped down next to her.

"He had a pulmonary hemorrhage." Dion braced his forearms against his knees, dropping his head into his hand. For a second, Sophia saw him as a little boy, lost and lonely in the orphanage, desperate for someone to love him. "He'd coughed up some blood and had a tight feeling in his chest, so they called the ambulance, but..."

Tears plopped onto her cheeks, and she brushed them away angrily. It wasn't her time to feel sad.

"I'm so sorry." She felt as useless as anything. Worse than useless. "I know how much you loved him."

He looked at her, his face like stone. "He was my mentor, not my father. I didn't love him."

They both knew it was a lie. But if he needed to say that now to help him get through the day, then fine. She wouldn't argue. Grief needed time, and when he was ready to talk, she would be there.

"You should go." He didn't look at her. "There are things I need to take care of."

"Dion, I'm here for *you*. This isn't something you have to do alone." She reached for his hand. "If all I'm good for is just to sit here and be quiet, fine. But you are not alone now, even if it feels like it. I'm your wife, and I'm going to hold your hand."

A tired half smile drifted over his lips. "Literally?"

"And figuratively." She knocked him with her elbow. "Smart-ass."

After a moment, he closed his eyes. "I knew it was going to happen soon. I just… It wasn't supposed to happen yet."

"You're never prepared for it, no matter how much you know it's coming."

He nodded. "Yeah."

They sat together in silence, leaning back against the wall with hands entwined. She remembered losing her grandmother ten years ago, the pain that had felt like nothing else she'd ever experienced. It had been at that point that she understood mortality and loss and what it was like to truly love someone and know you could never see them again. Her grandmother had been her lifeboat at times—her home away from home. She'd been a buffer between Sophia and Cyrus, been the only person who could pull Dorothy from one of her spells. When she died, Sophia felt like the bottom had fallen out of her world.

"It doesn't get easier," she said.

Dion let out a humorless laugh. "Thanks."

"I know that sounds bad, but it's not. You don't forget them, which means you never really get over it. But I'd rather feel the pain than lose the memories, you know?"

He looked at her as if seeing her for the very first time. "You continue to surprise me, Sophia."

"You, too." And she meant it.

The peace was shattered when the doors were thrown open a few feet away, a dark figure storming into the ICU. Theo. His hair was wild, but his eyes were wilder. A feral snarl pulled his lips back as he charged toward them.

"Were you going to tell me?" Theo was on them so quickly that Dion barely had time to get out of his chair before the other man's hands curled into his T-shirt. "It should be me getting that call!"

"Stop!" Sophia tried to grab Theo's arms, but he knocked her back as if she were no more than a mosquito buzzing around his head.

"I had to find out by accident because I decided to visit." Theo looked like he was about to spit fire. "Why are you even here? He's *not* your father."

"Please, stop," Sophia begged.

Dion said nothing—his grief had morphed into something dangerous. Something glinting-edged that twisted his face in a way that made Sophia's stomach roil. "I'm here because I'm next of kin."

"You're not blood."

"I'm here because he *wanted* me here. Can you say the same?"

Theo pulled his arm back and slammed his fist into Dion's face. Sophia screamed, clawing at Theo's arm as two security guards came rushing into the room. It took them plus another doctor to get Theo off Dion.

It all happened so fast, Sophia hadn't even realized that she'd slammed her wrist against the wall when Theo had pushed her. She cradled it against her chest, her heartbeat thundering so loud it distorted her hearing.

The security guards shouted something in Greek and held the two men apart. Then they were all ushered out of the ICU and into the foyer. Theo was enraged, yelling at the guards and at Dion. When his eyes locked on Sophia all of a sudden, she felt a chill run through her.

"You think you're so high and mighty, both of you," he spat, looking at the ring on her finger. "You're as good at playing the fake husband as you are at playing fake son. You're going to have to keep your eye on her."

Dion's eyes burned, but before he could say anything they were cut off by the guards and ushered out of the hospital.

The two burly men stood by the doors, and one talked into a radio.

"What the fuck is that supposed to mean?" Dion asked. Sophia's stomach rocked so much she thought she might vomit right there on the ground.

"I know you had us followed that day. I'm not a fucking idiot." Theo's eyes were black like coals. "She came to me, asking for my help to get her out of your bullshit arranged marriage. I asked her to get my father's ring."

"I wasn't going to do it." She shook her head.

"No, but did you tell your husband that you asked me to make it look like we were having an affair, huh?" Theo snarled. "She wanted out so bad she asked me to be her fake fuck buddy."

Dion's face blanked. All the emotion he'd shown earlier had gone. Replaced by the mask of a man who knew better than to show himself. "We're going. Now."

He stalked away from the hospital in the direction of the car, leaving dust in his wake. Overhead, the sun was bright, and the sky was mockingly blue. But Sophia suddenly felt like she'd been thrown into the pits of hell.

"You two deserve each other," Theo said, his face hard.

Sophia didn't say a word as she hurried after her husband, the band on her wedding finger suddenly feeling tighter and tighter, like it might strangle her to death.

Chapter Seventeen

"I wasn't going to do what he asked," she said. "But it's true I asked him to pretend to have an affair with me. It was before I got to know you, and now I'm glad we didn't do it. I would have regretted it so much."

Dion stared at the road ahead as his car ate up the miles between the hospital and his house. He white-knuckled the steering wheel, holding it so hard it was like he was trying to snap it in half. "I don't care."

"Yes, you do," Sophia replied. Out of the corner of his eye, he could see how intently she watched him. But he wouldn't turn his head. "Otherwise you wouldn't be giving me the silent treatment right now."

He scoffed. "We're two weeks married, and you're already using words like 'silent treatment.' I guess all marriages have clichés, even the fake ones."

"I know what you're doing."

Of course she did. If he was any more obviously pushing her away, then he'd have been wearing his intentions in flashing neon. But the pain was too real now, and he didn't have time to take a delicate approach.

Elias was gone.

His mentor was gone.

His only semblance of a family was gone.

The void pulsed inside him like a beast, waiting to devour him whole the second he allowed it. In some ways, he'd welcomed Theo's punch. Because the bruise forming on his cheek would give him something to focus on. A way to redirect the pain away from the inside and into something tangible. To something that he could control.

The important thing here was that he remembered what Elias had said: *we cannot learn without pain.*

Even in death, the old man continued to teach him. The reason he was hurting now was because he'd opened himself up to love. If you love, you can lose…and he'd been bankrupted in one shot. He couldn't let it happen again.

"This isn't about the thing with Theo," she said.

"Don't you dare say his name!" His throat was scraped raw, and the sound of his pain echoed in the car. "I don't want to hear it."

"Dion, I know you're hurting, but I don't expect to be yelled at." Sophia's voice wavered as she spoke. But that was his wife in a nutshell—she spoke clearly and concisely in the face of anything and anyone. She said her mind, spoke her truth. And she didn't shy away from the difficult things. "What Theo said is bullshit. Elias *was* your father, in all the ways that count. And, in the same way, you were his son."

"Stop it." He barreled down the road, desperate to get home so he could lock himself away.

"And I was never going to take the ring from you," she said. "One, because I am not a thief. And two, because I know how much it means to you."

A fucking ring. That's all that was left after more than a decade of friendship. Of love. How was it possible to pour so much time into something and be left with so little?

"Dion..." The way she said his name made his chest squeeze. Any other person would have turned away from him. He was like a wounded bear, lashing out, and still she spoke to him like she truly cared. Did she care?

He wanted her to. The realization made him feel ill. He was already too close, and he already knew that she would leave. By caring, he was simply setting himself up for failure. For more pain.

"I don't know what you want me to say," she said eventually.

"I want you to say nothing. I thought I made that clear." He pulled up into the driveway and got out of the car, disbelief and anger and turmoil filling his body with nervous energy. He stalked toward the house, and Sophia followed him, her sandals slapping against the stone path.

"Don't talk to me like that."

He raked a hand through his hair. Fuck, he was being an asshole. But the black emotions swirled inside him with such force that it felt like he wasn't even in control of his own body anymore. And the thought of her going to Theo, asking him to concoct an affair...it burned him up inside.

"Please." She approached him, one hand outstretched. "I'm here for you."

"I don't want you to be here for me." He had to lie, because it was the only way he could protect himself now.

It was incredible how much the truth came to light in moments of intense pain. Like the mind suddenly wiped away all the noise so that all that remained were the important bits.

Like the fact that Dion liked his wife. A lot.

He liked waking up smelling her hair. He liked going to sleep with her body tucked against his. He liked all the bits that happened between them getting into bed and going to sleep. He liked the movies and puzzles and that one evening where she spent two whole hours showing him the Pinterest board for her dream cottage.

He liked how she didn't take his bullshit and she called him on his behavior. They challenged each other, supported each other. They loved pulling pranks and being playful with each other.

Yeah, he liked her *way* more than was safe.

"I'm on your side. We're a team, remember."

"We're a piece of paper." He kept his face neutral. The road ahead would have a lot of difficult things—he was the executor of Elias's estate. Which would mean dealing with Theo, organizing the funeral, going through all of his mentor's things.

Being reminded over and over and over that they *weren't* family.

"We're a piece of paper and more," she said. "I know we didn't start out the way most people do, but—"

"No." If he heard the rest of that sentence, he might crumble, and he couldn't afford to be weak right now. "I want you to go into that house and pack your things."

"What?" She shook her head.

"Pack your things. Iva will organize the company jet to take you home." Each word was like swallowing acid. "We got married. I bought your father's company because I have every intention of destroying it. End of story."

"Why would you do that?"

"Your father's old boss, Aristos Katopodis… He's my real father." Saying his name was enough to make Dion want to smash something. He vowed to never speak it aloud again.

Sophia stared at him, her dark eyes unblinking. Staring vacantly. "That's why you didn't care that you had to marry me. It was all about your revenge."

The way she said it was like a knife in Dion's chest—like she was disappointed that he wasn't the man she thought him to be.

"What does it matter, if he's dead?" she asked, confused.

"I never existed to him, so I'm making sure he doesn't exist to me." He felt the darkness swirling inside him—the black tar of toxic anger. Resentment. "Or to anyone else."

"That's not who you are, Dion. You're not a hateful person." Her cheeks were pink, and tears glistened in her eyes.

"You don't know me."

"Yes, I do. But I'm worried you don't know yourself."

"This is your official permission to stop caring, okay? I got what I needed."

She rolled her eyes in an exaggerated way, but it didn't stop a tear dropping down on her cheek. She didn't deserve this. Not one little bit.

It's better this way. You're protecting her as much as you're protecting yourself. She'll move on, find someone who deserves her.

He hadn't felt this much self-loathing since the day he watched yet another family walk away with a little boy who wasn't him. The day he decided that he would choose to be alone, because at least then it was his decision.

"That's all you care about, even now. Even after all the time we've spent together?" She shook her head. "You don't care at all if I walk away?"

He knew saying it again would be like swallowing thorns, but he was angry. Hurt. Grieving. And he didn't *ever* want to go through this again. "Like I said, I got what I needed."

"Screw you." She looked at him like she was hoping he'd spontaneously combust. "I know we shared something, even if this wasn't a real marriage. Because I can be honest with myself, even if you can't."

She turned and walked toward the house, her arms swinging forcefully by her sides. A second later, the front door slammed, and the loud noise sent birds scattering into the sky. He was alone again.

Just like he was supposed to be.

• • •

Sophia couldn't remember a time when she'd slept so soundly or so deeply. She woke early, while the sun still had that buttery quality that she'd loved about Brooklyn before the city truly woke. But despite the small hour, it felt like she'd slept for days.

Unsurprising, since she'd stolen one of her mother's sleeping tablets. Not her best move, admittedly. But after two full days on home soil and still being unable to sleep, she needed some reprieve. Her mind was exhausted from running through her fight with Dion over and over like a bad movie stuck on a loop.

But it was clear after coming home that this house wasn't *actually* home. She'd never felt cherished here. Never felt as though she belonged. It was a good thing, Sophia had told herself. It cemented why she could never live here again.

Her father had been circling like a shark since she set foot into the house, and she'd been doing her best to avoid him. But that would have top stop. She needed to deal with this situation so she could move on. It was time to break free. For good.

"Sophia!" her father called. "Come and see me in my office."

Sucking in a breath, she went to see her father. The early light spilled into the room crammed with his social trophies. The sight of the fake Eames chair turned her stomach because it immediately reminded her of what Dion had looked like in Paris, long legs stretched out while he worked on his laptop early in the morning so they could spend time together during the day.

Cyrus pushed out of his chair and came toward her, his large frame casting a big shadow. It had been a long time since she'd viewed him as anything but the villain of her story.

"Mrs. Kourakis." His smile sent a chill through her. "How does it feel to be married?"

"I still feel like me." She turned to gaze at the window, willing the soft, rolling clouds to soothe her.

You can do this.

"I'm assuming the honeymoon is already over, since you're here at home instead of being with your new husband. Am I right?"

"He's away on business," she lied. "And I missed Mom."

Cyrus narrowed his eyes at her. "I need you to do me a favor."

One day, she'd need to tell her father the real definition of a favor…and that it implied reciprocation. "What's that?"

"Find something on him." Cyrus folded his arms over his chest. "Something juicy."

She almost wanted to laugh. Her father had no idea that she already *had* something juicy—that Europe's most beloved billionaire had a father who'd turned out to be a thug and a deadbeat dad. It was no reflection on Dion, but the tabloids didn't need much to splash across the front of their papers. It would be negative press. A *huge* breach of Dion's privacy and an embarrassment. Sophia's father would gobble it up.

But she had no intention of telling a soul. She would *not* betray Dion's trust.

"You want me to dig up dirt on my husband," Sophia said. "So you can blackmail him into giving us the company back?"

"Smart girl." Cyrus put his arm around her shoulder. "We'll kill two birds with one stone. Get the company back, get you an annulment so you can come home and be with your family for good. That way you won't have to miss your mom anymore."

Some part of her wished she could be shocked by her father's devious plan—but she knew him too well. *Of course* this was what he'd planned all along. "You never intended for me to stay married to him, did you?"

Her father shook his head.

"Why didn't you tell me?" She could already guess.

"Apart from the fact that you would have kicked and screamed like an insolent child?" He raised a brow. "Well. Even more than you already did?"

"Sorry I have a conscience," she said, straight-faced.

"You would have blown it. I'm proud of the fact that I raised such an honest daughter, but that means I had to keep you in the dark." His hand tightened on her shoulder.

Honest…yeah, right. She'd been lying to Dion from day one. First by letting him think she was this wild, kooky person, and then by not telling him what Theo had asked of her. Not being honest that she was failing to keep her distance from him.

She'd been lying to herself, too.

"You should look happier, Sophia. You said you never wanted to marry him in the first place, and now I'm giving you the perfect solution."

"Only if I rifle through his secrets and find something for you to hurt him with." She looked up at her father. Had there ever been any good in this man? Had there ever been anything real that her mother had fallen in love with? Or had she been so desperate for survival that she overlooked his need for control?

Mom, why did you do it? Why do you love him?

"It won't matter in the end. Whatever you find will be kept a secret, anyway. It's not like we'll go public with it." He looked genuinely baffled by her response, and for a moment

Sophia wondered if maybe he had no idea how much his actions hurt others. How unhappy his steamrolling made her. "I really don't see what the problem is."

"Shocker." She rolled her eyes.

"What's *that* supposed to mean?"

She couldn't help herself. Maybe living away from her father these past weeks had amplified his bad behaviour. His bullying. Or maybe it was that Dion helped her believe that she *was* a strong person, a determined person…despite everything her family had ever told her.

"It means you only ever see what benefits you," she replied, her voice sharp. "Not our *family*, like you claim."

This time, she couldn't find the strength to swallow down the resentment. Was having a father like Cyrus really better than not having one at all? Was having a mother who was unable to prevent her daughter from being manipulated better than having no mother at all?

Guilt stabbed her in the gut. She loved her mother, even with her flaws. But she could no longer shoulder the responsibility of trying to make this family whole. They were broken. She had to accept that.

"Shouldn't this be a chance for you to change your ways?" she asked. "You've got a fresh start. No debts, no boss. You could be a good man."

"I *am* a good man." Her father's indignant response told her everything she would need to know: at no point, ever, would Cyrus Andreou change. "I put food on the table for you and your mother. Even when business was slim, I found a way to feed you. I put a roof over your heads, paid for your schooling, and gave you everything you could ever need. Regardless of what you think, *everything* I do is for this family."

For a moment, Sophia saw that her father really believed himself. He really believed that he had their best interests at heart—that every dirty trick he pulled was for the betterment of the three of them. Maybe this was the only way he knew how to show love.

Her father swallowed. "I never wanted you to go through what your mother did when she was young. Her father didn't take care of his family properly, and they suffered. I will never let that happen."

Her heart ached. Her father *could* have been a good man—a caring man. But his obsession with controlling every aspect of their lives was so deeply ingrained he would never change. He saw control as his duty, his responsibility…and he would not relinquish it.

But she refused to continue bending to his warped ideas about loyalty and family.

"Control isn't love, Dad." Sophia couldn't regret the words, only that it had taken her so long to say them. "I'm done letting you make decisions for me."

The morning of the wedding had proven to Sophia that Dorothy Andreou would only see the light if she chose it. Nothing Sophia could do would ever make a difference. And at some point, she had to take responsibility for herself. She couldn't be a prisoner forever.

"What do you mean?" he scoffed.

"I mean I'm done." She felt the power rise up in her, power Dion had helped her to find. He'd changed her, helped her to be in this position. "I'm not going to help you bring him down. I won't do it."

She stood rooted to the ground while adrenaline pumped all through her body. The thought of betraying Dion made her sick to her stomach. It would have been easy to cave to her father, especially after Dion banished her from his house. But he didn't deserve it. Anger and grief had made him lash out, but that didn't make him a bad person.

They both had pasts that had given them scars. Flaws.

Neither one of them was perfect. But they'd become better together. They'd learned to talk and share, and she knew that if they kept trying, maybe they could overcome the twisted beliefs gifted by their fathers.

The thing *her* father didn't understand, however, was that now *she* held the power. She would never give up Dion's secret about who his real father was—not to her father. Not to anyone.

Her heart fluttered like a butterfly trapped under someone's glass, but she wouldn't let it show. "I came home to say goodbye. I'm going to pack my things and leave tonight, and that's the last you'll ever hear from me. I'm done being part of this family. Mom can call me whenever she wants, but consider yourself free of your ungrateful daughter."

"You're making a huge mistake." Cyrus's dark eyes flashed as he stared her down.

But Sophia had a revelation then: the man was all bark and no bite. He had nothing but bluster and words to do his bidding. She'd let those words beat her into submission her entire life, leaving her small and unable to breathe from where she lay trapped under his thumb.

She was far from helpless now.

Sophia lifted her chin, confidence roaring through her blood. "No. I'm not." She pinned him with a glare, something she'd never dared to let cross her face in his presence before. "And don't even *think* about hurting Mom, because I've been doing the books for your business the last few years. I know how much money you've squirreled away. And I'll be happy to share that information with your business associates if you do anything to upset her."

It was a bluff. She had only suspicions, rather than facts. But she ran laps around him when it came to administration, so he wouldn't necessarily know it was a bluff.

"You wouldn't." He tried to maintain his angry demeanor,

but his face had turned white as a sheet. Sophia's instincts were clearly on the money…no pun intended.

Difference was, now she had the confidence to face him down. To not buckle under the weight of his control. She wouldn't be his puppet any longer.

"Best you use the money Dion gave you to pay those men back," she said. "I hear they're very determined when they think someone is dodging them."

Masking the tumultuous combination of relief, victory, and lingering terror, she walked out of her father's office and up the stairs to the bedroom that had been her prison for twenty-six years.

She paused at the doorway, her body almost trembling with emotion. She'd done it. She'd *really* done it. After years of saying yes, she finally had found the courage to say no. It felt so freeing she wondered if her feet might actually be hovering above the floor.

She was her own woman now. A free woman.

And all she wanted to do was celebrate with Dion, the man who'd given her that courage. Who'd shown her how strong she could be.

It wouldn't take long to pack—she didn't own much beside her wardrobe of "good-daughter" clothes. She would use her savings to book a flight back to Corfu. Dion might not want her back, but she *had* to tell him how she felt, even if he would likely turn her away.

The fact was, she cared about her husband. A lot. He'd changed her for the better, made her into the person who *could* stand up to Cyrus Andreou. Who *could* see that she didn't have to be a victim of her mother's choices. Who *could* take the life she'd always wanted instead of wallowing in fear. That was the woman he'd helped her become, and she was damn proud of it. Of them both.

Wasn't that the mark of real love? Growth and change

for the better? She'd forever bear the imprint of him, bear the influence of him. He'd made her better, and she wanted him to see that.

Because Sophia Kourakis was *not* Sophia Andreou. And that was a damned good thing.

Chapter Eighteen

Dion stood on the beach, staring out at the ocean. He must have looked a strange sight, dressed in all black, right down to where the polish on his dress shoes was currently being assaulted by grains of sand. The sun beat down, relentless and merciless, cooking him inside his suit.

But Dion was numb to it all. The cavernous nothingness had grown inside him with each day since Elias and Sophia left within a span of a few meager hours. He remembered this feeling too well, no matter how hard he tried to forget.

He twisted the signet ring on his little finger as the waves rolled in. How was he supposed to go on tomorrow like everything was normal? Today, he'd buried one of the most important people in his entire life. And he'd thrown out the only person who'd managed to get close to him. His only true friend was Nico, and as much as he was like a brother, he had his own stuff to deal with: his growing young family, keeping Precision Investments going while Dion's mind was elsewhere.

"This was what you wanted," he muttered to himself.

"Now you're not vulnerable to anyone."

Then why did it feel completely and utterly wrong?

"Talking to yourself, Kourakis? That's not a good sign."

The familiar voice made Dion snap his head to one side. Theo walked the last few steps toward him, looking equally ridiculous on the beach in his all-black outfit. The funeral had ended some time ago, and Dion had skipped the gathering afterward, unable to bear the thought of facing Elias's loved ones. Sharing in their grief would only make him feel worse.

So he'd come here, seeking solace. Instead he was now face-to-face with the last person he wanted to see.

"You're not in a position to judge anyone's behavior," Dion replied, turning back to the ocean.

The two men stood silently for a moment before Theo broke the ice. "We're getting strange looks. People probably think we're about to carry out a hit."

Dion snorted. "You might look like a hitman in that suit. Mine fits too well for that."

It was a lie, of course. Theo was nothing if not as impeccably dressed as a Savile Row devotee, but some childish part in Dion wanted to lash out. They'd stood on opposite sides of the church that morning, and then on opposite sides of the grave. Between the bandage on Theo's hand and the sickly bruise on Dion's cheek, it wouldn't take a genius to figure out what had happened.

"What do you want?" Dion asked. "If it's about the estate, you need to direct all questions—"

"I'm here to talk to you."

"What could you possibly have to say to me? Or did you want to take another swing and even me up?"

Resentment bubbled under his skin. It was like all those times he'd tried to fight fists with words as a kid because he never had the inclination to raise his hands to another human being…as much as it would be satisfying to give Theo a matching bruise.

"I had a complicated relationship with my father," Theo said, raking a hand through his dark hair. "I know you thought the sun shined out of his ass, but the family you choose is different from the family you don't."

"You're going to speak ill of your dead father the day we put him in the ground?" Typical Theo. Always wanting to have the last word.

"No. Actually, I was going to say that I'm glad he had you."

Dion frowned. That was *not* what he'd expected Theo to say.

"I understand you've only ever heard the things about me that he told you. You think I'm a thief and an ingrate and a bully."

Dion raised a brow. "Have you given me any reason at all to think otherwise?"

"No. Frankly, I haven't given anyone a reason to think otherwise. Not even my father." A seagull squawked overhead, and the sun glimmered on the water's shifting surface. "I let him think I stole the money because I knew he wouldn't believe me. And I chose to protect someone I cared about… someone I probably should never have protected because I was only enabling her."

"Your mother."

"We do terrible things for the people we love."

He didn't have any proof of Theo's story, but something deep in his gut told him the man was telling the truth. "Did you tell Elias before he died?"

"No. I came home with every intention of doing that so I could mend the bridge, but in the end, I couldn't do it. It was easier to let him hate me than to say I'd wasted all those years letting our relationship rot based on a lie." He let out a sharp, humorless laugh. "I couldn't let him die with any regrets."

Except he had. Elias regretted turning his son away and had told Dion in the days before he died. He'd changed his will to reinclude Theo, against Dion's advice. Because the bonds of family were stronger than people realized, and Elias loved his son. And god that had made Dion jealous.

"I think he knew," Dion said. "Deep down, I think he knew what you did. And why you did it."

"You might be right."

"So why are you here? Your relationship with your father is none of my business."

"I don't even know." Theo jammed his hands into the pockets of his suit pants. "I have no idea why the hell I came here. I guess… I don't know. I guess I thought you'd understand because you knew him better than anyone. I fucking hated you for it."

Past tense? "He was a great man."

"Yeah, he was." Theo's face was hard as marble. And though Dion had known Elias to be gregarious and charming, he was also of a generation where men were raised to show emotion only if it fell on the "right" side of the masculinity equation. Anger was fine. Tears were not. Showing your pain was not. Perhaps he'd never had the skills to be the father Theo needed when he was young.

Dion ran his thumb over the signet ring.

"Where is she?" Theo's astute eye missed nothing, and Sophia's absence at the funeral had been noted.

"In America." He didn't have any energy left to make up a story. There had been plenty of questions today, which he'd dodged with his usual slickness. But now there was no charm left. He'd been rubbed raw by the day's events. The sadness chafed at him in a way he couldn't ignore.

"Women." Theo shook his head. "I know a thing or two about those problems."

"By which you mean you know nothing at all." He

laughed. "Yeah, me, too."

"I know one thing." Theo yanked at the tie around his neck. "If I could start over, I'd do it differently."

Dion kept twisting the ring, around and around and around. What would he do, if given the chance? Would he be like Theo one day, standing here wishing he'd mended a bridge instead of creating one? Sophia immediately popped into his head. If he had the chance to do things over with her, what would he change?

The image of her walking down the aisle filled his head—how he'd been desperate for her to get to him. *Walk faster!* he'd shouted in his head. He'd wanted nothing more than to take her hand and pull her away from the man who'd hurt her so badly. But that made him a hypocrite, didn't it? Because he'd turned around and hurt her, too.

You were trying to protect both of you.

But it was bullshit, because he was only protecting himself. The only thing Sophia had ever wanted was the chance to make her own decisions. To be her own person. And he'd done exactly what her father had always done—made the decision for her.

He was such an idiot.

She probably hated him now. It hit him with the force of a tidal wave that he'd done everything wrong. Here was this amazing woman, who'd tested and challenged him, who'd brought him more fun and joy than any of the artificial shit he filled his life with. And he'd pushed her away by doing the one thing that would hurt her the most.

"What would you do differently?" Dion asked.

"You really care?" Theo looked at him skeptically.

"Getting to hear you relive your life's mistakes doesn't sound so bad." The quip lacked any of the usual sting he had when talking to Theo. Because now he'd started to understand the guy, to see that by doing what Dion had perceived as him being a bad son, he was really trying to protect his mother. He'd made a great sacrifice.

Dion might not like him, but he had to respect him.

"I would have told my father the truth, let him decide whether to believe me or not instead of deciding for him. I would have let my mother make her own mistakes instead of trying to clean up after her."

Dion nodded, his thoughts starting to become clearer and clearer. The extent to which he'd fucked up was becoming more apparent—excruciatingly apparent. Sophia was more than a piece of paper to him; she was more, even, than his revenge plot. Because in all the time they'd been together, he hadn't thought about actually dismantling the company. The satisfaction it might bring him. How he would actually do it, from a business standpoint. Literally nothing beyond the acquisition of the company.

Instead, he'd flown to Paris for a week to convince her to marry him. And the whole time he was there with her, he'd been entranced. Nothing would ever be the same, because now he knew that by not letting himself open up to a person, he *would* be like Theo, standing on a beach with nothing but a head full of regrets.

He didn't want to live his life like that.

Realization crystalized in his mind, sharp and clear as a blade made of ice: destroying his father's company wouldn't change a damned thing.

It wouldn't change that his father had been an asshole. A deadbeat. It wouldn't change that Elias had meant everything to him. It wouldn't change that Dion had built himself an empire from nothing. Dismantling his father's company would simply be…paperwork.

Revenge wasn't going to achieve anything, and Dion knew now that it would leave him hollow. It wouldn't solve a damn thing.

"Too late now," Theo muttered. "The chance to talk has passed."

Dion twisted the ring off his finger and handed it over to Theo. "Here. You deserve this."

The other man eyed him with suspicion. "What's the catch?"

"No catch," he said, laying a hand on Theo's shoulder. "I have the memories, so you should have the ring."

Something flickered in the depths of the other man's eyes, but it was swallowed before Dion could properly read it. "What changed?"

"I just realized I'm not going to make your mistakes."

He left Theo standing by the water, looking bewildered, the ring held tightly in his fist. Dion had no idea if he could even start to untangle the mess he'd made, but the longer he left it before he took action with Sophia, the less chance he would have of winning her back. Because he knew what he wanted now, and it was clear as a perfect summer morning—Sophia had changed him. She'd opened him up to the possibility of love and family, she helped him to see that striving for a goal at the detriment of another person was *not* how he wanted to live his life.

And he knew exactly what he needed to do to show her that.

• • •

Sophia had arrived in Corfu wrung out and heartsick over leaving her mother. It was the right decision, but that didn't make it any easier. Dorothy had held her tight at LaGuardia Airport, trying to soothe her daughter's worries, but no words would make it better. Only one person held that power now.

Herself.

She hoped that her mother would come to her senses

eventually, but for now, it needed to be Dorothy's concern. Not Sophia's. Dion's assistant, Iva, had very kindly organized her a hotel room and a driver for the week. Iva hadn't questioned her desire to stay in a hotel instead of with Dion. Likely, she knew *exactly* the reason why.

Sucking in a breath, Sophia strode into the shining building that housed the Precision Investments office. The fine heels of her black stilettos clicked over the marble floor. The building had once been a bank, and though the outside was delightfully old, the inside had been redone to modern perfection. Everything radiated success—from the polished chrome finishing on the reception desk to the glorious paintings hung on the walls.

This was it. Time to step up.

Sophia was feeling sick over seeing Dion, because she knew it was going to hit her like a ton of bricks how much she'd missed him this past week. But living one's own life meant acting like an adult and dealing with the difficult bits. She hoped he'd at least give her a few minutes alone in his office so she could talk to him about her decision to leave home. He was the only other person she wanted to tell.

She took the elevator to the fourth floor and was greeted by a woman with cropped dark hair and a quick smile sitting behind a small desk that looked like a replica of the one on the ground floor. "Ms. Andreou?"

"Yes." It appeared that Dion hadn't instructed the staff to call her by her married name. It could mean something, or it could mean nothing at all.

"He's stuck in another meeting at the moment." The woman led her through to a smaller waiting area, outside a room with a closed door. "But please call out if you need anything."

"Thank you."

Sophia took a moment to collect herself, smoothing her

hands down the front of her skirt. Everything would land where it was meant to land… She had to hope they landed together, instead of apart.

Wrapping her hand around the doorknob, she was about to open the door when she caught sight of the plaque beside the room. It was shiny and silver with elegant engraving. *E. Anastas: Boardroom.*

Elias. Dion had named the boardroom after his mentor. Her heart squeezed. They must have had the funeral by now, and she knew Dion would be hurting. She also knew he was a good man underneath the layers of his exterior. Under the charm and wit, under the anger she'd seen recently. He had a huge heart, and she wanted to get to know him even more.

Sophia pushed the door open. Behind a long, white table was a view of Corfu Town. The old buildings seemed to glow shades of cream and peach and white, contrasted by the perfectly blue sky overhead. There were clear vases with white and yellow flowers dotting the length of the table. Precision Investments knew how to set up a classy boardroom, that was for damn sure. She turned and was putting her things down in front of one of the seats when a surprised squeak shot out of her.

At the head of the table, wearing a tie—an actual silk tie—was Baroness Sasha Foxington III.

"What in the hell…?" Sophia placed her things on the table and walked over to the stuffed fox. Whoever had placed it here—she assumed Dion—had set it at the head of the table, with an envelope in front of it which said *Sophia Andreou* in printed letters.

Swallowing against the lump in her throat, she picked it up and tore at the seal. Inside was a folded stack of paper, a form of some kind. Divorce papers.

Her heart sank. Well, at least she knew where she stood. But then she frowned. That didn't make sense, since her contract with Dion stated that she would get the company if they divorced. It had been her father's ill-conceived contingency plan, and she knew how badly Dion wanted to see it destroyed.

And why bring Sasha into the office if he wanted it over and done with?

Sophia had the prickling sensation of being watched, and when she looked up, Dion was standing in the door to the boardroom. Attraction hit her like a punch to the gut. He wore a pale gray suit with a white shirt and a yellow-and-white tie. All those light colors made him darker by contrast—his hair gleaming like night and his sun-tanned skin looking even richer.

"I didn't even get the chance to submit the name-change forms," she said benignly. "And I'm assuming you're going to sue for custody." She inclined her head toward the fox.

"I want Sasha to be happy, and that means her mother needs to be happy." He came into the room and let the door close softly behind him.

"How do you know what makes her happy?" she asked. Tears threatened, but she wouldn't let them flow. She'd wanted this responsibility, and now she had to woman up and deal with it.

"I know what makes her *unhappy*. It's a process of elimination." The closer he came, the less strength she seemed to have in her legs.

Sophia planted a hand on the back of one of the chairs to ground her. "And what makes her unhappy?"

"Being controlled."

Wow. He didn't beat around the bush.

"Feeling like she doesn't get to make important decisions in her own life."

And he was on the money, too.

"Am I close?" He took another step toward her, closing

the distance that she'd been feeling with every beat of her heart for the past week.

"You're very astute." She bit down on her lip. "But there's a slight problem with your plan."

"What's that?"

"You lose the company if we divorce."

He nodded. "I know."

"The company you *paid* for. The company that was the whole damn point of this marriage to begin with."

"Yes, I'm aware."

She shook her head, trying to figure out what in the hell was going on. "And you're willing to throw all that away?"

"For you? Yeah, I am." Dion was finally standing in front of her without his mask. Without the charming smile that he used to deflect and distract. Instead, he looked so sad that she wanted to throw her arms around his neck and hang on for the rest of her life. "And you helped me realize something."

"What?"

"When we were in the hospital and you were telling me about your grandmother passing away, you said: 'I'd rather feel the pain than lose the memories.'" He looked at her intently. "After it all blew up, I thought about this. A lot. Destroying my father's company wasn't going to change anything—not the pain *or* the memories. It might feel good for a second, and then I would be looking for the next thing, trying to forget. Trying to…move on."

"But you won't forget."

"No, and maybe that's a good thing. The pain has made me who I am, and while I always thought that was a weakness, maybe it's actually a strength."

"Of course it's a strength."

"I never saw it that way. But now that I know, I can learn from what he did. Use the pain to make me a good husband one day. A good father. A good friend." He raked a hand through his hair. "My birth father is gone, but the truth is… he was never actually my father. He contributed to my DNA, and that's it. I learned more from Elias than I ever did from him. But all my life I've tried to make myself untouchable. I wanted to be the toast of the town, the most successful. I wanted to be liked. And, in doing that, I made myself into someone who puts business deals before people. I built business relationships and made connections all over Europe, but not one of those people knew me. Only Elias. And you."

He had been as isolated as her. Only he hadn't realized it for so long.

"When you came here, you saw right through all the gloss to the person I tried so hard to hide away. I didn't want anyone to see the real me, because the real me would bleed when cut. I would bruise when punched. I would crumple when I lost something I cared about."

"Anyone would," she said softly. "It's called being human."

"I know that now…thanks to you."

"And yet you still want a divorce?" She wrung her hands in front of her.

"There was no way this marriage was ever going to work the way we started it. Because we didn't come in on equal footing."

She thought that very thing herself, and hearing him voice that concern filled her heart with hope. He understood her.

"I have a chance to make things right with you." He reached out to touch the soft ends of her hair, rubbing the glossy strands back and forth between his thumb and forefinger. He looked at her like he had the moment she'd walked down the aisle—full of wonder and intensity. Full of possession, but the good kind. "I'm asking for a divorce because I don't want to force you into something. You wanted your freedom, you wanted control over your life, and this is the way I can give it to you."

"And where does it leave us?" She wanted there to be an "us" more than anything. Because *this* Dion was the man she could love. This Dion was the man she could grow old with. The man with whom she could have the kind of marriage she deserved. "If we get divorced."

"It will leave me thinking about you for the rest of my life, whether you're by my side or not." He swallowed, his dark eyes boring into hers. "I want to have this amazing life with you, Sophia. I want us to go to bed every night and wake up every morning together. I want us to build your wild cottage among the trees and listen to the birds sing. I want to play stupid games with you, like hiding this fox in ridiculous places. I want us to do puzzles and grow vegetables and live a life full of the important things."

She laughed, tears making her vision hazy. "I want that, too."

"You have changed the course of my life, Sophia. You have changed me fundamentally and irrevocably. I cannot ever be the man I was before I went to the airport that day."

"You've changed me, too. I left home, and I'm never going back." The pain was still sharp, like a fresh wound. But it would heal. *She* would heal. "I don't know what's going to happen there, but I need to take charge of my life. I had hoped to tell you something important today."

"Tell me now." His voice was heavy, smooth. It sent a thrill through her.

"I want to be your wife."

She took the divorce papers and tore them in half. And then in half again. And again. And again. Then she threw the pieces of paper up in the air like confetti. They drifted down to the floor, fluttering this way and that, the fine black print rendered inconsequential.

"You make a messy point." The cheeky smile was like a warm hug. She'd missed it so much.

"I never do things the right way."

"Good." He brought his lips down to hers, the kiss so soft and fleeting she wondered if she might have imagined it. But the second kiss left no such wonder—it was as hard and real and powerful as the man in front of her. "Doing things the right way is for boring people."

"And we're certainly not boring, are we?"

He back her up against the wall, pinning her with his hips. "Not even a little bit."

"So you think we can make this work?" She tilted her face up to his. "Even with such a rocky start?"

"I think we'll make it *because* of the rocky start. We battled the demons up front." His hands were firm at her hips, and when they slid up her rib cage, she melted. "Now all that's left is the good stuff."

"Thank you for believing in me."

Dion stilled and pressed his forehead to hers. She loved his sexy side, but this unexpected tenderness was even more of a delight. "Thank you for believing in *us*."

"Always." She turned to where the fox still sat at the front of the boardroom table, watching on with its unmoving eyes. "All three of us."

Epilogue

Three years later

"How is she?" Dion sat on the arm of the couch, hands knotted tightly as his wife padded barefoot out of the bedroom. Sophia had been checking on her mother constantly since her arrival. "Did she finally get off to sleep?"

Sophia sighed, interlacing her fingers underneath the growing bump that pressed against the flowing cotton dress. "Yeah. Took a lot of reassuring her, but she got there."

Tears glimmered in his wife's eyes, but her shoulders were back, her chin up. Her lip trembled only for a second before she reigned it all in, strong as a warrior. She'd made that promise to herself before her mother came: she would be the rock Dorothy needed. And Dion had no doubt in his mind that she could do exactly that.

All of this stress couldn't be good for the baby. He stretched his arms out, and Sophia came straight to him, without hesitation, like she did every day. There was nothing between them now, no holding back. No reluctance to being vulnerable.

He stroked her hair and pressed a kiss to the top of her head. They stayed like that for a while, finding comfort in each other. The day wasn't over yet, but it already felt like they'd crammed a year's worth of worry into it.

That was why they'd come to the cottage. It had been Dion's first wedding anniversary gift to Sophia—perhaps a little bigger than she'd envisaged, with its sprawling open-plan living space and multiple bedrooms. But it had all the things she wanted: trees for miles around; space for a vegetable garden, which was now teaming with ripe, red strawberries and zucchini and beans. Birds chirped, and sunlight slanted in at the perfect angle, dappled and shifting. It was the place they came to get away from it all—from Precision Investments and Sophia's growing virtual-assistant business, which now had staff and more clients than she'd ever dreamed possible.

This was their haven. Their safe place. Their private place.

Now, they'd brought Sophia's mother here in the hopes it might help her heal the way this place had helped to heal them.

"Apparently, Dad told her that if she came to see me, she wouldn't have a marriage to come home to." Sophia looked up at him, her eyes red-rimmed. "He threatened to change the locks. He even tossed some of her clothes out of the bedroom window. She's devastated, Dion. I didn't know what to say to her."

Dion had to fight the instinct to roar. Cyrus Andreou was a bully the likes of which he'd never seen, and it had only gotten worse once he lost his control over Sophia. But his anger wouldn't help her or her mother now. There was no point in being angry over the past—that was the lesson Sophia had taught Dion. "Maybe this is exactly what needed to happen. Maybe now she'll see."

"You think?" Her hope sliced right through his chest.

"I do. And when our little girl arrives, your mother will have even more joy to help her through the pain." Dion tucked her hair behind her ears. "There's so much love in this house, she'll want to be part of it."

"I hope so." She rested her cheek against his chest. "Thank you for letting me take her in."

"You don't need to thank me for that. She's family. There will be a bed for her here as long as she wants it, and one back at the house, too." He kissed the top of her head.

"Are you nervous about the baby coming?"

"Yes." Sometimes when she asked him these important questions, he still found there was a shadow inside him that wanted to shy away. Like muscle memory that kicked in whenever he was asked to open up. But he never gave in to it. "I'm nervous about not sleeping again for the next eighteen years."

She laughed. "Me, too."

"But it will be worth every second of sleep deprivation. I can't wait to see what a wonderful mother you'll be." He knew she needed to hear it—over and over and over. There were parts of his wife that still doubted herself, doubted that she'd know how to be a good mother, since her own was so imperfect. She loved Dorothy with all her heart, but she didn't want to repeat her mistakes. "I have so much confidence in you, and our little girl is going to be fierce and loyal and powerful, like her mother."

"We need to settle on a name soon." Sophia placed a hand over her bump.

"I know." It was such a big decision. They'd gone back and forth, crossing off names as quickly as they wrote them down. But he'd been toying with one that felt right. "Elia is a pretty name."

He hadn't wanted to push the idea on Sophia, but the

more he thought about it, the better it felt. It had been three years without his mentor, now. But Dion still thought of him daily. And now that he was about to have a child of his own, he missed the man even more.

"That's beautiful." Sophia's face broke into a serene smile as she looked up at him. "And I think the baby likes it, too. She's kicking up a storm."

She grabbed his hand and pressed it to her belly. Sure enough, the flutter of strong, tiny feet vibrated against his palm.

"Elia," she said. "We can't wait to meet you."

"Everybody who loves you is going to be there." He pressed a kiss to her belly. "You're going to have a whole room of people so excited for you to join our family."

"Our family." Sophia pulled her husband close and pushed up onto her toes to try and kiss him, which was difficult with her belly in the way. "I never thought I'd love that word so much."

Turn the page to start reading the brand new Romantic Comedy from *USA Today* bestselling author Avery Flynn!

PARENTAL GUIDANCE

An Ice Knights Novel

AVERY FLYNN

Chapter One

Just when Caleb Stuckey thought it couldn't get any worse, his mom walked in.

Now, some people might think getting an ass-chewing by the Ice Knights' coach, Winston Peppers, and the team's oh-my-God-our-players-fucked-up-again public relations guru, Lucy Kavanagh, was about as bad as it could get. They would be wrong. Having his mom join the ass-chewing party in Lucy's office on the fifty-sixth floor of Harbor City's Carlyle Building brought the entire shitstorm to a whole new level of misery.

Britany Stuckey—AKA Brit the Ballbuster, according to some of her players—wasn't just a state champion high school boys' hockey coach and one of the handful of female boys' hockey coaches in the country, she was also the Stuckey family titleholder for taking absolutely, 100 percent no shit from anyone. The anyone, in this case, being him. And the fact that he was a grown man and a professional hockey player with the Harbor City Ice Knights meant nothing. He would, as she often told him, forever be her little Caleb

Cutie—a nickname that proved a mother's love blinded her to her offspring's physical flaws—and she would probably treat him as such until the day one of them got hit by the number six crosstown bus.

He turned to Peppers, a man he thought would have his back despite the video-recorded smack talk that had been blown all out of proportion. "You called my mom?"

"Yes," Peppers asserted, not bothering to slow his pace as he marched from one end of the room to the other as if he were still in the locker room giving his team a what-for in between periods. "Because she is a crucial part of this rehabilitation plan to fix your fuckup."

Caleb slouched down in his chair. "It wasn't that bad."

"Really?" Lucy asked from her seat behind her desk, snark dripping from her voice. "Do I need to play the video again? I can, because every media site on the face of the earth has posted it. Bad Lip Reading even did a mockery of it."

Yeah, and he would have laughed his ass off at anyone else who'd been caught running his mouth like an idiot. Objectively, it was funny. It wasn't every day almost the entire first line of a hockey team got caught bitching and moaning about the team, their playing, the coaches, and the quality of puck bunnies they banged. They'd sounded like spoiled assholes, which he totally admitted wasn't 100 percent not the truth.

Fuck, the next words out of his mouth were going to hurt.

"Okay," he said, avoiding eye contact with every person in the room. "It was dumb. I should have shut it down sooner."

"Dumb?" his mom said, how-in-the-hell-did-I-birth-this-idiot thick in her voice. "You were the most senior player in that car, and you let the younger guys trash their own team!"

He flinched. Yeah, that was not a good look. Still… "I'd had some beers, and they were letting off steam. And it should be noted that I did the right thing by taking an Uber instead of driving."

His mom rolled her eyes. "That's called doing the bare minimum to adult properly."

The room went silent except for the mental buzz saw revving in his ears so realistically that he could smell the diesel fumes. He clenched his teeth hard enough that his jaw ached so he wouldn't snap off a nasty retort at his mom. That wouldn't get him anywhere. She hadn't gotten where she was because she backed down from fights. He'd inherited the trait, but he'd learned that sometimes the best way to win was to appear like he wasn't fighting at all. Guerrilla warfare. Psyops. Subterfuge. When it came to winning a war with his mom, those were the only ways to go.

Never mind that he was an adult with a mortgage, a retirement plan, and a degree in sports management. Sure, he'd had a lot of help from a tutor to earn his degree, but he'd still use it to open his own company when it came time to hang up his skates for good. To his mom, though, he would forever and always be Caleb Cutie who'd fucked up again. And again. And again.

It was fucking exhausting trying to meet Britany Stuckey's expectations.

Lucy, who'd been uncharacteristically watching the goings-on with her mouth shut, broke the tense silence. "Here's what it comes down to, Stuckey. You embarrassed yourself by not stopping the smack talk. You embarrassed the team. You embarrassed Harbor City. This has to be fixed. You are going to have to change the narrative and give everyone something else to talk about besides what dickheads you all are—that is, if you want to keep playing for the Ice Knights." She gave him a second to digest that bit of *yes, it's been confirmed you're an asshole, and if you don't fix it, you'll be playing in the reindeer league at the North Pole*. "And that's why you're going to give the media a story they won't be able to stop talking about.

You're going to let your mom be in charge of your dating profile on Bramble, and you're going to tell her about each date so she can film video segments that the company will use in ads that will begin running immediately."

He couldn't breathe, and a throbbing started in his head right behind his eyes. "That's not gonna happen. I didn't even say anything about the puck bunnies. Why do I have to be part of a date PR nightmare?"

"Because you didn't tell your teammates to shut the fuck up, either," Lucy said. "And because you were the senior player in the car, and you have to set the example or pay the price, whichever the public decides needs to be done for the team as a whole to move past this."

She wasn't wrong. His silence had spoken just as loudly as if he'd made any of the dumb-ass comments.

Still, there was nothing in the world they could say that would make him give in to this bizarre plan. Him? The center of all that attention? No fucking way. Even the idea of it had his stomach doing a triple spin.

"If you don't," Lucy said, "they're going to trade Petrov to reshuffle the first line. This isn't just the possibility of you earning a spot as the Ice Knights' assistant captain on the line."

One of those silences fell that was so heavy, there was no way the news Lucy had just delivered wasn't true. Reshuffle? It had taken two seasons for the team to really gel with their current lineup. Sure, Petrov was coming back from injury, but he would only miss a few of the new season games, and they needed him. He wasn't a player who scored a lot, but he was the glue for the first line. Without him? The team would be fucked. Damn, why was the front office such a bag of dicks?

"They can trade him, and for a guy just off his peak and a couple of early-round draft picks," Peppers said. "I'm not for it, but it's the GM's call."

Guilt squeezing his throat and expanding his lungs, Caleb turned back to Lucy. The look on her face wasn't recrimination so much as an ice-cold warning that actions have consequences—and not just on the person doing the acting.

Okay, so Caleb had heard the rumblings about Petrov—but that had all been before they'd turned the last season around. Then he'd gotten injured. Training camp was a week away, then it was preseason games and the new season. Petrov was at the gym rehabbing every day to get back for it.

The Ice Knights were going to be unstoppable this season. And people would realize that if the Harbor City sports media would focus on the team instead of his viral fuckup. He sank down in his chair as the old familiar you're-failing-again gut punch landed with a solid thud against his solar plexus.

Way to go, fuckhead.

Lucy let out a sigh and shook her head. "Here's what we need to know. Do you want to make the perception problem that you're a team full of privileged rich whiners go away so you can earn the A and the front office will stop eyeballing your boy Petrov?"

Caleb pinched the bridge of his nose, hoping it would stave off the ache making him think his head might explode, and nodded. "Yes."

"Then this publicity stunt is gonna happen," Lucy said. "Lucky for you, Bramble is totally on board with using you to promote their dating app. As the founder told me yesterday, if they can make you datable, then anyone is game."

Ouch.

"So here's how it works," she continued. "Bramble requires a five-date commitment so that everyone really gets a chance to know each other. However, each party must reconfirm their interest on the app after each date. Bramble will set up the first two dates, and after that it's up to you, your date, and your parents."

His headache was only getting worse. "Five dates?"

"Stop whining, Caleb." His mom gave him the look. "What's that in comparison to being able to reach your goal?"

"Got it," he muttered. "Five dates."

"After each date, you'll do a little here's-how-the-date-went chat with your mom. Bramble will interview her and your date's mom. That footage will be used in their latest ad campaign to show that anyone can meet their match using the app."

Oh God. Would this nightmare ever end?

"And I already filled out most of your profile for you," his mom added, handing him an iPad with the Bramble app open on it.

God's answer? *No. It's only gonna get worse. Enjoy your time visiting hell, sucker.*

He didn't want to, but he looked down at the screen anyway. Just like they had for as long as he could remember, the words bunched together on the screen, overlapping and squashing in on one another as the letters jumped. It wasn't a quick scan—but then again, it never was when it came to reading—but he managed to get through what was on the screen.

The backs of his eyeballs were aching by the time he got done, and the anxious fear that someone would realize how slow he was going twisted his gut as per usual. A quick glance around Lucy's office confirmed that either it hadn't taken him as long to read as his clammy palms testified or the others were working hard to pretend they hadn't noticed. The uncertainty had him chewing the inside of his cheek, but it was better than the mocking looks and full-on taunts of "hey, stupid" he'd gotten in school. He'd take a puck to the face before living through that ever again.

"Do we have to add a picture?" he asked.

"Nope." Lucy shook her head. "They don't have photos in an effort to eliminate unconscious bias in dating, on the theory that users will be more open to the person on the inside that way."

And what was inside him? A fuckup dating a chick as a publicity stunt. Yeah, he was a real catch. The whole thing just kept getting more and more messed up.

"So how do they match people?" he asked.

The grin on his mom's face should have warned him of a fresh, new level of hell. "So glad you asked."

She reached over and clicked on a question mark icon. A new tab opened filled with—he scrolled down and down and down—at least a billion questions. Yeah. This was Brit the Ballbuster, not Mom right now. She knew his weakness and had been convinced since forever that all he needed was to push harder, and by some sort of miracle all the letters would stay in the right order when he looked at them.

Kill me now.

"You fill out those, the app will match you with a few possibilities," his mom said. "Then I'll pick out your new girl."

That buzz saw in his ears? It turned into mortar fire, deafeningly loud and almost certain to fuck up his world. He looked at Lucy and Coach Peppers, desperate for another option that wouldn't include him having to get the letters on the screen to stop moving the fuck around when they shouldn't or putting his mom in charge of his dating life. When Lucy and Coach met his gaze without blinking, he turned back to the woman way too happy to have her control-freak fingers all up in his life.

"Whoever you pick, I'm not going out with her past date five," he said. "This is a publicity stunt only. Nothing more."

"No one is saying you have to or that you should," Lucy said. "The point of those little exercises is to change the narrative and clean up your image. What is more wholesome than a boy's mother helping him pick out a date?"

Had he fallen into a parallel universe where it was the total opposite of reality? His mom in charge of his love life? "That's not wholesome. It's creepy and wrong."

"Well, unless you have a better plan to fix this disaster so you have a chance at a leadership position within the team and Petrov isn't sent packing," Peppers said from his spot across the room, "then you're stuck with it."

Having his balls dipped in battery acid sounded like a better idea to Caleb at the moment, but he had no real alternate plan to offer. This parental-guidance-type date looked like the best option.

His toes itched as badly as that time when he'd skipped using his shower shoes at hockey camp when he was in middle school, and his headache went from rumba-throb to death-metal hammering.

He turned to Lucy. "And you're behind this plan? Really?"

"You dating a woman your mom picked out is a story that will grab the media's attention away from that stupid viral video of you and your teammates being jackasses. This is a plan that will work—for everyone," Lucy said.

Translation: *You are so screwed…so very screwed.*

He couldn't agree more.

• • •

Zara Ambrose was neck-deep in one-twelfth-size alligators, and all of them looked like shit. Okay, to someone who didn't spend their life devoted to the care and creation of miniatures, the alligators probably looked normal. Cute, even. To her, though, they were an abomination.

"I'm gonna have to toss them all and start again," she said, accepting the shot of sympathy tequila her bestie, Gemma MacNamara, handed her. "There's something wrong with their eyes. They just don't look right."

"No, there is something wrong with your work-life balance," Gemma said, tapping her paper Dixie cup against Zara's. "And it's time you do something about it."

It was the same line she'd been feeding Zara for the past two years—basically ever since her friend had met and fallen for the accountant next door. Yesterday, he'd proposed. Tonight, Gemma had shown up at Zara's apartment with a bottle of tequila and a smile that sparkled almost as much as the diamond on her left ring finger. They were holed up in Zara's miniatures studio, otherwise known as her loft apartment, supposedly celebrating Gemma's impending wedding. Too bad, with that last comment, this was starting to feel like a well-laid trap.

"What is this, the Gemma MacNamara version of an intervention?" she asked.

"Yes," Gemma said without hesitation.

She took a sniff of the liquid in her little paper cup, and her eyelashes nearly melted off. "Isn't Patrón the wrong thing to be serving at one of those?"

"Not for you." Gemma shot back her tequila like it was Dr Pepper and eyeballed Zara's shot. "Girl, you need to loosen up and stop working like your life depends on it."

Her tequila days were long gone—her dad always said she was the oldest twenty-eight-year-old he'd ever met—but that didn't mean a little revisiting of the old days wasn't warranted. Zara could let loose. She went out gambling. So what if it was bingo night with her grandma? She went out for girls' night dinners with Gemma. That still counted even if she was back home at eight so she could curl up with a book while her Great Dane, Anchovy, snuggled up next to her on the couch. Then there was… Her mind went blank. She really couldn't think of anything else she did on a regular basis that didn't involve work. Fuck. She didn't want to have to admit that to Gemma—as if her bestie didn't already know. Bringing the cup up to her lips, she threw back the shot, the alcohol burning its way down her throat in the best possible way.

"Well, my life does depend on my ability to work hard if I want a roof over my head and food in the fridge."

"Okay, I'll give you that." Gemma nodded in agreement. "You're one of the best miniatures artisans in Harbor City. It's gonna happen for you. I know you're going to break out."

"I love you for thinking that, but you're the only one who does."

She poured another shot for both of them. "Then the rest are idiots."

They drank to that. Then they drank to true love—well, Gemma did. Zara drank to her good luck to never have that particular curse befall her. Then they drank to Gemma's brand-spanking-new engagement. Within the hour, they were giggling like they always had together.

"Oh my God, you won't believe what my dad's latest get-rich-quick scheme is." Her dad was a legend in their neighborhood for being the greatest guy with a million plans, none of which ever panned out. She loved the man almost as much as she hated seeing him go off on another quixotic adventure to line his pockets. Growing up as Jasper Ambrose's daughter would have been amazing if it hadn't been for the fact that their rent money always seemed to disappear in a multilevel marketing scheme, or drinks for all at the neighborhood pub when his pony came in first, or training for a job that was going to be huge in the future like becoming a pig whisperer. "He's decided that he's going to be a character actor. The fact that he has no experience? A minor molehill. The real problem is that he needs to get on TV to earn his Screen Actors Guild card, and—get this—he wants me to do this online dating reality TV thing where parents pick out their kid's date and then offer advice about finding true love. Can you imagine? I need another shot."

"It's not a bad idea."

"More tequila?" She poured them both a half shot. "I agree."

"No, the dating thing," Gemma said. "You should totally do it."

Zara snort-giggled. "Not gonna happen."

"This is a total win-win here." Gemma tossed back her shot. "Your dad will get his SAG card, and you'll get to go out on five fabulous dates with a somewhat normal human being."

"We both know I don't have that kind of luck. He'd probably be some distracted dreamer just like my dad." She took her shot, the tequila burning its way down to her belly. "Hard pass."

"I can get you in the same room with Helene Carlyle." Gemma did a little shimmy dance move across the living room with Anchovy, obviously thinking this was a fun new game, following close behind with an oversize tennis ball in his mouth. "I have tickets to the Harbor City Friends of the Library charity gala, and you can be my plus-one, but only if you agree your dating life needs help and do your dad a solid."

And then, the next thing Zara knew, Gemma had her phone and was downloading the Bramble dating app. When she tried to grab her phone back, her friend easily held it out of reach. That was the problem with being barely five feet tall and being besties with an Amazon.

"Gimme my phone," she said, stretching up and reaching for it. "I don't want to date. Anyone. Ever. I like being in full and complete control of my life."

Gemma held the phone high and shot her a questioning

look, the tequila-induced haze in her eyes giving her a comical look. "Don't you want to meet someone like Hank and fall in love?"

She shook her head. "No."

"What do you want, then?"

She didn't even have to think about it. "To have Helene Carlyle fall in love with my work."

In addition to being one of the richest women in Harbor City, Helene Carlyle was also the metro area's biggest collector of miniatures. If she signed off on someone's work, then the entire art world paid attention. And that meant showings in galleries and private commissions. That, in turn, meant she would be able to create her art, which she knew full well wasn't paying the bills as opposed to creating the commercial miniatures that she sold in her Etsy shop which is what kept a roof over her head now, and use the resulting cash to turn her single Etsy shop into a miniatures-making empire. If everything went according to plan—and she'd make damn sure it would—then she could finally put to bed the nagging worry that it was only a matter of time before she'd miss a payment and the debt collectors would be at her door.

"Zara, I love you, but you are going to put yourself in an early grave if you don't allow yourself to have a little fun every once in a while." Gemma sat down beside her, put the phone on the coffee table, and draped an arm around her shoulders. "I'm seriously worried about you."

"You don't understand what it's like. If you grew up the way I did, you'd be all about work, too."

To make sure the lights stayed on. To guarantee eviction notices didn't appear on the door. To not open the fridge and find only a few ketchup packets. Jasper Ambrose might have been the life of the party and the entire neighborhood's favorite charming dreamer with a million ideas for how to make a billion, but that hadn't made living with him any easier. She loved him—everyone did—but she couldn't shake that feeling even now that the debt collectors would come knocking at any moment and she'd lose everything.

"I know your dad pulled a number on you. I was there to watch a lot of it," Gemma said, her voice wavering with emotion and probably tequila. "However, you can't let your past rule your future. You're an amazing person, and no, you don't need a man to complete you, but you also can't look to work to be the only thing that defines you." She shifted on the couch, turning Zara's shoulders so she had to look her friend straight in the eyes. "You, Zara Ambrose, are so much more than teeny tiny alligators—even if they're the best teeny tiny alligators in the whole wide world. Go out there, meet people, maybe get laid for the first time in forever, and let yourself have fun for once. It doesn't have to be for the rest of eternity, just five dates."

Tomorrow she'd probably be blaming the tequila, but at this moment, Gemma's outrageous plan made sense. "You're killing me, Smalls."

Gemma smiled at the use of her grade-school nickname. "But you know I'm right, Biggie. Your dad's a mess, but he's a good guy. You can help him out, and who knows, this just might be the dream that comes true. Plus, you'll get to meet Helene Carlyle and maybe even have some fun of the orgasmic variety."

Yeah, that wasn't going to happen. Orgasms that she didn't make happen herself—with or without a partner present—never happened. Literally. She had the world's most shy clit ever that never responded to anything but her own fingers and vibe. Still, if she knew going in that it wouldn't be love or climaxes, she'd at least be prepared. Plus, she was getting two things she really wanted: meeting Helene Carlyle and helping her dad get his SAG card.

"Fine." Zara held out her hand, palm upward, knowing she'd been beat. "My phone."

Dating was so far down her priority list that it came after cleaning the dust bunnies under her dresser and defrosting the freezer. However, if going out on five dates could get her what she really wanted and could make her dad happy and got her in to see Helene Carlyle? She'd suffer through listening to some guy ramble on and on about himself over never-ending breadsticks.

Gemma swiped the phone off the coffee table and gave it to her. Since she'd already filled out most of the personal information, all that was really up to Zara was to finish the introductory part. Thumbs hovering over the screen, she tried to figure out what to say. She wasn't looking for love. She had no interest in finding forever. Gemma wasn't wrong about the getting-laid part, though—it had been too long. Waaaaaaaaay too long.

However, the last thing she wanted was to play games or deal with someone who really was looking for Miss Right. She might be a workaholic, but she wasn't a bitch, and she wouldn't do that to someone. How in the world was she supposed to finesse that into an introduction?

And that's when inspiration flicked her on the nose. If she was going to do this, she was going to be 100 percent honest.

Assholes Need Not Apply

I don't believe fairy tales of happily ever after, but are a few not-self-made orgasms with a guy who makes my heart race and isn't a total asshole really just a pipe dream??? I work hard and hardly play. Now I'm ready for a little—really, a lot of—fun with the kind of guy who isn't a total lost cause and can clear out the cobwebs in my vagina. Too honest? Too bad. Life is too short for jerks who don't know their way around a lady garden. Forget being Miss Right. I just want to be Miss Right for Five Dates.

She handed her phone over to Gemma, whose eyebrows went higher the more she read until they were completely hidden behind her bangs.

"If no one answers, Gemma"—and who would respond to that kind of ad—"you still have to take me as your plus-one."

Her best friend nodded. "Deal."

They sealed their agreement with a pinkie shake and another shot of tequila. And by the time Zara curled up in bed hours later, she had almost convinced herself she hadn't just made a huge mistake.

• • •

Acknowledgments

I wish I could remember who sent me the link to the Bad Taxidermy website that inspired aspects of this book–inspiration comes from the most unusual places. Whoever you are, thank you!

Huge thanks to both Liz Pelletier and Heather Howland for helping me to bring this story and these characters to life. Your editorial input and the push you gave me to keep digging into the emotion is what made me love this book so much.

I must thank the team at Entangled for being a great group to work with. Thanks to Hannah for your incredible attention to detail during copy edits. Thanks also to Jessica, Holly, and Katie for always being super friendly and responsive.

Thank you to my incredible agent, Jill Marsal, for always keeping me on track and for helping me grow my career. And to all my writer friends, especially Taryn. Our Skype sessions and FB messaging marathons really keep me going when the words get tough.

As always, thank you to my husband for who supports

me endlessly by brainstorming ways to torture my characters, helping me wade through plot holes and listening to me whinge whenever I hit the “I hate this book” part of the editing process.

Lastly, thank you to my coffee machine. Without you, I would not function.

About the Author

Stefanie London is the *USA Today* bestselling author of contemporary romances and romantic comedies.

Stefanie's books have been called "genuinely entertaining and memorable" by Booklist, and her writing praised as "Elegant, descriptive and delectable" by RT magazine. Her stories have earned accolades such as the RT Top Pick and have achieved bestseller status with USA Today and iBooks.

Growing up, Stefanie came from a family of women who loved to read. After sneaking several literature subjects into her 'very practical' business degree, she worked in HR and Communications. But writing emails for executives didn't fulfil her creative urges, so she turned to fiction and was finally able to write the stories that kept her mind busy at night.

Originally from Australia, she now lives in Toronto with her very own hero and is currently in the process of doing her best to travel the world. She frequently indulges in her passions for good coffee, lipstick, romance novels and anything zombie-related.

Also by Stefanie London…

THE RULES ACCORDING THE GRACIE

PRETEND IT'S LOVE

LOVING THE ODDS

MILLIONAIRE UNDER THE MISTLETOE

TAKEN BY THE CEO

BETTING THE BAD BOY

TROUBLE NEXT DOOR

THE AUSSIE NEXT DOOR

HOW TO WIN A FIANCE

Discover more category romance titles from Entangled Indulgence...

69 Million Things I Hate About You

a *Winning the Billionaire* novel by Kira Archer

After Kiersten wins sixty-nine million dollars in the lotto, she has more than enough money to quit working for her impossibly demanding boss. But where's the fun in that? When billionaire Cole Harrington finds out about the office pool betting on how long it'll take him to fire his usually agreeable assistant, he decides to spice things up and see how far he can push her until she quits. But the bet sparks a new dynamic between them, and they cross that fine line between hate and love.

An Accidental Date with a Billionaire

a *Wrong Bachelor* novel by Diane Alberts

Samantha Taylor turned her back on her wealthy family to focus on social work. She finds herself at a charity bachelor auction, of all place. But oops, she was supposed to bid on her bff's brother as a favor and accidentally bid on the wrong guy. Backstage, she goes to tell him not to worry about having to go through with a date or anything, but the oafish billionaire hands her a card with his assistant's contact details, and reminds her that sex is definitely off the table. Oh, she'll call the assistant all right. The only "hammering" this guy is going to be doing is at Habitat for Humanity. Too bad he turns out to be nothing like she expected.

A Limited Engagement

a *Limitless Love* novel by Bethany Michaels

Racecar driver Derek Sawyer needs a fake fiancé to deter his sponsor's daughter, and childhood friend Lilly Harmon fits the bill. Lily used to dream about Derek proposing…but not like this. Money. Family. Love. It's all in danger if the truth gets out.

The Penthouse Pact

a *Bachelor Pact* novel by Cathryn Fox

Billionaire software developer Parker Braxton knows everyone wants something from him. That's why he made a multi-million-dollar bachelor pact with his friends to never marry. But he never counted on running into, literally, the quiet but sensual Layla Fallon. Sparks fly. Hearts flutter. But falling for Layla could cost Parker more than just several million dollars.

Manufactured by Amazon.ca
Bolton, ON

13602775R00152